UNCOVERED

Megan Rizk

Uncovered

This book is dedicated to those that have loved and lost and have found the strength to move forward. Tomorrow presents you with another opportunity to do your best with what you've been dealt. Make sure you take the chances, take the risks, take every single opportunity given to you.

To my family and friends, for continuing to listen to me ramble about this crazy dream I had. For all of you standing by me as I turned a dream into words on a screen.

For my mother- God bless her- for always listening and helping me with all my grammar mistakes from start to finish.

To my Aunt Dawn, I am beyond lucky to have your expertise. You have been the best thing to happen to this entire experience! I can't thank you enough for all the editing hours you've put into this novel and making sure everything was as perfect as possible. You have helped me turn my crazy dream into a reality, and I do not have enough words readily available to express my gratitude. Thank you!

Love you all.
Megan Rizk

Megan Rizk

Chapter One

EMILY

Evan! I scream his name again, choking on the words. *Evan, come back!* It's always his hands that I see, though my eyes are not yet open. The warmth of his hands clasping mine is real. The tender heat that radiates from Evan's hands is undeniable, it's as if he were right here next to me! *No! Evan!* I yell again as his sweet hands are now, cruelly ripped from my grasp! I want to hold on, but I can't as I wake from this incurable nightmare with tears escaping, calling his name over and over until my own shrill voice wakes me at 6AM like an alarm going off.

More than *any*thing, I want to change the ending of that dream. Because in truth, it's not a dream at all. It's the daunting reality that I live day in and day out. Sleep *was* typically my only escape, but now even *that* was haunted.

Wide-awake now, lying in sweat-drenched sheets and easing my tightly clenched fists, I stare at the ceiling and remember. The nightmares had been ramping up this past month. I should have known this would happen eventually. The three-year anniversary was coming up. The day my life changed forever. The day I learned from the officers standing at my door that my husband Evan was missing. The day my questions turned from, *where is he?* to *what do you mean you have no further information available?*

There were answers out there. I felt it in the pit of my being that there was more they weren't telling me. No matter who I spoke to, or how many letters I'd written, I was always met with roadblocks. The news of Evan's disappearance was the worst day of my life. Missing in Action! Lost! And still, after nearly three years he hadn't been found. I could still feel the hope I held onto those first few weeks. I remember thinking this was all one big misunderstanding. A misunderstanding would surely be better than this.

I stretched as I rolled out of bed in the pre-dawn gloom and shuffled my way to the safety of my quiet living room. In my old suburban fixer-upper, the month of June was always miserable and this one was proving to be the hottest of the year. I had time this early morning to clean up the house a bit before the heat became so unbearable that I'd have to turn up the air conditioner yet again.

"OUCH!" I yelled as I stepped on a stray Lego. These damn things would be the death of me. My daughter Tillie was only two and a half and still not the best at clean-up. To be honest, neither was I.

I opened the curtains to let in the cool morning air and caught the first line of sun coming up over my neighbor's willow across the street. Before Evan went missing and when he was home, we had started making plans to renovate our 20s Craftsman bungalow. It had such great bones … high ceilings with crown molding people dream about, and a wonderful large kitchen that needed more than a quick cosmetic makeover. We even talked about filling these four bedrooms with kids, though maybe just a boy and a girl would be enough.

But for now, I was in my happy place once again. My early morn retreat from reality, as well as my sweet active toddler who would still be asleep for at least another hour if I were lucky. That is, until the morning commuters heading downtown would start honking and shouting two blocks away on Center Street like restless roosters waking up the dead.

Uncovered

I always thought of myself as a pretty easy going soul and let life happen as it may. However, the last few days felt off. Like something big was about to happen. Whether I liked it or not, something different was in the air. I suspected it had to do with the black Escalade camped out across the street in front of my home for the past two days.

In most bigger cities this would be nothing to think twice about. I probably would never have even noticed, but in the cozy suburb where I call home, you literally knew anything and everything about everyone. It was both a blessing and a curse.

With the last curtain drawn, I peered out to see the Escalade still there, and was sure I saw the driver look in my direction! He slowly diverted his eyes from his newspaper and again gazed up into my window straight to my eyes! The piercing stare caught me off guard, and I quickly moved behind the curtain. That had to be a coincidence, right?

With this early dose of intrigue, it was now time for some much-needed coffee. I must be way overtired to think some stranger was watching me from outside my home and laughed to myself as I poured a steaming dark roast into my favorite *US Army Wife* mug. My curiosity, nonetheless, had escalated to about a level nine.

Moments later, I found myself perched at the window sipping my morning brew. With a sidelong glance I peered again at the SUV. The driver was still looking in my direction! This was indeed becoming rather strange. He then appeared to shuffle about and promptly opened his door and stepped out. He was walking straight towards my house!

My heart rate increased the closer he came. This was no ordinary guy; this was a man, and he was beautiful in every sense of the word. I didn't know much about men's clothing, but from what I did, he was wearing a very expensive suit, and he clearly knew what he was doing when he put it on this morning. I couldn't help but watch him and notice how great the suit fit in all the right places. His perfectly framed features were shadowed by his tousled brown locks, which I'm sure he must have purposely styled to look effortless and unkempt. His broad shoulders demanded my attention, and I couldn't look away. Even if I wanted to. My eyes were practically glued to the man.

The attractive stranger was now making his way to my front steps and onto my front porch! He projected such confidence and determination that I was convinced he knew what he was doing, and he knew it well. But what was he doing *here*? Did I have a meeting with someone?

I quickly glanced down at my yoga pants and thin tank top, not the most flattering outfit to meet Mr. Gorgeous in. Catching my breath, I checked the mirror in the foyer, mortified to speak to anyone in this state, especially someone as beautiful as he. I hurriedly twisted a handful of my unbrushed hair and looped it into a bun on top of my head. A few blonde curls were already dropping around my face. And then, a persistent knocking rattled my entire life.

Was this really happening? What could this man want with me? Do I even answer the door? *Yes, of course I need to answer. If I don't, I'll be thinking all day about what this could have been about.* I reached for the doorknob and took one last look through the peephole to see what I was getting myself into. Peering out at this man calmly standing on my doorstep, I had a strange sense that this guy was both terrifying and yet captivating, all wrapped into one beautiful package. If Evan were here, he would've never let me answer this door.

Cautiously I opened it with the brightest smile I could muster. I hoped the stranger wouldn't notice I'd been spying on him almost as much as he had been with me.

"Hello?" I managed, tilting my head to the side. "Can I help you with something?" The strange man eyed me up and down and I couldn't tell if it was out of disgust or desire. I was hoping for the latter given how attracted to him I had become in only a few short minutes. I felt a blush and swiftly crossed my arms as I waited for him to speak.

"Sorry to bother you, ma'am, but I have some serious business to possibly discuss with you." His deep voice sounded raspy, yet calm, like a voice you'd love to fall asleep to. *Who the hell was he calling ma'am?*

Before my mind got too caught up in his charm, I blurted out the words, "Excuse me, I'm no ma'am, and sorry, but I've already found Jesus and I don't need your prayers."

He laughed but caught himself before I could continue with my rant.

"I'm sorry, that's not what I'm here for." He fumbled for a badge and held it up. "My name is Officer Kai Taylor, and if you have a moment, I would really like to speak to you … you're Emily Decker, right?"

How did this gorgeous man know my name? I wasn't about to let my fascination get the best of me, so I invited him to sit on my front porch.

Joining him, I motioned to a seating area where my two vintage Mission style chairs flanked a small side table. "Yeah, I guess I should hear you out, seeing how you've been spending so much time outside my house the past few days, and somehow know my name." My mocking undertone seemed to have made him slightly uncomfortable.

"I'm really sorry about all that. My team wanted me to make sure I'd found the right person before I spoke with you, and I'm pretty sure I've found the right person."

He talked in such a soothing, confident manner it was hard not to be swept away with the absolute utter nonsense he was saying. My eyebrows raised and I felt my cheeks flush. I'm sure this stranger noticed my growing intrigue. "I'm ... I'm sorry, what?" My voice sounded weak, but I wanted to hear him out before losing it completely. "Who are you, again? And what are you talking about?"

The officer took a deep breath and seemed to calculate his next words. "Like I said before, my name's Kai, and well, I work for Senator Greyson. He wanted me to–"

"I'm sorry!" I interrupted. "Did you say Senator Alex Greyson? Like the Top 20 eligible bachelor's senator? *That* Alex Greyson?"

Kai stopped himself from laughing at my response. Clearly, most women had this response when hearing Greyson's name.

"Yeah, that's the one." He half-laughed with an exaggerated eye roll. "Can I finish now, or would you like a moment or two to compose yourself?" There was a slight pang of annoyance in his tone.

I straightened and leaned in toward him, a bit embarrassed for my minor fangirl moment. "I'm sorry. Yes, please tell me how anything involving the senator could possibly do with me!" I set my mug down on the table and gave him a smirk.

It was obvious Officer Kai was beginning to lose patience with me. He smiled and then seemed to carefully choose his next words. "We have privileged information of your involvement with the senator, and it's been confirmed that your affair with the senator resulted in a child."

My hand flew to my throat as I gasped. My eyes would have popped out of my head if physically possible. Should I laugh or slap the man across the face? He was so confident in his statement that I found it impossible not to react.

"CONFIRMED?" I shouted and jumped to my feet, shaking my head in an obvious indignant manner. "Please tell me how on earth you have confirmation of this absolutely ridiculous idea!" I knew I needed to hear him out before asking him to leave in a totally mad rage.

How could someone think my baby girl could be anyone but Evans? Her deep dark eyes were completely her father's. Even her smile was one that could not be mistaken. The freckles that wisped across her nose… Evan would have been entirely wrapped around her finger … had he ever had the chance to meet her!

Chapter Two

KAI

Majority of the time I consider myself an expert at reading people and was shocked to see this raw and honest response. I was so sure of myself, so sure I'd found the right woman. There could only be so many who fit her description. The description I had memorized for the last few months was engraved in my mind: dirty blonde, brown eyes, single mother with a two-and-a-half-year-old child, gave birth all alone at St. Luke's in October, initials ED.

I was eager to explain myself but knew anything I said right now would go in one ear and out the other. Instead of speaking to the wind, I waited for her to calm down and finish her incessant shouting. Once Emily finally sat down and composed herself, I got the courage to speak to the feisty woman. As hard as it was, I had to keep catching myself from looking at her in ways I know I shouldn't.

"I do apologize for the way that must've come across. I should've approached it a little better. It's just that I've spent months tracking you down and was so excited to finally be speaking with you. I'm sorry if I blurted it out all wrong. Will you let me explain the situation better?"

What was I thinking, approaching this woman's house without concrete evidence? Yet, there was something about her that drew me in. This morning when our eyes met, the gravitational pull toward her was too much to ignore. And before I knew it, I was walking to her front steps.

I knew I'd never hear the end of this from the guys back at headquarters … oh god! Alex! He'll be so upset if I ruined his chances to get this settled once and for all.

From the way she was looking at me though, I was sure this couldn't have gone any worse. How did we get to *this* point when things started off so great? The way her eyes lit up when she saw me! I don't know who she thought I was when she opened the door, yet I'm sure she noticed me staking her out, so I had no choice but to make my move.

"Emily Decker, right?" I asked again, making sure not to call her ma'am this time. Didn't want to start *that* argument again. She sat back down and kept rubbing her forehead and staring off somewhere, obviously reeling from the information I so casually threw her way.

"Yes, it's Emily, but you have to know one thing! I'm not the person you're looking for. I don't know who the hell you think you are, but you've practically been stalking me for the past couple days! And now you come up here telling me I slept with *the* Alex Greyson?" She was on her feet again shouting and throwing her hands in the air nearly knocking over her coffee mug. Then she began laughing almost hysterically.

I didn't know if this was the wrong woman or not, but for Alex's sake, I sure hope she's not. This woman seemed to have some issues and it wasn't our business to fix them. Yet, why did I find myself observing her every move for the simple satisfaction of catching her tight tee caress her hips and watching how it fell right above her belly button? *Alright Kai, stop looking at your best friend's possible baby's mother like this.*

"Okay Emily, I understand that all this may have been startling to you. But we really did think we had the right person. The best intelligence we had to go on was the initials ED from the same hospital as yours and the date matched up as well." She sat down again and appeared more relaxed and eager for more information.

"It's Kai, correct?" she questioned, as she delicately tilted her head, looking straight at me with an intriguing expression.

"Yes, Kai Taylor, but please call me Kai." I leaned forward, angling my shoulders to her. Hoping to gain some sort of a relationship with this wild woman. I wanted her to understand that I wasn't here just as a private investigator, but as a friend. Thank you to my years of police service for this small tip of advice.

"Okay, Kai, please explain yourself better, and do it fast cause I'm sure you'll be interrupted by my daughter any minute now."

She was looking at my hands, and I saw her linger there for a minute. I stopped with my nervous thumb-twirling and carefully chose my next words.

"Emily, I really do apologize for any awkwardness or confusion on my end." I'd better phrase this well or I could really mess things up for Alex. "This may come as a surprise, but I not only work for Alex Greyson, but he's actually a really close friend of mine. Well, he had a relationship with a woman who we assumed was you. Like I said before, all we had to go on was the name of the hospital, the date, and her initials. Hence, me showing up here today." She had to know all the signs leading to her couldn't just be a coincidence.

What was it about this woman giving me the eyes again? Why did she have to be so beautiful, so captivating? Why did her honey brown eyes have to look me up and down as if I were making this all up just for a chance to talk to her? Would I really be camping in my car for days just for an excuse like this? Surely, I could've come up with something a lot better than *this* crazy story.

To my relief she spoke with a different quality this time. Softer and more understanding.

"I'm truly sorry you've wasted your time here, Kai, but my baby is one hundred percent not the senator's child. I've never even met the man. I feel bad for the guy, really, I do. It would be horrible to not be able to find a child you've fathered." Then she looked off past my left shoulder and whispered, "Believe me, I understand … being a single mom and all."

There she was again, trailing out into space with that same look as before. Was she coming up with her newest lie? Now that I heard she's a single mom, one more piece of the puzzle completed. "Emily, I hate to ask, but if Alex isn't the father, would you mind telling me who is? I know it's none of my business, but I can't help but notice there are still some rather large coincidences." I hated myself for asking, the second the words came out of my mouth. I had no right to question her about something so personal. I felt like an idiot. She sat there, looking upset with my question. But to my relief, her face softened yet again.

"Kai, yes, I'm a single mom, and yes, there *are* coincidences to whoever birthed the senator's child, but that's not my problem. My problem is that I have some man at my house wanting me to prove some ridiculous theory he has about who fathered my child."

Emily's words were spoken with grace, but the fire in her eyes spoke of an unresolved fear. Her eyes were beginning to well up with tears. There was no denying now that I had made a huge mistake. This poor woman had a past, and my gut was telling me it did not involve my friend Alex Greyson.

Chapter Three

EMILY

Do not cry, do not cry, do not cry!
Maybe if I kept telling myself this I wouldn't. Who was I kidding? Still to this day, every time I thought of Evan, I got emotional. You would think it happened yesterday by the way I was acting in front of a total stranger. The look on Kai's face was soft and different now. It was almost as if he knew I was moments away from breaking.

"I'm sorry, you've caught me off guard. This is just a bit much right now," I calmly said. Hoping I kept my composure for a few seconds longer.

He appeared as though he wanted to swoop me up, hold me in his arms and take back the hurtful accusations. The look in his eyes made me miss the familiar sensation happening deep in my stomach. This look, it was one I instantly remembered, a look from someone who cared for you, someone who wanted to help when you were upset. Someone near when you needed a shoulder to cry on.

"Emily, please don't apologize. I've come here making crazy accusations, and I've obviously made a horrible mistake." His eyes looked full of regret. "I'm the one who should be apologizing, coming in here without concrete facts. I've been on this case trying to find this 'ED' for months now."

He paused just in time to catch my attention. My eyes still had tears on the edges waiting to fall, but I hoped that Kai had seen through my tough exterior into the pain hiding behind my tightly guarded walls.

"Alex is my best friend, and you have to understand I'm just trying to help him find this woman. I promise this will be the last time I bother you."

I tried to answer him this time with less temper and more grace. "I see where you're coming from … Kai … and if I could help, I would. The point being, I have no idea who gave birth to Alex Greyson's child. I have issues from my past… but he is certainly not one of them."

Before I could say more, there was a loud cry from inside the house. I turned and saw my bubbly haired toddler dragging her Pooh blanket across the living room over to the two of us. She pushed open the screen door and came over to my side and leaned her head on my lap.

"Well, hello there little one," Kai whispered. "You look just like your mommy."

As I swooped up my beautiful, curly-haired daughter, and noticed the tenderness in Kai's eyes, it dawned on me that maybe he really *was* here just as a friend to Alex Greyson. There was hopefully no malice behind this whole ordeal.

"Well, Kai, it's been great meeting you, even under such strange circumstances, but like I said before, I can't help you. I really do hope you guys find your "*ED*" person."

Kai was doing that thing with his thumbs again. It seemed a bit silly, but it was quite charming how nervous he appeared. Here was this strong, incredibly built man, obviously flustered as he reached for something in his back pocket. He fidgeted with his wallet and finally pulled out a flashy business card. "Here's my card. I really would love to take you out for coffee or something to apologize for today. I should've been more professional with the whole thing."

The picture on the back showed off his strong jawline and broad shoulders. The light hit perfectly on his pretty blues, and his soft chocolate curls were perfectly styled. One look from this man and any woman would feel charged. How could someone take that fine of a photo? Mine always turned out looking like a mug shot. I picked my jaw up off the floor and searched his enticing blue eyes.

The awkward start to my morning could not have been weirder. First, I find out I am not imagining things, and someone ... a very sexy someone, has been parked outside my house, only to realize it's because he thinks I'm the mother of his friend's child. Alex Grayson's even! Yeah, things couldn't get any weirder.

After being practically single for almost three years, this early morning surprise was almost too much! I definitely wanted to take Kai up on his offer for coffee. I knew it was time to put myself out there again, but I couldn't help thinking this wasn't the best way to go about doing it. Even so, with all the red flags and my mind telling me no, I casually reached out and accepted that beautiful card from him.

"Thanks, I don't know when I would find the time to take you up on that coffee, but now I have your card." I shrugged with a smile as I wiggled Tillie on my hip. Incredibly, I was now turning down a beautiful man on my front porch. The need for more caffeine was strong, and I needed to warm up my now cold cup. I couldn't miss the disappointment on his perfectly groomed face, and if I hadn't known any better, I would have thought I put it there.

"Well, Emily, again, I apologize and promise I won't be parked outside your house anymore. I will fill Alex in as soon as I get to my car ... you won't be bothered with any more of this nonsense ... anyway you have my card, so if you think of something or I don't know, whatever ... um, you have it ..."

18

He was twirling his thumbs again and I couldn't help but smile. The way Kai stumbled on his words almost made me giggle, but I knew he was being sincere. I gave him a smile as I nodded my head and watched as he walked down my steps. Just before he reached his car, he turned one last time and gave me a million-dollar grin. My heart skipped a beat.

"Bye, Emily. Thanks for being so understanding," he called out and gave me a rather awkward wave. I had to hold in a laugh.

I watched Kai get into his huge vehicle and pull out his phone then thought, *was this the last time I would see this intriguing and charming man?* If I knew any better, I would listen to that tiny voice of reason, and my answer would be *yes*. But then again, I have never been one to listen.

Chapter Four

KAI

What was I thinking, asking her to coffee ... let me know if you hear anything? What was she going to hear? Sometimes I wonder how I even do this line of work. Apparently, I can't even talk to a beautiful woman without sounding like a complete idiot. However, Emily was not just a beautiful woman, she was our prime lead, and yet she had an elegance about her that you didn't see much of these days. Sophistication mixed with a thread of feistiness. I found myself thinking about the way a stray lock of blonde hair fell at her collarbone. I found myself daydreaming of ways I could get closer to that collar, closer to those lips. Just then, my phone vibrated. The lit screen and the ringing woke me from my lustful imagination.

Well, here it goes, time to upset one more person this morning. "Hey, Alex. Thanks for calling. I–"

"So, was I right? Was it her? You got the picture I sent, right?" he interrupted.

I struggled to answer. I could hear the excitement in his voice. He had been so eager to find this ED ever since he got that cryptic letter earlier this year. Who waits nearly two years to tell someone they'd fathered a child? This was the complicated story of a one-night stand that resulted in a pregnancy. Alex was just starting his career as a senator when the rumors started flying. It was my duty, as head of his security team, to find this woman and child and get things settled once and for all. Even if that meant taking someone like Emily Decker down.

"Alex, I know I said this had to be her, but it's just not, man. I hate to say it but we're back at page one. I have a couple leads I'll get working on, and we *will* find her."

I needed Alex to believe we could do this; I needed him to trust me that I had his back … that I would do anything in my power to get to the bottom of this. However, the silence on the other end was unnerving. After six months of dead leads, I knew this was his only light at the end of the tunnel, extinguished now as fast as it was lit.

"Alex, I know what you're thinking, but we *will* find her."

I heard him huff, and after knowing him for over twelve years, I waited for the yelling to begin.

"Kai, honestly, I'm not even worried about this woman, she obviously doesn't want to be found, and clearly doesn't want me to be included in raising *my* child. But that's just it, it's my child too. I have every right to know my kid! Hell, the hospital won't even tell me if it's a girl or boy. My mind's been racing so much the past couple months I thought for sure she had to be the one."

He got quiet, and I felt my heart crush for the guy. I can't even imagine the anguish he'd been in with all this coming out and still no answers.

"How sure are you that it wasn't her? Did she look anything like the picture I gave you?"

I knew the answer he wanted to hear and the answer he *needed* to hear. "Alex, the picture you sent me was in a poorly lit room. But from what I could see, this wasn't your girl. She was beautiful, but not your girl. She denied ever even meeting you. Her shock when I dropped your name was definitely genuine." I laughed to myself, remembering the look on Emily's face when I mentioned Alex's name.

"Well, did you get a picture of her? I would know if I saw her. Please tell me you got at least that." He sounded as though he might throw a punch across the phone if I gave him the wrong answer.

"I'm sorry, man. No, I didn't get a picture, but I did see her daughter and sorry, but there was no resemblance to you."

"Daughter ... I have a daughter?" Alex whispered.

I could hear the wheels turning as he became quiet. "Alex, Alex, Alex! That's not what I'm saying man. I think ... I believe her, and I don't think she's the one." I struggled to break the news to him. "That child is more than likely not your daughter. You may have a daughter out there, but I don't think it's with Emily Decker."

"Oh, so her name's Emily. That sounds familiar ... this is all just too much. I need to see her for myself. I need to see with my own eyes if this is the woman from the club. We need a new approach, and if you're not willing to do things my way, I'll be taking this situation into my own hands."

Dammit, I was afraid of this. If Alex tried to do any of this on his own, the press would have a field day in two seconds flat. I knew he was desperate, but we had to come up with a better plan, and fast.

"Hey man, I know you want to find them, and believe me, I do too. I hate that you have this hanging over your head. We all know you need closure but, if you were to barge into this woman's life, like I did today, we'll have a story on our hands to deal with and you and I both don't want to deal with *that* right now."

Alex got quiet again and I knew he understood. This was a damn awful situation, and I had no clue where to continue. The closest thing I had to a lead was joining *tinder* myself and scrolling the pictures of women that could possibly resemble Alex's blurry photo.

Just then I had an idea that might clear his mind and help us move forward. I also had a few selfish reasons of my own as to why I wanted to see Emily again, but I wouldn't let on to Alex. "Dude, if you want me to contact the woman I spoke with today and set up a meeting, I can do that. She seemed pretty levelheaded. Want me to do that?"

Right then, Alex's mood shifted, and I could hear him take a deep breath.

"Yea, Kai, if you could set that up, I'd be forever grateful. I know you say it's not her, but I just can't get past the similarities. I have to see her for myself."

"Alright, send me your schedule and let me make a few calls. I'll let you know when we can meet up."

We said our goodbyes and within seconds my phone pinged with Alex's schedule. And just like that, I was once more looking toward the front steps of Emily's home... Here I hadn't even started my vehicle before needing to walk those steps again. I smiled at the prospect of seeing her again but quickly reminded myself as to why I was there. With that thought, I really hoped she was willing to meet up, and not just for Alex's sake.

Chapter Five

EMILY

As I spread some sticky raspberry jam on one of my homemade biscuits for Tillie and me, I kept a watchful eye on the black SUV still parked outside my house. I could see Kai in his front seat, phone in hand, having what looked to be a profoundly serious conversation. He appeared to be bothered by something. Could it be that this crazy morning actually upset him, as well?

I had a full day of baking ahead if I was to have my latest order ready by tomorrow, and I would be lucky if Tillie let me finish before naptime. Baking was always my escape, and after a morning like today, I was grateful for my little side hustle.

Just then, Tillie spilled her juice, and I was thrown back into reality. As I was cleaning the floor from all remnants of her sticky mess, I heard my doorbell ring for the second time this wild morning. I hurriedly pressed my cheek against the window to see that it was yet again the tall dark and handsome man who I hadn't stopped thinking about, and who had stolen my attention all morning.

Without hesitation I opened the door so quickly I think I may have startled him. With widened eyes, I found myself eagerly staring at not only his inviting, captivating eyes, but his full appetizing lips.

"Hello, I am so sorry to bother you again this morning, but I have a huge favor to ask of you before you slam this door in my face." A slight devious grin formed on his pursed lips.

I couldn't imagine any favor this man would ask that would make me want to slam a door on his beautiful face. I nodded my head not knowing how to answer as I was still trying to check my overactive imagination.

"Okay, I will take that as a yes?" he questioned.

His confused look gave me all the reason I needed to take care of whatever it was he wanted. I had to be an adult here and help this incredibly gorgeous-looking man. The chiseled jaw, the towering broad shoulders, the brown wavy locks just asking to be messed up. I hoped my taunting thoughts were not too transparent on my face. My expression must have looked a bit odd as Kai began to speak in a way that made *me* nervous.

"So, I'm completely aware you don't owe me any favors, but my friend Alex … Alex Greyson, well, he's desperate to find his child. Not only his child, but the child's mother, which we both know *isn't* you. He won't take my word for it, and he wants to meet you … to see for himself."

His eyes made strong contact with mine and I couldn't mistake a hint of hope in them. Hope that I might be able to ease his friend's distress, hopeful to find answers. I knew this look all too well. I myself was hopeful once. This was the type of situation that happened in the twilight zone, not on my front porch before noon on a Thursday morning.

I knew I couldn't do this favor he asked of me. I was not the woman he was looking for, and I couldn't go off and meet the senator. The man had been the object of lust to every housewife I'd ever come across plus the gossip of all three of my baby yoga classes. I tried to hide my laugh, but it slowly escaped.

"Kai, I understand how you would want to help your friend, but not only am I not the senator's type, but I don't think I could even find childcare for at least a couple days." *Was that the best I could come up with? Childcare … really?*

"What if I found you certified childcare for this afternoon? The sooner we make this meeting the sooner you could get rid of me. What do you say?"

What do I say? Well, I say no way in hell would I even consider letting my child go with some random person … but how could I say no with those eyes giving me that heartbreaking stare?

"I don't think you understand, I really can't do this. This is too weird and look at me. You can fend for me. The senator would never go for someone like me to begin with. I'm clearly not *his* type." I responded as I motioned to my attire.

His eyes widened. "Emily, and I say this with the utmost respect, but you're every man's type." Kai quickly countered as he looked me up and down.

I couldn't hide my discomposure when his words finally registered. Luckily, Tillie was now pulling at my leg, and I had an easy distraction from the blood rushing to my cheeks. His words floored me. I was never the woman men were drawn to. Sure, Evan and I had hit it off almost instantly. But he was the only man I had ever been with sexually. I was never sought after, then or now.

Before I could catch the words flying out of my mouth, they were already out there reaching their destination. "Ok, I can step away for a few hours. If I can review the candidates you have for childcare, I'll do it. I'll meet him, and your friend will see once and for all I'm not who he's looking for." What had I just said? These were no longer my words! I hadn't a clue as to why I'd spoken them. Perhaps it was because I so desperately wanted my meeting to be with Kai instead of Senator Greyson.

Tillie began pushing at my hip and wanted to be put down from my calculated attempt at a distraction. She ran to the living room and began playing with her toys.

Kai's expression changed from a look of desperation to a boyish grin, and I couldn't help but return the favor. He pulled out his phone and began scrolling through his contacts. "I have a couple different ideas for childcare. If you're more comfortable with a single person versus a daycare, I have either option. A couple of our staff all use the same woman to watch their kids, and she does this at the office. We have a playground and a nap area and everything. I could easily set that up for you, but if you would like a single person to watch your daughter, I would be more than happy to get that scheduled, as well."

He was now rambling, and I could tell he really wanted to make this meeting work.

"I think the daycare at the office sounds great. Tillie really loves to be social, and that seems like the best option. Maybe we could just meet there, if possible?" I turned to see Tillie deep into her Legos and thought leaving her just seemed too strange, but if we were in the same building, I'd be okay about the crazy situation I was getting into.

"Yes, definitely, I'll make that work. I just want this to be easiest for you. I'm completely aware we're putting you in an uncomfortable position, and I want to do all I can to make it easier on you and your daughter."

His calming and compassionate demeanor gave me the confidence I needed to follow through with this outlandish idea that I could ever have had a secret love child with Alex Greyson.

Chapter Six

KAI

I don't know how I was able to get Emily to agree to this, but standing there in her spacious living room, I felt like I needed to pinch myself to believe it was real. Part of me was hoping Emily *wasn't* the woman we'd been looking for, but honestly, it was for entirely selfish reasons. I knew Alex quite well, and this woman was far too good for him.

Ever since his election, he let the fame go to his head and he slept with anyone indiscriminately. But this whole child scenario had definitely calmed him down, and he was now around two or three women a month instead of his many one-nighters.

Emily, on the other hand, had a grace about her that told me she would never have slept with Alex. The fact that she thought she was not his type was almost comical. A woman as beautiful as she was would have easily been swept up by Alex, then spit back out within a few weeks … maybe months, if she were lucky. For some reason I couldn't quite understand, I wanted to protect Emily.

A thought occurred to me: what if Alex really were the father? And I found myself questioning the outcome. Would he then step up and marry Emily and would they raise the child together? Even though I had just met Emily, I didn't want to see her get hurt. And if I knew anything about Alex, it was that he could hurt a woman without batting an eye.

Emily entered the living room just then. She had changed her clothes and stepped out looking radiant in a white sundress. I had to catch my breath.

"You really didn't need to get dressed up for this meeting. I'm sure it will only take twenty minutes tops." I didn't like to think about the effect Alex had over most women. Sadly, Emily wouldn't be the exception.

"Well, it's not every day you get to meet the senator. I couldn't go in my yoga pants now, could I?" She smiled apprehensively, causing the skin around her eyes to crinkle.

Her wide eyes curved slightly when she laughed, and I couldn't help but want to see more of that magnificent smile. And it would have been fine by me if she were to wear her yoga pants.

"Guess you have a point there. I just see him as my old college buddy who just happens to now be the senator." I wanted to change the subject pronto. "So, I was thinking you could follow me to the office downtown. Luckily, it's still early in the day so there won't be too much traffic. I already texted our daycare and they're ready for us."

She smiled again and I couldn't help but think what idiot would have left this beautiful woman all alone for nearly three years.

"That sounds perfect. I just need to change Tillie and get her ready really quick. If you want to wait around in here, please have a seat. I'll only be about ten minutes." She motioned to the plush sofa to my right. I knew I couldn't stay put for ten minutes without getting antsy, so I told her I had a call to make. It wasn't a stretch as I needed to fill Alex in on the newest development. Thursdays were not so busy, because he typically went to the gym around eight and stayed till ten. It was eleven thirty, and he'd be on his way back to the office by now.

"I actually need to make a few phone calls before we go, so I'll just be outside waiting." When she smiled again, the curve of her lips was so honest, I found myself eager to make her smile once more before we left the house.

"Okay, that's fine, I'll meet you outside."

The steps leading out from her old fixer-upper were a bit old and weathered. I walked carefully down and got to my car. I had to call Alex, but why was I being so weird about a woman I'd just met? Why should I care if they hit it off? Nah, they wouldn't! Emily seemed far too smart to fall for Alex's charm. I dialed his number and said a silent prayer that Alex would not recognize Emily as the woman we had been searching for.

He answered on the first ring and without pause, questioned me. "Will she meet?" He sounded desperate and needy, something Alex was not.

"Yes, she's coming down to the office today. We should be there in an hour or so. She's going to follow me there and bring her daughter to the office daycare while we meet with her."

I could hear the excitement on the other end. "Thank you, Kai, I couldn't have done this without you. And I know you said it's not her, but I just have to see for myself and know that I tried."

He would never let this go if I didn't get her to agree to a meeting, so I was glad to make it work for him. For Emily's sake, I really hoped this went well and wouldn't be as awkward as I was anticipating it to be. We spoke for a few more minutes and I quickly ended the conversation when I saw Emily coming down her steps about to load Tillie into their small sedan. She was struggling with her daughter, and I had a strong urge to help the poor woman.

"Have to go now, Alex. Emily just got here, and I need to help her load up the car." He said something I couldn't quite make out as I pushed the end call button on my screen. I went over to Emily to assist in any way I could.

"Do you need a hand with any of that?" Her arms were full of bags, bottles, and toys. Tillie was walking behind her, throwing a bit of a fit about getting in the car.

"That's ok, I have a method to this madness. I've had to learn to do it all by myself from the very beginning."

She must have noticed my questioning look when she said, "I know what you're thinking, so I'll say it again … not Alex's child!" This time she laughed and began to buckle her little girl in the car seat. I couldn't help but laugh with her. This was going to be an interesting meeting with Alex.

"Well, I didn't say a word, but if you'll just follow me, I think we should get there in less than an hour. Do you two need to stop for anything before we get on the highway?"

She shook her head and pulled out her car keys.

"I feel like I should offer to drive you, I didn't even think about it. Would you like to all drive together? I can take you back here later?"

I could see the wheels turning in her head and liked the fact that she trusted me enough to actually give it thought. I continued with my reasons why I thought it would be a good idea, hoping to get an hour alone with her for the drive. "I'm just worried about the traffic, and I'd hate to lose you and risk you getting lost." I could tell that might have done the trick.

"You're right, I have no clue where I'm going, and I'm not the best with directions. I wouldn't mind not driving for once." She smiled and began to unbuckle her daughter but then hesitated. "However, it's going to be a pain getting this car seat in and out of the car though … so on second thought, maybe I *should* just drive."

"Well, I may not know much about kids, but I did learn one useful thing in the police academy, and that's how to properly secure a car seat. Let me do it, it's the least I can do. This will take me five minutes tops." I was confident I would definitely earn some brownie points in the car seat department. I could remember like it was yesterday how to get these things in and out of a car.

She picked up her daughter, and I swooped in and grabbed the car seat to take to my much larger SUV. With a couple of tugs and a few clicks, the seat was installed and ready to go. She had a wide smile as she took a step back, obviously amazed at my prowess. I could get used to her looks of approval.

"Wow! I've never seen anyone install a car seat so fast and so efficiently. Let me guess, you have some kids of your own?"

And there it was, I could tell the moment she finished the sentence she was eager to hear my reply.

"Nope, no kids for me. Just a full-time job and Alex to keep me busy."

She seemed to have no response at first and I noticed a touch of pink rush to her cheeks.

"Oh … that's why Alex … are you two …?"

I didn't let her finish the sentence before I burst out laughing. The thought of anyone thinking Alex and I might be anything more than best friends was too comical.

"No, that's definitely not the case. He may dress the part, but no, he keeps me busy with his issues and business to take care of. Hence, me making a fool of myself today here with you."

We laughed together, and I was pumped with anticipation that even with such weird circumstances to our meeting, we may actually have a chance to get to know each other a little better.

There's never much time to go out and meet women with my schedule. And like I mentioned to Emily, Alex keeps me pretty busy. But if today had taught me anything, it was that I was plainly in need of some female companionship. I couldn't help but be honest and hope it was with Emily.

I tried to hide my thoughts as we all got settled in my SUV and began our departure. To put it mildly, I was more than eager to spend the next hour with Emily, and hopefully give her more reasons to smile again.

Chapter Seven

EMILY

Sitting in the passenger seat of Kai's massive SUV, I couldn't help but picture what a future with someone *like* Kai would have looked like. Me, Tillie and my significant other going on little drives, simply enjoying the little things in life. Unfortunately, with Evan missing, and not having the chance to meet Tillie, I never had the opportunity for support during any stage of her life, other than from my parents who lived not far away, and a few close friends. I glanced back to see how Tillie was doing and was relieved she was amused and easily distracted by the stuffed animal we brought. I welcomed the time alone with Kai.

"So, how many women have you had to stalk for this endeavor you're on?" I asked. I was trying to be playful and the light in his eyes and kindhearted grin told me he knew.

"Actually, you're the only one. We haven't known about all this for very long. It's still pretty fresh. Hasn't been much of anything to go off of really."

I could detect disappointment in him, probably over the fact that things didn't pan out with me. "Well, I wish I had better news to deliver to you both, but I think I'd know if I had slept with the senator." I laughed, trying to keep things light.

"Emily, I don't know why, but I wholeheartedly believe you. I'm sure once Alex meets you, he'll understand that we just need to keep the case open. If I'm being honest though, I'm happy I was able to meet you. I couldn't have picked a better subject to stalk."

Uncovered

As soon as he said this, I think he was sorry he'd let that slip, as I heard a heavy sigh and saw a pained expression shoot across his face.

"Well, well, well, so you do admit to stalking me," I casually flaunted.

He shot a smirk back at me. "You know I'm kidding, but really, thanks for being so great about all this. Not everyone would be so open to changing their plans for the day and agreeing to meet with some complete strangers."

"Ok, when you put it that way, I hope I made the best decision by agreeing to this." I looked over at him and had no doubts that he was being sincere.

He nodded his head and placed three fingers in the air. "Don't worry, you made the right decision. Scout's honor." I couldn't help but smile and continue to stare into his soulful eyes. Now and then, he would look over and I could tell he liked the idea of me staring at him. He must have women staring at him all the time.

"So, I have to ask, what were you in the middle of when I knocked on your door this morning?" Kai asked as he kept his attention to the road.

Confused, I answered. "What do you mean?"

"Without sounding like a complete jerk, I couldn't help but notice you were covered in flour ... or at least I'm hoping that white powdery substance was flour," he laughed.

Mortified was one word for the emotion I was currently experiencing. Now that I was completely embarrassed by my occupational hazard, I found the words. "Yes, of course it was flour. No need to go all cop on me, I'm a mom by day and a baker by night. Or whatever time of day really. Just depends on the order and my availability." I answer as I shrug my shoulders. Baking was always more of a hobby, but once I needed to find a way to bring in an income, I put my hobby to work.

"That's cool, where could I find some of your goods?"

"My Goods?' I laughed.

"You know what I mean, where do you sell? Farmers Markets? Bake Sales? Do you have a Bakery you run?"

"No, no bakery, at least not yet. That's the goal ... someday. But for now, I bake per order. I have a couple bakeries in town that use me for their pastries and such. It works out nicely for me and my schedule."

Kai looked over to me as we slowed to a stop on the freeway.

"Good for you, do you enjoy it?" He asked.

I had to think about his question, sure I enjoyed the freedom my job provided, but it was still nothing I had envisioned for myself. Evan and I had grand schemes of turning our home into a Bed & Breakfast. His business savvy expertise, and my baking skills were going to be the foundation for our new endeavor. but again, that was another thing lost once Evan went missing.

Without getting too caught up on the emotions the past seems to bring to me, I knew I needed to answer. "Yeah, I guess you could say I enjoy it. It allows me time to be with Tillie and still make a living. I consider that a win."

Kai nodded in my direction, and I had to look away from his piercing blue stare. It was strange the excitement his stare provided. As the minutes kept pushing on, I found myself anxious about having to end this car ride. Kai was more than fascinating. He seemed so interested, so invested into all of my answers to every random question he asked.

This car ride had proved to be a great idea. In a short amount of time, we had covered almost every first date topic you could think of. Too bad this wasn't a first date. Someone as beautiful as Kai had to be dating someone. There was no chance that a man as gorgeous as he could be living the single life alone. There was also no chance a man like Kai would want to date someone like me, especially with the baggage I carried.

As we passed through the city, we came upon a large four-story government building of some sort with flags flying near the guarded entry. Over the years when looking for answers about Evan, I'd been to buildings similar to this. After a while, they all begin to look the same. Yet today, here I was squirming in my seat as we approached, trying hard to calm my anxiety. Kai flashed a badge and drove past the security gate.

I was about to meet Alex Greyson! My gut told me this was going to be uncomfortable, but nothing could have prepared me for the moment we parked, and I caught sight of Senator Greyson standing under a shade tree. The sun was shining through the tall maple spotlighting him as if he were a gift from God, and my oh my, was he a gift from God. I straightened in my seat, barely able to smile at this stunning human. He had a penetrating stare or was it just my imagination? Kai definitely noticed my reaction and somehow, I could tell he was less than thrilled.

"Let me get Alex back inside to the meeting room. I know you want to get your daughter to the nursery before we meet with him."

It might have been my look of disappointment, but I had every intention of meeting the senator right then, right now.

"No that's fine, maybe it's better this way. Once he sees me and Tillie, he'll know he's got the wrong girl. Now, seeing him in the flesh, I'm sure he'll know for a fact that any girl but me could be the mother to his child."

From the look on Kai's face, I think he must have liked how confident I sounded. "As you wish," he said. "But let me talk to him before you get out. Is that okay with you?" I was puzzled by the expression on his face. Was it merely concern?

"Yeah, that sounds perfect, thanks," I replied, trying again to understand what this strong connection was that I suddenly felt to Kai.

But now, I needed to prepare to meet Alex Greyson. Which from the looks of it, he seemed rather eager to meet me, as well. The dark stare of Alex's intense look in my direction caused his grin to deepen and a single dimple form. He then locked eyes on me, and within an instant I found myself wanting to know more about this intriguing man.

Kai got out of the car and casually approached his friend, and if not for the slight crease on the senator's forehead, you would never have known how nervous he was to meet me. I saw Alex shaking his head, and I sensed that Kai was tense. What did Kai have to say to Alex, and why did it appear as though he was now alert and agitated?

Finally, Kai looked back at me and motioned for me to join them. I unclicked my seatbelt and hastily went to the backseat to grab Tillie. She was giggling and eager to get out and run around. I set her down, held her hand and began to walk toward two of the most incredibly beautiful men standing right there in front of me.

Chapter Eight

KAI

Why was I so irritated at the fact that Alex was grinning from ear to ear, especially when we both knew Emily was not the right woman? My warning to Alex to not make a fool of himself only backfired. The moment their eyes met, I immediately regretted making the meeting happen for them. Alex approached Emily straight off. He extended his arm out to her and then quickly closed the space between them.

"Emily, thank you so much for meeting with me this afternoon. I'm sure Kai has filled you in on the severity of this situation."

Alex had a way of speaking to the general public. Cool, calm, and calculated. With me, his way of speaking was casual and relaxed. But to Emily he was mixing the two, and I wasn't impressed. She offered her slender hand to Alex, and they held each other's hands longer than I thought necessary.

"So nice to meet you, Senator. I'm sorry for the circumstances." There was a little quiver in her voice, and an all too familiar glimmer in her eye.

Alex smiled and drew his hand back. His gaze slowly drifted to Tillie on Emily's other hand and lowered himself to her level. "Hello there, my name is Alex. Aren't you the cutest little girl I've ever seen? Well, besides your mommy of course," he winked as he looked up at Emily.

I tried to hide my eyeroll, but not Emily. She was eating it up, like most women when it came to Alex. Even though Emily was embracing my friend, I sensed she was beginning to feel uncomfortable. After so many years on the police force, you learn to recognize body language.

"Well, let's let Emily get Tillie settled and we can meet in the conference room. Emily, if you follow me, I'll show you where the nursery is."

She looked at Alex and then at me with a light in her eyes that wasn't there moments earlier. I sure hoped Alex wouldn't find a way to corrupt the innocence this woman somehow still possessed.

"Oh, that sounds great. Come on Tillie, we're going to go play on a playground!"

As soon as Tillie heard the words, she was running towards the entrance. Emily shot a back glance at Alex as we left him standing in the shade with his phone in hand. They actually smiled at each other much to my dismay. I felt a gut punch, one that I brought on myself. Why did I always have to put Alex before myself? Oh yeah, because that's my damn job.

As soon as the door closed behind us and we were alone again, Emily let out a huge sigh. I couldn't help but feel it was a sigh of relief.

"Well, that was intimidating as hell," she laughed.

"Really? I thought you handled yourself pretty well. At least you didn't straightaway fall at his feet, like every other woman."

Her head jerked back, probably at my bluntness. "Gosh, I can only imagine, with a face like that ... hard not to," she laughed. "I'm so happy to not be with someone like that. Always in the public eye. I could never handle the jealousy."

Uncovered

She looked up at me and we locked eyes for only a moment before Tillie noticed the small playground behind a clear glass door. In the nursery I introduced Emily to Brenda, our in-office caretaker. There were only three other kids in the nursery today, and they were just heading outside to play. Emily gave Brenda Tillie's diaper bag and essential information. Brenda was kind and very knowledgeable in child development and I was happy to have this opportunity available for Emily. Tillie barely noticed when we exited.

"I'm glad that was painless. She is so social she barely even noticed I left." Emily smiled, but I could see she was a bit apprehensive.

"Honestly, you have nothing to worry about. Brenda came to us highly recommended. You'd be star struck if you saw her references and background check."

"I can see that." She smiled and seemed to let down her guard some more. "Tillie already looks like she is having such a great time out there." Emily had been watching the two of them from the viewing window when she turned to me. Her eyes settled on mine.

"Alright, let's go get this settled once and for all," she whispered with a look of determination all over her flawless face.

"Ok, I just wanted to make sure you're ready and comfortable."

She nodded but as I turned my back and began walking towards the hallway, I felt a tug at my elbow. I quickly turned to see Emily with tears in her eyes. I wasn't ready for this and didn't expect what it was doing to me. I was trained to handle every type of situation but seeing this beautiful woman shed tears tugged at every emotion in me. "Emily, what's wrong? I promise Tillie will be perfectly fine here."

She shook her head and managed to speak. "It's not Tillie. She is obviously doing better than I am in this whole situation. I don't know how to say this, Kai, but today has brought up a lot of emotions for me that I'm only just now realizing I've never fully addressed."

I was as confused as ever and had no idea how to respond.

"Kai … Tillie's father, Evan … he's missing. He's never even had the chance to meet her. So, coming here and proving that Alex isn't the father is simply crazy. I don't even have my husband around to go along with my story."

I knew Emily had mentioned she was a single mother, but I never anticipated this being the back story. As much as I wanted to believe her, and be as understanding as possible, I couldn't help but notice how many red flags were being waved in my face. I knew at that moment I had my work cut out for me. For now, I was not only working for Alex, finding the mother of his child, but I knew I had to help Emily find Tillie's father as well...if that really was the truth.

"Emily, I had no idea. When I investigated you before approaching your house, I never saw any Missing Person report, or any public announcement linked to your name. What happened?"

She slowly blinked and two more tears fell from her long, wet lashes. Her next few words were barely audible, so I found it hard to make out what she was saying. "Evan was in the military. He had been training in some form of special ops before he went missing. There's never been a formal report made on what actually happened. He's not even legally declared deceased. He's still considered just missing." Her tears were still falling, and I knew if anyone could get answers it would be Alex.

So maybe, just maybe, this whole situation happened for a reason. It seemed Emily had been living in a hell of a limbo for all of

Tillie's life. I needed to know the truth, and I wasn't going to give up on her like the system so clearly had done. I hated the fact that I needed Alex's help for this to work. But as my best friend, I knew I could count on him to use his connections to help Emily. Even if she was not the mother of his child like he had hoped.

Chapter Nine

EMILY

What was I thinking just blurting all that out for Kai to hear? A man I had only known for less than a couple of hours! And here I was baring my soul to the poor guy. I could hardly believe this happened. I don't easily open up to people, let alone another man. After a few excruciating seconds had passed, I began to compose myself and realized Kai had not said anything yet. I was mortified for him to see me in such a vulnerable state.

"I'm sorry, Kai, I know that's a lot to process. Please don't give this a second thought. This is my own problem. Give me a minute, and I'll be fine." I struggled to finish my thoughts and looked down at my aching feet squished into my peep-toe heels that I hadn't worn since before my pregnancy. Before I could blink, I felt a firm hand at the small of my back pulling me in for a gentle embrace. He held me there without releasing his hold and for some reason, I didn't pull away either. For the first time in I can't remember how long it had been, I felt safe. I felt protected. I felt wanted.

Sure, the impulse surprised me, but I wasn't ready to let whatever this was end. Kai took a step back, and I could feel myself already desiring more. His eyes were deep and full of concern. I had only told our story to a few people, besides those closest to me that knew firsthand about Evan. And now for some reason, Kai was one of them.

"No, Emily, please don't apologize for having emotions. This would be a strange scenario for anyone to be in. You have every reason to be upset about all this."

I cherished the words I was hearing from him. They were full of genuine concern, and it took everything in me not to grab him and return the gesture once more.

"I've had almost three years to process, you'd think I'd be better than this." I shrugged trying to appear casual about the whole situation. "I thought I was, but I guess not."

Kai seemed to see past the charade, and I had to admit, I was happy to not have to pretend with him. He placed his warm solid hands on my shoulders and briefly rubbed them with assurance. "I know we don't know each other very well, but after all this, I feel it's my obligation to help you get some answers. It's the very least I can do after bringing all this up again for you."

Kai had a way of spotting my concerns and giving me answers to questions I'd not even formed in my head yet. Evan and I had a connection that was similar. He could finish my sentences and it both infuriated me and turned me on all at once.

"I can't let you do that Kai. I promise you I'll be fine. I just had to let you know why I'm extra emotional about all this."

He had a look centered right on me that told me he was not going to just let this go, but I couldn't know for sure. Kai was hard to read, and at times I couldn't fight the feeling he was using his police background tactics on me. However, settled there beneath all that was genuine concern, and for that I felt safe.

"Emily, I want to help. Consider it my apology." He smiled now and revealed a grin that was impossible to say no to.

"I don't know what more you can find out that the United States Government hasn't, but who am I to say no to help," I shrugged. It seemed like centuries since I'd felt even a small glimmer of hope for receiving any answers at all.

Kai smiled again, revealing his kind spirit. I was starting to feel lucky that this bizarre situation was happening. Even if Kai was not able to discover *any* information, I was thrilled to have met this fascinating man.

"Great! Then it's settled. After the meeting we can discuss what should happen next."

I nodded in response knowing his intentions were good, as he motioned for us to head down the hall. We went toward the conference room that we passed on our way to the nursery earlier. As I walked in front of Kai, I felt for the second time that afternoon, his hand on the small of my back as if it had never left.

Chapter Ten

KAI

I pulled her in, and without even realizing what I was doing, I was holding her there in my arms. Her delicate body pressed against me, and her sweet floral perfume engulfed my senses. As I breathed her in, I would be lying if I said I wanted this to end. I knew that this wasn't professional and that it went against every protocol imaginable, but truthfully, I didn't care. Emily was hurting and holding her was the first and only option I could come up with. When the time came, I would have to help her get some answers. But for now, what I needed was to get this meeting with Alex over and done with.

As we started down the hall, I placed my hand again on her lower back to guide her to the conference room. When my hand settled there, I could feel Emily relax and ease into my touch. To hell with protocol!

Before we entered the room, I leaned down to Emily and whispered in her ear, "Don't worry, I won't mention any of this to Alex, unless you want me to."

She turned around, this time she placed a hand on my chest as if to stop me. I was relaxed and in her control. She took a step back and looked up at me with those beautiful honey eyes and spoke in the softest whisper. "Thank you for that. I don't really tell this to anyone, but given the situation, I may have to reveal this to Alex as well. You've been so helpful, and I'm incredibly grateful for your kindness."

The pureness of her words melted my strong-man exterior. Too bad kissing constituents in the State Building was definitely against protocol. I smiled instead and opened the door to Alex. Opening the door to a man that I knew could and would complicate whatever feelings were igniting within me.

Alex grinned as we entered; there was not enough air in the room to accommodate his inflated ego. He knew the effect he had on women and fearlessly used it to his advantage. I looked at Emily and could see that she was appreciating his eyes locked on her. I knew Alex was aware that this was not the woman he had me searching for. I knew with every mistrustful cell in my body, that he was gearing-up to get to know Emily and add her to his collection. If I had anything to do with it, that would not become an option.

Chapter Eleven

EMILY

As the heavy door to the conference room opened, there was Alex front and center eagerly waiting for us. He stood immediately with one of the most beautiful smiles I had ever witnessed. A pair of brown eyes that seemed to grow darker as the moments passed, followed me as I entered the room. His smile had grown deeper, triumphant.

I knew that smiles didn't always indicate joy and pleasantries; I could recall a few myself at the most inappropriate times in my life. Some people may shed tears when happy, and smile when they are not. However, this one was without a doubt, a smile formed purely by need. There was a slight hint of arrogance settled beneath the lines of his perfect lips.

The warmth of Kai's hand was still on my lower back, but before I knew it, the warmth had slipped away, falling to his side. Kai pulled my chair out for me, and I was seated in a plush tan leather conference chair. Kai sat down next to me, and Alex sat directly in front of us.

Without waiting another minute, Kai began the meeting with purpose. "Alex, I know you have questions for Emily. And Emily, if you could answer these questions to the best of your ability, that would be great. If at any time you would like to end the meeting, just say the word and we'll be finished, and I'll take you and Tillie home."

Kai never once let his eyes leave my gaze. He spoke with such poise and determination that my attention was completely his. I almost forgot Alex was in the room until he cleared his throat.

The senator spoke with authority and charm, "Emily, I want you to know I have your best interest in mind today, and now that I've seen you, I will admit I find it difficult to place you." He was precise and to the point and it wasn't like he had asked a question, so I didn't know if I should respond or wait for him to continue, which he did before I had a chance to figure him out.

"Emily, I want to give you a little bit of background on the situation and explain this strange predicament." He repositioned himself in the chair and continued. "A little over three years ago I was awaiting the election results. I had every intention of remaining professional during the festivities. I was ahead in the polls, and I let the excitement get the best of me one night."

His gaze trailed off as if recalling a distant memory. I recognized a look of regret or was it just plain misery in his eyes, and it felt all too familiar. I was surprised at my urge to comfort him and touch his muscular arm tightly settled beneath his tailored suit.

He continued with his memory. "Well, it was the night the results were announced. My team threw me a party to celebrate and wait for the final count. I can recall receiving drink after drink from some of the campaign workers." He looked over to Kai with a blank expression. "Well, I reached the point where I couldn't even see who was handing me what. I do remember when the results were posted, however, and hearing the crowd cheer my name as I won the seat."

He cleared his throat and continued. "I can recall seeing her across the room, slowly making her way over to me. She had her eye on the target, and I was the prize. It was all a blur for the rest of the evening, so much so that I never even caught her name. I know her face though; I see it every night before I go to bed now. And you, Emily, are not the face I see."

As Alex finished his account of the evening, I truly felt sorry for the man. He was telling me everything I already knew. I knew Alex wasn't Tillie's father. I'd agreed to come today to meet the infamous Alex Greyson, the man that most of the women I knew would invariably swoon over. The tabloids loved to gossip about his latest sexcapade. I selfishly wanted to meet the man for myself and to see him up close and in the flesh. My greedy reasons had probably given Alex the false hope that I was the woman, and I couldn't help but feel responsible for some of the disappointment resting in his eyes.

"Mr. Greyson, I'm truly sorry that I'm not who you are looking for. I'm sorry you weren't able to get the answers you were hoping to get today." I could find no other words of comfort to give him and that I felt he needed. He looked at me with a certain gentleness and warmth. As I returned the look, I saw something familiar I hadn't noticed earlier. His expression shared the same concern that Evan would always give me whenever something was bothering him. Alex was no Evan … not by a long shot, but there were eerie similarities in those eyes.

Caught in the moment, I forgot Kai was in the room. It wasn't until I felt his hand brush against mine, as he slid some papers in front of me, that I turned and looked up into the eyes I had so effortlessly grown fond of.

"Emily, we have a non-disclosure document we would like you to sign. The three of us in this room are the only ones that know of Alex's involvement with this mystery woman. It appears as though this woman knew what she was after that night and succeeded when she gave birth to Alex's child."

Kai glanced at Alex, and they both gave a slight nod. It was obvious their years of friendship gave them an advantage of knowing each other's thoughts. He continued, "Alex received an anonymous letter back in April stating that unless we resign and pay … whoever they are, two million dollars to an offshore account, they would release images to the public and claim this woman was raped and given a gag order."

Kai gave me a serious look and I now knew there was more to this situation than I believed before meeting with them here today. I looked back at Alex just in time to see the desperation form on his face.

"I had no idea this was such a serious meeting today, of course I'll sign. To be honest, I thought it was a strange meeting in general, but now that I know some of the background, I see the severity." I was sure they could see how tense and confused this made me.

Kai was reading me like an open book. He instantly reached for my hand as I was fidgeting the pen. "Emily, we're both incredibly grateful that you've been so understanding with this entire ordeal. Believe me, when I met you this morning, I thought we would get this whole thing settled once and for all. But now after hearing *your* story, I have more questions than ever."

He grimaced and looked down as soon as he spoke the words and I knew right away that Kai regretted saying them.

Alex perked up. "I'm sorry, but am I missing something? I know you both had the extra time during the drive and what not, but I'd like to be in the loop with everything you've discussed involving the matter."

Kai let out a heavy sigh and looked at me with obvious remorse. "Alex, it meant nothing. I just meant that this whole situation has me questioning everything. Nothing here makes sense."

I grabbed Kai's arm and gave him a reassuring smile. Instinctively, I trusted Alex and wanted to give him what peace I could. "Alex, I myself have a rather interesting story when it comes to becoming a parent. My husband, Evan, was in the military training for special ops. However, he went missing before my daughter was born."

As if a bomb just went off, Alex's eyes bulged, and he jerked his head back. I hated telling people my story for this very reason. I was grateful Kai didn't give me the usual look of shock. Kai's expression was warm and concerned. Not an ounce of pity flashed beneath the surface.

In such a short span of time, I found myself craving more time with Kai, and wanting to discover all the quirks that made him tick. I hadn't a clue that today would end up like this, but I was pleased that it did.

Alex was still staring at me, and I began to feel my cheeks flush. "Emily, now *I'm* finding the need to say sorry. I don't have the words to help you. But if I'd known prior, I wouldn't have brought you here today and questioned you like this." Even though his eyes held pity, his words were warm and appreciated.

"There was no way you could have known. Everything revolving around my husband and his disappearance has been hush hush. I'm not exaggerating when I say I've had no answers given to me. I tried for months, which unfortunately now has turned to years. They ended up simply writing it off and seem to have given up on him."

I knew I would cry, dammit. I hoped I wouldn't, but I knew I would. I hadn't spoken of Evan in some time, and it felt as fresh today as it had almost three years ago. As soon as I began, Kai slid me the box of tissues from the center of the table. I could feel their eyes on me. Oh, how I wished I had had a tougher skin!

Kai turned toward me in his seat. "Emily ... please, I'm speaking for both of us when I say that we want to help you get answers. We're the ones who brought you here and had you rehash all of this. But Alex here couldn't be a better contact for you to get some answers." Kai had yet again delivered the hope I needed right then. In fact, it was both Kai *and* Alex that brought me hope, something that I had lost for so very long.

Chapter Twelve

KAI

I didn't care if Alex was upset with me for signing him up to help Emily. He got me into this uncomfortable position to begin with. I told Alex earlier this was a bad idea. We both knew Emily was not the woman in question … yet here we were.

Seeing Emily break down in that meeting room had to have been one of the most heart-wrenching sights I have had to witness to date. It took everything in me to not reach out and hold her and to hopefully remove a small fraction of her pain. Gradually, instinct took over and I found myself rubbing her back.

I slowly looked up to see Alex giving me a strange look. He seriously could not be upset with me. I had every reason to help Emily. I was currently responsible for bringing this hurt back to the surface. Alex could, at the very least, use his connections and help Emily in any way he could.

As I looked into her eyes, I saw the light that so easily captivated me, returning. In my time as a police officer, I had always made it a point to never let my emotions get the best of me. I never let a charming woman control my actions. However, I knew Emily needed help, and I knew I was the one to do it. I looked over at Alex, and saw his smug grin widen as he watched Emily and me interact.

"Alex, do you have any more questions for Emily?" I gave him a stare hoping he would get the hint that we needed to be done for the day.

Alex, of course, did not catch on in the slightest. Or maybe he chose not to. "Well, I don't have any more questions, but I do want to mention that I have connections all over. And I already have a few team members in mind that I can give a call to as early as today to hopefully get some information for you."

Alex, now looking at Emily, smiled his million-dollar smile and basked in the potential of becoming Emily's knight in shining armor, which for some odd reason I despised the idea of. Although Alex was attempting to be comforting, Emily now seemed to have a newfound sense of hope in Alex and his connections. I wondered if this could blow up in our faces. As much as I wanted Alex to be right and help Emily with her dilemma, I feared that either way it went ... Emily would get hurt. And that wasn't something I wanted to be a part of. I needed this meeting to end.

She was now gawking at Alex as though he had given her the world. "Alex, that is too kind. I'm not going to lie, I want to be the gracious girl here and say don't worry about me, but I will definitely take you up on your offer."

Her eyes were no longer wet with tears, but wide open and engulfed in everything that makes Alex ... Alex.

"Please, it's the least I could do. You came here today, fully knowing I was a fool to think you were the woman I was searching for, yet you showed up anyway."

Alex looked as though he thought Emily still held the answers to his problem. There was something lurking beneath his grin. What plan was he hatching?

Emily quickly responded. "With this document signed, I promise to not mention a word of this meeting to anyone. You have my complete silence. I don't know where we go from here, or what I did to deserve your kindness, but I'd like you both to know I appreciate this so much. I have more hope today than I've had in months, if not years."

Emily looked to Alex and then at me. She gave me a smile that lit up her entire face. She truly was the most beautiful woman I had ever had the good fortune of meeting.

I decided it was time to cut the meeting short, since there was nothing more to be done at that point. Anyway, I'm pretty sure it would not align with protocol to just sit there and stare at Emily all day!

"Emily, I'm sure we will be in contact soon, and I will personally fill you in on anything we uncover. Again, I'm sorry we brought you into all of this." I began shuffling the paperwork into my folder and glanced over at Alex for a brief moment. It was enough time to see him staring at Emily with the look he gets when he wants something. And typically, Alex gets what Alex wants.

Being his friend had its benefits, especially when it came to women ... there was never a shortage. I had learned something early on in my friendship with Alex, that women had a way of forgetting the fact that he had been on every tabloid the day before with another woman. Being his best friend, and practically bodyguard, meant I was always there beside him to pick up the pieces and help the last girl he hurt in the pursuit of his newest conquest. I know he'd hate me for thinking of him in this way, when the truth was, he was a great guy. Lost when it came to women and relationships, but a great guy, nonetheless. In the entire time I'd known him, he had had only two serious relationships, and he ended both of them before the women became too attached.

While working for Alex had its perks, having a relationship for myself was not one of them. I was different from Alex; I was a commitment dater and hated the thought of having a new girl in every city. Call me old fashioned, but I didn't like the idea that if I were off with multiple women, that my partner could be as well. Monogamy dating was nearly impossible with the amount of work I had to tackle on a daily basis for Alex.

My life revolved around Alex, and until this very moment I was okay with that. Alex giving that particular look to Emily had quickly changed my mind. I knew the time would come someday that I would be done living in the shadow of Alex's life. Did I think it would happen because of a woman? … hell no!

Emily was looking at Alex with such innocence, she was full of pure excitement that we might find her long lost husband. I knew from experience that anytime a case was covered up with no conclusion, you were better off not knowing the details. Still, Emily had every reason to know what had happened to her husband. However, for her sake, I hoped and prayed the answers she was looking for would not crush her completely. I'd never be able to forgive myself for uncovering more heartbreak in this poor woman's life. Raising a child on her own for the past three years must have been so tiring. I just wished I could have met Emily under different circumstances.

Emily stood and gathered her things. I met her at the door and opened it casually before catching a glance at Alex once again. He was still staring at her, but this time he was appreciating her every curve.

Standing in the doorway, I said to Alex, "I'll call you on my way back from dropping Emily off. Call Ryan and tell him it's a no and that I'll email him tonight with more intel."

Alex hated relaying messages and always demanded it was beneath him to be the middleman. Knowing this I chuckled underneath my breath and watched him give me an annoyed glare as he nodded.

"Of course, drive safe you two. Emily, would you mind if I gave you a call later to discuss things in more detail with you personally?" He gave her his sly smile, and Emily fell right where he hoped. Under his spell. I knew he was doing this to get under my skin just by the smirk he threw my way.

"Yeah, of course that's fine. Here's my personal cell." She leaned down and scribbled her number on a small yellow post-it.

Alex was appreciating the view, and I was getting more annoyed each passing moment. Emily handed the number over to him, and he held her hand in his ... longer than necessary.

"Thank you," he said as he looked into her eyes. "Emily, I give you my word that I will personally get you the answers you deserve."

I couldn't tell if he was trying to be diplomatic or flirty. But whichever it was, Emily appreciated it and fell for his charm yet again. I moved quickly to exit the room and Emily followed me. I wish I could get inside her head to see if she truly fell for the Alex Greyson act.

Chapter Thirteen

EMILY

Have I woken in the twilight zone? Meeting two men in one day? What woman wouldn't be thrilled to have two gorgeous men looking at them the way Alex and Kai had been looking at me? I would pinch myself if it would help me grasp this new reality.

For years I thought this was my fight and my fight alone. A year into my growing questions, I began to accept the fact that I would never get the answers I sought when it came to Evan's disappearance. A few days ago, I knew it was odd that an unmarked car had been parked across from my house, but never did I think it would result in this. Sure, it crossed my mind that it may have to do with Evan; I always think the unusual revolves around Evan, since it typically did.

Here I was walking down this quiet empty hallway with Kai by my side, wishing he would shed some light on his stoic expression. I was losing the sense of calm he once provided. His eyes met mine and again I felt the kindness through them.

"I'm sorry that was such a waste of your time. I somehow knew it would be, but that's Alex for ya." He wedged the contract we had just signed into his underarm. He was fidgeting with his thumbs again and I could feel the angst growing in him. He slowed his pace when I stopped and nearly grabbed him.

"Are you kidding me? Kai, this is the best hope I've had in years! You may see this meeting as a waste of time, but I see it as a silver lining. Twenty-four hours ago, I never would have thought that today I might be one step closer to some kind of resolution to Evan's disappearance. So, no … This is a huge victory. This, in no way, was a waste of my time!"

I tried to keep my voice from breaking and not show any more sign of weakness. I didn't mean to get worked up, but how could he think I would see this as a waste of time … that was unless *he* did, in which case I had misunderstood Kai this entire day. As we walked down the hall toward the nursery, I tried to shake the feeling Kai could sense my unease.

"Emily, you really have to know I want to help you find answers. Really, it's all I can think about doing now. I just never want to give anyone false hope, and you seem like a really good soul. You've clearly been screwed over by the people in charge of keeping your husband safe, but I'm not sure at this point what I, or Alex even, can uncover for you. This isn't typically one of our tasks." His voice was purely honest and full of genuine concern.

"Well Kai, I already know in my heart that this is a longshot, but you have to understand that for someone who has literally nothing to work with, this is everything to me. Anything at this point is more than I've ever had. Please understand, I've actually resigned myself to the fact that I'll never have answers to the hundreds of questions involving my husband's disappearance."

There was a softness to his eyes and without a moment to comprehend what was happening, he put his arms around me and pulled me into his solid, comforting embrace. Everything about this man was enticing to me. His arms, his smile, his eyes, his towering stature, and even his serious demeanor. I was appreciative of his simple gesture and yet despite the heaviness of the situation, my stomach fluttered at the feeling of my body pressed against his. His scent as I reveled in his warm embrace was dizzying. His touch made the empty hallway warmer somehow and made the seriousness of my plight less daunting. It was one of those hugs that tells you right down to your core that everything was going to be okay.

Kai had begun to pull back but showed no sign of letting go. He started to gently rub my arms with his thumbs and stared into my eyes with a connection that women only dream about. For a moment I thought I saw something in his eyes that I had only seen one other time in my life. He stepped back yet kept an arm gently around my shoulder as we made our way into the daycare center.

While we loaded Tillie into the car, I felt an air of excitement that was entirely new to me. I never had someone with me to help with Tillie, other than my parents. It was me, myself and I since day one. Watching Kai laugh and make Tillie giggle as he buckled her into the car seat was totally unfamiliar, yet welcoming, almost like foreplay. I was well aware of my emotions, and even though I tried to keep them in check, I found myself fantasizing about what it would be like to have someone like Kai as a partner. His broad shoulders and toned upper body definitely proved to be useful in wrangling a wild toddler, and Tillie seemed to like his goofy side as well. As he finished the challenging task of getting my toddler buckled and ready to go, he turned to me, only to catch me staring at him with a most definite awestruck gaze.

"Am I doing this right? Sorry, I've helped my sister with her kids for years and it's become a habit of sorts." He looked a little embarrassed as if he had just slipped up and I would be upset with the gesture.

"No, don't worry about it! I'm grateful for the help. I never get the luxury of watching someone else tackle the task. You continue to amaze me with your kindness Kai. Thank you!" I quickly replied as I grazed my hand on his forearm.

His eyes lit and his cheeks became flushed. *So that was how you made a grown man blush ... noted.* After I checked Tillie and made sure we were good to go, I situated myself in the passenger seat. Kai was still smiling as we left the parking lot, and I felt almost giddy knowing we had over an hour's ride ahead of us. More if we hit traffic ... please Lord, let there be traffic.

Chapter Fourteen

KAI

Something was definitely in the air and to be honest, whatever it was, I liked it. Emily was increasingly the star lead of my thoughts this afternoon. I found myself desiring to know more about this strong, determined woman. I was given the task to discover answers about her husband's strange disappearance and I knew just where to begin and fortunately who to contact to get intel. However, in the back of my mind I knew I'd never be able to break the news to Emily if it were to come to that. After three years, she likely already had an idea it could be bad news, but no matter what the outcome, Emily deserved answers.

Before the silence became uncomfortable, I looked in the rearview to see that Tillie had fallen asleep. "Looks like someone played a little too hard on the playground," I whispered, as Emily glanced back to see Tillie already fast asleep.

"Oh yeah, ever since she was a baby, car rides always knocked her out. It's both a blessing and a curse," she laughed. "When Tillie was a newborn, I had no idea what I was doing, and she'd cry almost daily around a certain time each night. One night I had tried everything and needed some relief, so I remembered reading somewhere that some babies like the feel of a car ride and that it helped them calm down. Sure enough, thirty seconds into the ride she was out. I can't even begin to count how many times I had to resort to driving around town to get some quiet time for myself."

Emily looked over to me and I could feel the world fall away in her eyes, I could envision a world where she didn't have to face parenting alone, where she had someone to share the journey of raising a child.

"Well, I'm no expert, but from the looks of it you've done a pretty great job raising Tillie. Brenda at childcare said she did great. My sister Allison has support from my whole family and a-work-from-home-husband and boy does she let me know any chance she gets just how easy I have it living the bachelor life."

I laughed inside because my sister liked to harp on me for being thirty-two and single. It wasn't that I didn't want to settle down and find someone, I just honestly hadn't had the time. My life revolved around my job ... and Alex's life of course.

Emily was giving me a look that could melt any man's cold exterior. "So, tell me, what's the issue?" she blurted out then touched her fingers to her mouth as if she hadn't meant to say it aloud.

"Issue? What do you mean, *what's the issue?*" I may have sounded a tad defensive, but I was curious to know what she was referring to. She stumbled for a minute and felt my heart rate increase.

"Issue. You know, like why are you still living the bachelor life? Some men's issue is commitment, some men love to go out because they love the single life, or some just don't like the thought of being tied down to one woman. So, what's your tick Mr. Taylor?" She peered over at me with her questioning eyes and sarcastic lips. I hadn't expected *this* conversation with Emily, but I needed to answer her, nonetheless.

"Well, if I'm being honest, I think it all boils down to my career."

She made a face, one that was to be expected. "Oh, you're one of those," she joked.

"Hey, you don't know the whole story. Alex is my best friend, and we've known each other since high school. So of course, when he asked me to lead his personal security, I quit the force and did whatever I could to keep him safe. And truthfully never looked back."

I could see the wheels turning in her head as she looked at me. "Okay, you're right, I didn't know you two had known each other for so long. That's very honorable of you to drop your career and well, everything for a friend. Has it been easy?"

I wasn't sure how to answer that. Of course, it was difficult at times, and stressful for certain. But emotionally, was it easy to see my friend be so successful while I hide in the shadows? Not exactly. However, I didn't think Emily was looking for *that* conversation.

"Well, it's stressful, if that's what you're asking."

Emily shook her head. Maybe she *was* looking for something more in-depth, but I wasn't quite sure.

"Not stress-wise," she continued. "I'm almost sure that's a given. Um … easy, like always watching Alex, and being his go-to for literally everything." She pointed to herself as she said, *everything*. She must have gathered pretty quickly that I did all of Alex's dirty work. Not that I would consider finding Emily dirty work.

"Oh, the stories I could tell." I laughed, trying to change the subject.

Emily was smarter than that and could see through my attempt to avoid having to answer. "I can only imagine the stories. I don't doubt you could write a bestseller from the things you've seen while working for the senator."

I appreciated a woman that didn't keep digging when it was obviously not an easy subject to talk about.

She smiled. "Ok, hit me with the best story you've got. I would love a good Alex Greyson tale." I may have stared at her smile a bit longer than necessary.

I didn't know if I should tell her a *funny Alex* story, or an *Alex is not someone you would want to pursue* story? I decided to tell her about the time Alex threw a party in college. It was the first time I had to bail him out of something and save his ass from going into the back of a cop car. Alex would have lost his scholarship, so I took the heat for his reckless night of celebrating. That was the first of many bailouts, and it had become a pattern to this day.

Once I finished my saga, I felt her eyes on me as I sat in traffic and pretended to be checking my blind spot.

There was finally a soft whisper from her lips. "Kai, you know Alex is a big boy, right? He's a senator for chrissake. He can take the heat once in a while. He probably *should* take the heat once in a while"

Emily was just trying to be kind and lighten the conversation, but she also needed to know our dynamic. "Unfortunately, you're wrong. Yes, Alex is a grown man, well, let's be real ... man-child," I added with a laugh. "But my whole job is to protect him, and sadly, at times that means taking the heat for the drunk girl leaving his hotel room in the early morning hours."

I really wished I hadn't said that last part. I didn't want to be the one to sour Alex's character to her, even if I did want to have her all to myself. "Sorry Emily, I didn't mean to lay that bit of information on you, that was unprofessional. Don't get me wrong, Alex is a good guy. He may not be ready or willing to settle down just yet, but this whole possibility of having a baby out there has really made him change his ways. It's been weeks since he's gone out and made a scene."

I could feel the awkward silence rising and saw Emily 's mouth scrunch to the side, "Well, I'm sure he has his reasons, but as a friend, he shouldn't be okay with letting you take the blame for everything. It's too bad you have to be the one to take the punches."

She looked out the window probably to avoid looking at me. I placed my hand on the center console right next to her small, slender hand. I could feel its warmth so close to mine. It took everything in me to not reach out, touch it, claim it.

"It hasn't always been this way between Alex and me," I explained. "He used to be a pretty clean-cut guy. He grew up in a rough home, so he worked hard in high school? to get this massive scholarship to the university. If Alex were to get in any sort of trouble, his scholarship would 've been jeopardized."

Emily glanced toward me now with a softer expression. Her kind eyes spoke of the years she had lived.

"I can understand as a friend wanting the best for him, but please don't tell me you've been covering for him since high school?"

She stared at me now and I couldn't look away. "Guilty. My father is a retired military sergeant turned police chief, and it was a whole lot easier for *me* to get out of things than it would have been for Alex." I hoped she would understand that I really just wanted to help a friend out all these years.

"So that's where your seriousness comes from!" She said playfully, and gently placed her soft, slender hand on my forearm. I didn't want her to ever take it away.

Her honey speckled brown eyes looked at me now with an unresolved hope. "Well, your dad had to have known all those years you weren't the one doing those crazy mishaps."

"I'm sure he did, but he knew better than to question my motives for helping a friend. He knew the upbringing Alex had." I hoped my response would make sense to her. My father and I might not have had the best relationship, but we knew each other enough to know when our actions spoke louder than words.

"I'm sorry your friendship with Alex hasn't been easy. It takes a good man to put others before himself," she said just louder than a whisper.

We were stalled in early rush hour traffic and Emily's eyes were mine once again. There was no chance I was looking away. That was until the excessive honking from the Corolla behind us forced me to break our gaze.

Chapter Fifteen

EMILY

Damn that Corolla for ruining our moment. In another world, I could have sworn Kai wanted to lean down and kiss me. I didn't actually believe he would, but if I were being honest with myself, at that moment I didn't know if I would have been able to protest. I really didn't know what came over me because reaching out and touching Kai's arm wasn't something I would have normally done. I hadn't even been with another man since Evan. Now that my hand was on his arm, I very well couldn't just remove it so abruptly. Out of the corner of my eye, I could see Kai looking down at my hand, and a very subtle grin formed on his supple lips. I could see him fidgeting in his seat. It was almost as if he were moving his forearm on the middle console to be closer to me. I couldn't help but enjoy the new development growing between us.

"Would you like me to pull over, and we can grab something to eat? If we stay on the freeway now, we're probably looking at another one to two-hour standstill," Kai asked as he glanced in my direction.

"Yeah, that sounds great. I could definitely eat something right now." I gave his arm a little squeeze and softly removed my hand from its place. His eyes lit up, and for a brief moment I saw the desire in his eyes yet again.

"Great! How does a burger sound?" He asked with a smile the size of Texas.

Yay! A man after my own heart.

"A burger sounds perfect. Do you want to know something funny? I gave up fast food for the longest time, but every once in a while, on those late-night drives getting Tillie to sleep, I would get a burger and a shake just to dip my bread into."

Kai made the same face most do when I tell them about my unconventional dipping procedure. Disgusted, yet curious.

"Okay, okay, I know what you're thinking, but you have to give it a try before you write it off," I laughed.

"I'm not saying you're gross, but you're gross! That sounds like something you throw up, not voluntarily create! I've heard of people dipping their fries into a shake, but the bread … where did you even come up with something like that?"

He smiled at me now, and I hated that my answer might sour our silly mood. "Actually, Evan used to do it, and I was always disgusted by it. But once he went missing, it sort of became a fun way to keep his silly side around. And now I love it. Tillie does it too. It's … It's just become this fun thing we do."

In just a single day, it had become so easy talking to Kai about Evan and the things we shared. My life rarely felt empty because I had preserved Evan's memory so well, and my sweet wild child Tillie kept me going. But spending today with Kai and sharing these bittersweet memories with him made me see what I had been missing these past few years.

From the way Kai was looking at me now, I could tell my response had not soured the mood. If anything, his expression was filled with something like desire and even more interest. How could someone as kind as Kai be single?

"I think it's beautiful that you've kept him and his spirit alive through everything. I'll say it again, Tillie is incredibly lucky to have you as her mother." His gaze could move mountains.

He reached out his arm and placed it on my knee then gave it a gentle squeeze. "Now, what do you say we try this monstrosity of a treat?"

The twinkle in his eye was enough to make me go weak in the knees if I hadn't already been sitting down.

"Okay, you're on! Believe me, it may not be your thing at first, but I promise it will grow on you." I laughed as I glanced at my knee, feeling a heat imprint where his hand had been placed only a few seconds before.

"Oh Emily, I'm sure it will." He laughed as we pulled into a local burger shop.

Thankfully they had a drive-thru and we were able to keep Tillie from waking. After we ordered and found a place to park in the shade, I was eager to share this silly tradition with Kai. I could barely hold my excitement as we unwrapped our food and I got the shakes ready for dipping. I caught Kai watching me ever so intently.

"So serious, Miss Emily. This is quite the experiment. And quite cute how excited you are about this," he chuckled.

My cheeks felt warm like I was a schoolgirl hearing a compliment for the first time. "Kai, I can assure you, this is a very serious matter; I need to make a believer out of you." I smiled as I tore off the bun from the extra burger we bought for this very experiment. I'd only shared this silly ritual with a select few friends in my life, and now Kai was somehow one of them. I dipped the bun in the vanilla shake and slowly lifted it up ready for Kai to take from me. Instead of grabbing it, he put his lips to my fingers and ate the bite of dipped bun and licked his lips. He winced as if eating something tart. His warm wet lips grazed my fingers, and without giving it away that this casual act had lit a small fire in me, I just smiled and waited for his full reaction.

"Well, that *is* something for sure. And now I hate to be the bearer of bad news, Emily, but that's one of the most disgusting things I've ever tried!" He laughed as he tossed a fry in his mouth.

I'd never been one of those girls that romanticized scenarios in their heads, but I felt almost certain that this dynamic we shared could evolve into something great. Being here with Kai felt real, it felt right.

"Well, you just wait and see, it'll grow on you."

"Oh, I'm sure it will," he quickly replied.

I smiled now and stared right into his deep blue eyes. You could get lost in those eyes if you stayed long enough. His smile now reached those blue eyes, and the twinkle in them was enough for you to know he had a streak of mischief to him.

"I'd love to know what you're thinking. You have an interesting look on your face," I asked, hoping he would open up to me.

"Well, if you must know, I'm thinking I sure hope that we can stay friends. Even if I think your taste in food is questionable."

He laughed and gave me a movie star grin. I had to remember to breathe because that grin was making me lightheaded.

"Hey! Who said we're friends?" I breathed lightly, and instantly regretted making the joke as his smile instantly disappeared. Even though I was just playing with him in my attempt to be funny, I was not successful in getting the joke across. Seeing Kai's expression could make any girl fall to her knees and try to help the poor guy out. "You know I'm just kidding, right?"

His eyes widened and relief washed over his face. "Of course," he said as he shrugged and threw a fry into his mouth.

We chatted back and forth for a while as we both finished our food. Kai watched me every time I dipped my bun in the shake. And I laughed at the face he made almost every time it reached my lips.

"We should probably get back on the road soon, so I can get you home at a decent hour," he said as he shoved the last bite of his burger into his mouth.

"Yeah, of course. Let me just throw this in the trash so it doesn't make the entire car smell like fast food." As I reached for the bag of leftover trash, Kai reached for it as well, and his fingers gently stroked the top of my hand. If I couldn't admit the chemistry before, our touch *this* time sent a rush of electricity through me that I couldn't deny. And the look on Kai's face, sure as hell, told me he felt it too. We locked eyes as if searching for answers, and then he quickly moved his hand.

"No, let me get it. You stay in the car with Tillie." He grabbed the bag and quietly exited the car.

I looked in the rear-view mirror and saw Tillie still passed out and cozy as ever. "I have a feeling we're going to have our hands full with this new development Miss Tillie," I sighed as I watched Kai return.

We drove for the next hour, and our conversations were meaningful and entertaining. Tillie woke up for the last half hour and Kai found a station of kid songs to entertain her. Everything felt so natural and so good. My heart became heavy the moment we pulled up into my driveway. Even though today had been one of the best days I'd had in a long time, I knew it was time to check back into reality, time to return to our normal, and I needed to say the words that had been floating in my mind the entire afternoon.

"Well, I can't thank you enough for today, Kai. It turned out to be quite the adventure. Thanks for driving and then entertaining Tillie. You must be a great uncle". I found it hard to look him squarely in the face. "I know you and Alex are busy men, so I would understand if I don't hear from you again."

I hated saying it, but I couldn't help but feel that my issues were mere bleeps on their radar, and I didn't want them feeling like they owed me any favors.

However, as soon as I said it, I wished I hadn't. Kai's face said it all. He was hurt that I thought of him in this way.

Chapter Sixteen

KAI

Is that what she thought? That she would not be hearing from me again? She had to see the way I had been looking at her all day. And that touch, that touch we shared could wake the dead. I knew she felt it too, and I would be damned if I let this girl slip away just like that. I made a promise, and I never backed out of a promise. My interest had been piqued and I needed to find the truth.

"Emily, I realize you don't know me very well, but when I give someone my word and make them a promise, I don't back out, and I have no plans to start now."

Emily's eyes were now fixed on me and my … mouth. I might be overthinking, but that was the second time today I'd caught her looking at me like this, and it excited me more than I cared to admit.

"Kai, I don't think you're the type to say something and not do it. That's the exact opposite of what I think of you. Heck, I've only known you for a day, and I would bet a month's pay you're one the of the good ones. I just also know that my issues have nothing to do with you or Alex. It was just some strange coincidence that our paths even crossed at all. Now don't get me wrong–"

"Emily! Emily look at me," I repeat, needing her to hear me out. "Emily, okay, first off, don't call this predicament an issue. You and I both know it's much more than that. Alex and I find this entire thing appalling! And you deserve answers! As a politician, Alex has the clearance to get you those answers."

I put my hand on the center console right next to hers. It took everything in me to stop from grabbing her and pulling her in for another comforting embrace. Emily looked so fragile, yet I knew down to my core how incredibly strong she was and would continue to be. She began to shuffle now, and I wondered if she knew just how much I wanted to reach out and touch her. She smiled at me and nodded her head as she opened her car door.

"Let me walk you in and help you get settled," I whispered as I unbuckled my seat belt.

"Okay, that would be great. I'll never be able to repay you two for your help. I hope you know how truly appreciative I am that you came into my life today."

I could not believe how lucky I was to meet this incredible woman. I opened the car door for her and started helping her with Tillie's things, then followed her to the front door.

"I think that's everything from the car. If I find anything, I know where to find you."

"Oh, I'm sure you do," she laughed as she began to set Tillie down and she ran to her toys in the corner of the living room.

Before she had a chance to close the door I blurted, "Can I have your number?" Her eyes had a sparkle. "For business purposes of course … so I can let you know as soon as I get more information for you."

"Of course, let me get some paper and write it down for you."

She turned and grabbed a pen and paper from the nearby desk and scribbled her number down for me. She reached out and handed the paper to me, and as I took it from her, she went in for a hug. Unable to resist, I hugged her closely in return. As my arms wrapped around her and her face was buried in my chest, I heard a small cry.

"Kai, I can't begin to explain to you how good it feels for someone to help me, someone to show me they care. It's been so long since I've had even a glimmer of hope. I'm not so naive to think it couldn't be horrible news, but either way I need to know … I'm so sorry for crying again."

She looked up with tears in her eyes. One tear started down her soft cheek and I instinctively caught the tear on my thumb. Being her comfort and support came as natural to me as protecting Alex from gunfire would be.

"Emily, please don't apologize. I can't pretend to understand what you've gone through over the years with so many missing pieces. I want to be there for you and help any way I can."

I realized we were still holding each other when Tillie made her way to us. She tugged on Emily's dress, pulling us from our trance. "Well, I should get going, I have lots of calls to make. Thank you for the interesting day. It was incredible meeting you, Emily, and you too little Miss Tillie." I tugged on Tillie's dress and gave her little hand a shake making her laugh and bringing another beautiful smile to Emily's face.

"The pleasure is all mine. Thanks again for everything. Hope to hear from you soon. Please drive safe."

She waved as I turned and headed down the steps to my now lonely SUV. I looked back one last time to see both of them smiling and waving as I got to my car. I couldn't help but hope I'd be seeing more of them very soon. As I got to my car and started the engine, I reached for my phone for the first time since our meeting with Alex. There was a text from him.

ALEX- *That girl is hiding something, and she thinks she already has you wrapped around her finger. Call me when you're alone.*

My heart raced. What could Alex be thinking? Everything about Emily was the real thing. I was the ex-cop for chrissake. I was the one who had a good read on people. I would eventually have to give him a call, but I knew who to call first and it was not Alex.

I tapped the name on my screen. The name that I rarely made a point to contact, my father. Within moments he answered with his commanding tone.

"Well look who's calling their old man! What drama has that friend of yours pulled you into this time?" he said as he laughed into the phone. I cringed at the tone of his voice, making me regret ever calling him. In a split second I was seventeen again and getting scolded for my choice in friends.

"Why do you have to assume it's always about Alex?" I asked, sounding annoyed.

"Answer me this, Kai. Am I wrong to assume this call will circle back to Alex?"

I hated that my father knew my calling would be because of an Alex issue. He was right, and he knew it. Over the past few years, I only called when I needed something. Most of the time our only interaction would be when I'd call my mom and my mother would tell me to say hello to him from across the room. I wouldn't lie to him but we both knew our relationship was rocky.

"You're not entirely wrong, but you're not right either. Yes, what I'm about to ask started from an Alex issue, but now it would be a personal favor at this point."

I knew I'd better phrase this carefully, I always made it a point not to share too much with my father. His military background always had a way of slipping into our conversations. He was a master at getting the information out of me that he needed.

"What is it, Kai? What favor could your old man help you with?" For once my father sounded sincere.

"I can't give you *all* the information because it's confidential, but right now I'm looking for a missing person. Don't have much to go on except his name, plus I know he was in the military but appeared to just vanish."

I looked over the notes I had made on the back of the contract Emily signed earlier. My father cleared his throat, and I could sense the shift in conversation.

"Who is this person to you? Did you know this soldier?" he asked, sounding concerned.

"No, not personally, it's more of a friend of a friend matter," I answered, hoping my father would not try to pry more information from me.

My father let out a huge sigh. "Is there a woman involved in all of this?" he asked, sounding smug as hell.

"Why would you assume there was a woman involved?" I asked.

"Because I only hear from you a couple times a year, and this is the first time you've asked me to look into something like this. We may not be close, Kai, but I can hear it in your voice that this is something different."

I couldn't tell him the details of Emily's situation. That was her story and hers to tell. Yet, I knew if my father were to uncover anything, he would need to know at least the basics.

"Yes, there is a woman involved, and yes, it circles back to Alex."

My father let out a low growl, and I couldn't quite pinpoint where he was taking this.

"So, tell me, how does this circle back to Alex? I'm guessing *that* may be the missing puzzle piece to this very cryptic conversation."

I took a deep breath and knew I had to tell him about Alex's dilemma.

"I guess if I need your help in this, I will have to tell you how it started." I went on to tell my father all about the threatening email Alex received and how I ended up on Emily's doorstep just this morning. I told him all about the devastating uncertainty this poor woman has had to endure because the government wouldn't tell her anything regarding her husband's disappearance.

"This all developed this morning?" The shock in his voice was almost comical.

"Yes, this all happened this morning. I've been tracking her for about a week now and noticed this morning she was on to me, so I made my move before she got too concerned. Are you going to help me, or not?" I held my breath, waiting for his response.

"This all sounds a bit fishy, Kai. First off, she fits your description rather well. Second, she miraculously has this insane story of a missing husband when questioned. Let me guess, she is absolutely beautiful too?" he laughed. I did not find humor in the situation. My thumbs immediately started doing their number and I found my foot tapping along as well. Had I been played?

"It's not like that. You and I both know I'm a good judge of character." Sure, my father wasn't as invested in the whole nine yards as I was, but I couldn't help wondering if maybe he was picking up on something I missed.

"Well, Son, I will look into whatever it is you need, but you should understand not everyone is as honest as you. They could have alternative motives. You need to keep an open mind to the possibility that this woman could be lying to you."

I was annoyed, but he had a point. From here on out I knew how I needed to act towards Emily. Strictly professional.

Chapter Seventeen

EMILY

Once Kai had left, the rest of the evening kept me busy getting Tillie to bed at a decent hour since her routine had been severely messed with. I still had to complete an order of my raspberry almond scones. They needed to be delivered in the morning, and I had missed my opportunity earlier today to get the order done. Since baking was typically my mental escape, tonight was as good as gold. I needed every distraction possible. My thoughts were racing as I rolled out the scone dough, careful to not overwork it. I felt like I'd been running uphill on a treadmill all day long, and only until now could I really catch my breath. When Evan first went missing, I found it nearly impossible to say the words aloud. I wanted to avoid the words, pretend this wasn't my life. There were so many days my heart struggled to remember what my mind already knew... He was still missing, and I still had no answers. There are still moments when I find myself holding my breath. Today was the first time in years I felt a rush of air in my lungs.

The scones were now out of the oven and placed on the cooling rack waiting to be drizzled with their almond vanilla icing. My version of scones was light and fluffy, and full of buttery flavor, nothing fancy.

Evan was similar to scones, thick and tender with a soft center. I missed him more than words could ever really express. Today showed me there was still hope out there, I just needed to stay strong.

As I laid in my bed and replayed the day's events, I was in a state of disbelief over everything that had happened in those few short hours.

Meeting Kai made me give some serious thought to the fact that perhaps there could be more to Evan's story, and how I could possibly be tied to this insane debacle. The way Kai made me feel is what turned me into a tailspin this evening. Could I be ready to date again? I hated the thought as soon as it came. It wasn't in me to give up hope. I always thought there was more that they weren't telling me given how strange it all seemed. And why? What could be their reason?

I smiled, remembering my last conversation with Evan. The last time his arms wrapped around me. The last time he was mine. Evan and I, we never had to try with our relationship, our love was always so natural. From the very start I knew he was the one. He had a light about him that could fill a room. I loved the way he never knew a stranger. He could make friends with anyone, and frequently did. Everyone was drawn to his light. Evan would lend a hand to anyone that needed help. He had a bit of a savior complex that was never really fulfilled until he joined the military.

He was quickly recognized and put into Special Operations. I remembered the day he got the call confirming his deployment. His eyes were filled with eagerness and yet, there was a slight hint of fear. In all our years together, it was the only time I'd seen any trace of uncertainty in his eyes. Evan was so ready and so confident; we were all so proud of our very own hero. Our future was planned, and our lives together had been well mapped out. I was not ready to change them just like that. But from the moment he stepped onto that plane after we said our goodbyes, it felt as though I had already lost him. And then, only a few short weeks later it appeared that I had.

As I lay there in bed thinking of Evan and the numerous calls I'd made those first few months begging for even a tiny bit of information, my phone pinged and a text lit up the room. Who would be texting me at 10PM? Everyone who knew me knew I would likely be asleep by now. Squinting at the bright screen, my heart skipped, and I found myself wide awake.

KAI: *Hey Emily it's Kai. I just wanted to let you know I just got off the phone with someone who has agreed to use their connections to help us with your case. They have a military background and are pretty confident they will get some answers within a few days.*

I couldn't believe how quickly Kai got to working on this and was shocked he was actually getting some answers. He was not kidding when he said he wouldn't back down from a promise. I liked a man who kept his word. From the moment I first saw him, I knew there was a kindness about him. There were many other qualities I admired about Kai. His smile and strong physique were definitely high on that list.

EMILY: *WOW! Kai, I can't believe you already made some calls...you weren't joking when you said you keep your promises! THANK YOU!!!*

I couldn't help feeling giddy. I may actually have hope once again! And then, it suddenly dawned on me that it had been years since I had had any sort of late-night chat with another man. It also didn't escape my mind that Kai was just helping me find answers about my missing husband presumed dead for the past three years. But *presumed* was not enough. Not only for me, but my entire family needed answers, and it was starting to look like we might be getting somewhere. Another text came through and I jumped to read it.

KAI: *Of course, like I said before, I don't back down! I really meant it when I said I am happy to help. Emily, you deserve so much more than how you've been treated. Incredibly, it's taken this whole screwy situation to get you answers.*

I knew Kai was just being a nice guy, but I couldn't help but be captivated by him. He said all the right things to make me believe him, and I did. We chatted for a bit more about his drive and what he planned to do once he heard back from his source. A few minutes later I found myself barely able to keep my eyes open. I knew I needed to cut our conversation short if I were to ever wake before Tilly in the morning.

EMILY: *Kai, it's truly been an interesting day, I am so happy this whole problem came about, it was definitely meant to be. Please let me know if I can help in any way. Unfortunately, I'm falling asleep and need to get my beauty sleep haha, Goodnight.*

KAI: *I don't think you need sleep for that, but goodnight, Emily. I'll let you know if I hear anything tomorrow. Sweet dreams!*

I had been out of the dating game for a while now, but that was definitely flirting, right? Great! Now I'll never be able to go to sleep. All I could think about was what if this crazy dilemma was actually meant to happen. What if this was how I would finally get the answers to finally move on with my life? Kai had come at exactly the right moment. No matter what the reason was, I needed to keep my head and heart strong for whatever came from all of this. Not only for Tillie's sake, but for my own sanity.

I was able to sleep for only a few solid hours and was soon awakened by a curly haired toddler crying for my attention. As I sluggishly pulled her into bed with me for cuddles, my mind wandered to what it would be like having a partner in parenting.

For two and a half years as a single mom, I had only let myself envision this a few times, knowing how fast that thought could turn to self-pity. When I first became a mother, it wasn't easy seeing families everywhere I went. Happy families just living life together, going to the park, grocery shopping, all the simple things I thought I would have as a mother and wife. But those fantasies were taken from me the day Evan went missing.

"Okay, Honey, let's get you some breakfast. How does Cheerios sound?" I put the coffee on in slow motion, while Tilly played with her Cheerios. With mug in hand, I picked up my daily devotional. I needed this to get my head on straight. Again, routine was the only thing keeping my sanity all these years alone. As I opened the devotional book to read the insert for the day, I instantly noticed the subject for June 19 was *Opening Doors* and I couldn't help but wonder if it was somehow prophetic.

Today we had plans to go to my mother's as she lived only a short drive away from the bakery I needed to make my delivery to. It would be a welcome distraction from the craziness of yesterday. I knew how lucky I was to have my family around me. God knew how much I needed them when we first heard about Evan. At first thinking it was a temporary thing, I never in my wildest dreams thought he would be missing for this long with absolutely no further word. My mom stayed over to help me with Tillie as I'd spent many nights crying myself to sleep. She'll be ecstatic to hear that we could possibly get some news in the near future. At the same time, I didn't want to give her false hope if we came to another dead end.

And just like that my phone pinged.

KAI: *Good Morning, hope you slept well. Can I give you a call in a few to go over something?*

My heart could not take this. I was normally fairly good at reading people and their tones through a text, but this text was vague. Did Kai have good or bad news? I couldn't wait a few minutes! Screw patience at a time like this! I hit the little green button and called Kai within seconds of receiving his text. He answered just as fast.

"Well, hello there. That was fast! I didn't know if you'd still be asleep or not."

His voice sounded thick, and husky all rolled into one sweet package. But I didn't have time for pleasantries. I needed to know what his sources may have uncovered.

"I was barely awake, but now I'm fully awake thanks to your cryptic text." I tried to hide with a laugh my eagerness to hear what he might have for me.

He let out a deep breath, but I couldn't tell if it was a good sigh or a bad one.

"Sorry if my text sounded cryptic, but don't be worried. I haven't much news for you, only that my dad was able to locate Evan's last known location."

Wait, did he just say *dad*? What could his dad possibly find out about Evan?

"Kai, that's great news! We've never even gotten *that* far in the past three years. You may think it's nothing, but it's huge for us to even know that much!" I was almost shouting into the phone. His poor ears! "But wait, did you say *dad*? How would your dad be able to help?"

Kai sighed again, and I almost wished I hadn't asked.

"My father has some pretty special connections. I called him last night and asked for a few favors. He and I don't have the best relationship, but he knows I wouldn't ask unless it meant a lot to me. And this does Emily," he murmured in a low soothing voice. I tried to keep my thoughts in check, but I needed to know more.

If someone had told me my life would change so drastically in only a couple days, and that I would actually be relishing the process, I never would have believed them. But right now, my anxiety was through the roof. Anxious, not only about the news I was about to hear, but who was delivering it to me, and the lengths he had already gone for me. It was time to buckle up and hear the news Kai and his father had uncovered.

"Okay, I'm ready. I know it may not be anything of importance to the two of you, but it's important to me. And I'm ready," I sighed. I was more than ready to hear the first piece of real details surrounding my husband's disappearance.

The fact that Kai's father was able to find this information in just a few hours led me to believe that there *was* information out there that they had intentionally kept from me. For what reasons, I had no idea.

Kai cleared his throat, and I held my breath.

"So, I want you to know before I get into this, that the information we found was a bit strange. Please don't get hung up on any one single detail, because we may find more information later that contradicts." He paused, and I wanted to leap across the phone to get him to continue.

"I understand, Kai, just please say what you've found," I mumbled, trying to hold back my growing fear and anxiety.

Kai began again, using what I would believe was his cop voice.

"Emily, we found that Evan was part of a special task force sent out to Yemen. There was a group of six soldiers on their way to an undisclosed location to help locate a missing soldier. Upon their arrival they seem to have been ambushed. Now we know that Evan and three other soldiers made it back to the base safely after the ambush, but that's as far as my father has gotten for now."

He stuttered on the last part as if sorry he wasn't able to give me more. I struggled to reply right away. Damn Evan and his savior complex! "Kai, you have no idea how great it is to know anything at all. I can't thank you enough for looking into this and reaching out to your dad ... Can I see you?" What did I just ask him? I was shocked that I let my desperate plea slip.

His reply was quicker than I had time to second guess myself.

"Of course, anything you need. I can come over as soon as hmm ... 45 minutes. Does that work for you?"

His voice was full of emotion and infused with concern. Kai wanted to be there for me, and I wanted him within eyeshot.

"I had planned to take Tillie over to my mom's house today so I could make a delivery. She lives just across town. I can drop her off and meet you at the coffee shop I'm delivering to. Do you know the old coffee shop Steamy Beans on Fairgrove?" I asked, hoping to hear the same amount of enthusiasm to see me as I was to see him.

"Of course, I know the one. I was a cop, remember? We love our local coffee shops!" He laughed using his strong voice that lightened the mood of our earlier discussion.

He had a way of putting my heart at ease, and I was grateful to have his company for a few hours.

"How could I have forgotten, officer Kai? Please excuse my slip in memory." I laughed and couldn't remember the last time I'd spent any amount of time alone with another man since before Tillie was born. I was nervous, yet happy it would be with a man like Kai.

"Oh boy, I asked for that didn't I? Well, I can meet you there in a half hour, if that gives you enough time for everything?"

Obviously, he had never tried to pack up everything for a three-year-old to spend the day away.

"Let's make it an hour and a half, and I'll meet you there." I laughed as we said our goodbyes. I gulped down the last of my coffee, packaged the scones, and began to get Tillie ready for a day with Grandma.

I sent my mom a quick text to let her know the change of plans, and she straight away had a million questions. I hardly ever dropped Tillie off to meet with friends, and never with a man. No matter how many questions she asked, she would have to be patient and hear the news when I got there.

I got Tillie settled in the car, and we made our way across town. I wondered how much I should tell my parents about yesterday. And how much I should tell them of what I'd just learned about Evan's last whereabouts. And most importantly, all that Kai and Senator Greyson were doing for me.

Even before Evan went missing, my parents helped me cope whenever he was just away in general. They always supported Evan and his dream to join the military. As I got to their house, my mom was at the door greeting us both with open arms. She took Tilly's hand and gave me a questioning look.

"What's going on Emily? You never drop Tillie off. Want some company for your drop off?" she asked, with her famous look of concern.

It wasn't unusual for me to have off days when coping was too much, and I needed a few hours to myself. Ironically, today was not one of them. Yes, the information Kai and his father found was concerning and obviously sounded dangerous, but he made it back to the base alive … so, maybe there *was* hope? However, negative thoughts played dodgeball inside my head. Would we soon find out more news that would prove much worse?

"No, mom, it's nothing like that. I do have something to tell you that may be …shocking."

She gave me *the look* again, as if bracing for something big. I gave her the short version of yesterday's strange events and told her the news Kai and his father had given me this morning. Tillie had already made her way to the backyard and was playing with Bradley, my family's golden retriever. My mom sat down in her white padded lawn chair and seemed as though words had escaped her for once. But she soon found plenty of them.

"Wow, who could have predicted this? This is the craziest thing I've ever heard. Do you trust these people? What if they have alternative motives for helping you, Emily? You never know nowadays what people have up their sleeves."

I should have known my mother would think of the worst-case scenario. She had watched too many drama movies in her spare time. The strange thing was, I trusted Kai. The kindness in his eyes equaled his kind actions. Undeniably authentic and true.

"No, Mom, I don't think there is anything alternative to this. I met with Alex Greyson, and there's no way he, of all people, would be conning me. There'd be no point. I do believe this was all meant to be, and I'm going to accept the help. If I don't, I might never have another opportunity like this again. And also, Mom, what makes me know this is a godsend is the anniversary of Evan's disappearance next month. There are no coincidences in the world anymore. Please, just let me be excited for this."

I let it all out, my own insecurities with the situation, the annoying tone my mom had about it all. I was going to listen to my heart on this, and my heart was saying to trust it. Trust it all.

She smiled and patted my knee. "There's my daughter, nice to see you. It's been a while," she laughed as she looked me in the eyes.

"What do you mean?" Had she seen through my tough-sounding exterior?

"You've been living in silence for too long now, and it's nice to see you fighting again. You have a new light in your eyes, Emily. I truly hope this situation brings you a better life. Whether that be a door closing, or a door opening … or maybe both. I just want to see you happy again."

There it was again, *a door opening*. Twice in one day. Was it a sign? My mom always knew I couldn't go on forever living with what-ifs hanging over my head. I smiled at her confidence and her pure intentions.

I kissed Tillie goodbye and made my way to the coffee shop bursting with anticipation. I couldn't keep from wondering what we would even talk about. Kai didn't have any more information for me.

Could it be that I just wanted to see him, even if just for a few moments? If I was being honest with myself, I knew the answer, but still felt conflicted with it all. If my desire to see Kai meant I had given up hope on Evan, what did that say about me?

The coffee shop was only a half block away now and I questioned if I should turn around and back out now. That was until I saw Kai standing next to his SUV waiting for me. He wore a beautiful smile the moment he saw me pull into the parking lot. That smile was for me, and I had my answer. I was enamored.

His brown locks had a new touch of curl to them this morning, as if he was eager to get here as quickly as possible and had forgotten to do any brushing at all. I could see the confidence he possessed in the way he stood firmly against his car. His strong jawline and near perfect cheekbones were speckled with a bit of a five o' clock shadow. Everything about this man was inviting, he was built like he meant business, and I could only imagine he did. Now, what I needed was to be truthful with myself and figure out what the hell I was doing!

Chapter Eighteen

KAI

The second I saw Emily with her blonde hair falling to her shoulder in a loose braid and her honey speckled eyes locked on me, I forgot what I had just been asking myself. Almost. I'd been asking how could I even remotely begin to have feelings for a woman like Emily who had only been looking for her missing husband? A woman who I didn't know much more about other than that? As she made her way closer to me, it was as if we were two magnets needing to touch. Without thinking, I reached for her, I couldn't stop myself from holding her tight in my arms. We stayed there for mere moments, but it was a heaven's length of time. Just enough time to absorb every curve, every scent ... every inch.

When we each pulled back from our newly developed attraction, she smiled up at me. But behind those beautiful eyes I detected a hint of unease. Could she be feeling what I was feeling? Scared to be having such a strong attraction given the situation we were in? But as awkward and new as it was, I wouldn't change it for the world if it meant more time with Emily.

"I'm glad you suggested this. Can I help you with anything? Please let me buy you a cup of coffee," I whispered to her, hoping to not break our gaze.

"I've just got to grab a few boxes from my car, give me a second." She turned around, and I tried to keep myself from watching her with pure fascination.

"Please, let me hold some for you." I stepped forward and without letting her oppose I grabbed two of the boxes she was stacking on top of each other. The smell coming from the boxes reminded me I hadn't had any breakfast, and whatever these were, they looked amazing. "I'm going to have to buy one of these, they smell incredible."

"Thanks, they're raspberry almond scones, personally one of my favorites. Steamy Beans has a standing order of 4 dozen a week." She was obviously proud of her baked goods, and it was a good look on her.

As we each carried two boxes, we began walking to the door when she spoke just loud enough for me to hear. "Kai, I wanted to see you today because I need you to know just how grateful I am for everything you're doing."

The light in her eyes that moment made me wish I could pursue her each and every day like this. Unfortunately, it was something I wouldn't be able to do until we both found some closure to the dilemma, we found ourselves in.

"Thanks, Emily, I won't be leaving any time soon. You're stuck with me till I get you the answers you've been looking for."

I must have said something right because that light in her eyes just got brighter. We made our way into the nicely decorated coffee shop where all types of people filled every corner. I guess all my senses were heightened because even though I'd been here several times before, I'd never noticed how cozy the shop was like now with Emily beside me. It had everything you would look for in a coffee house. Large fluffy couches, eclectic tables and the sweet scent of coffee filling the air.

Uncovered

After Emily delivered her scones to the barista, we each ordered our drinks. I ended up ordering two of her scones, and I insisted on paying for her drink. She was no match for my persuasive skills and gave in quickly. We chose a pair of blue velvet wingback chairs, and I found myself staring as she brought the straw of her iced caramel latte up to her full red lips. She was watching a couple across the room play chess as they indulged in each other's presence. I wish I could hear her thoughts behind that sweet smile as she looked at them.

Within seconds after receiving, I finished devouring one of Emily's scones. I was met with a laugh from Emily as she took a sip from her coffee. "I guess I'll take that as a compliment?"

A bit embarrassed, I made sure there was no crumbling evidence on myself. "Emily, those are amazing! Do you do this professionally?"

"Thank you, it's more of a hobby than anything really. It would be great to someday do it professionally, but right now it just helps pay the bills." She took another sip from her coffee.

"Well, you can count on me as a repeat customer when that day comes. I happen to have a few friends in mind that would love a new bakery in town." I laughed as I began to devour another tasty scone yet again.

"So, do you come here often?" I asked, trying to bring her eyes back to mine.

She quickly provided me with a shrug and the warmest gaze. "Well, I make my delivery weekly, and I used to stop for a drink sometimes. Before Tillie this was my favorite place to people-watch. I honestly forgot how therapeutic it was to just sit in silence and watch the world around you go about the day."

"You'd be a great cop," I laughed. "But no, really, I agree it's quite entertaining at times. Have you ever played the game where you guess what people are talking about, or what they could be thinking?"

She shook her head, and I knew this could get fun. "Okay, well let's choose someone. You go first."

She looked around the room and her eyes settled back to the original couple she had been watching moments before. "Okay, those two, they look like they're having a good time together," she whispered loud enough for only me to hear.

"Would you like to do the honors and come up with what they're thinking?"

She nodded and then started with her assumptions. "Okay. So, the girl actually hates chess. But she knows he loves it. So, she pretends to love it just as much. He's actually waiting for the game to be over though, so he can sit back on the couch next to her. He has something he wants to give to her. He's just waiting for the perfect time to surprise her with some flashy new present."

She stopped now, and I couldn't tell if she was finished or thinking more about the couple. After a few moments passed, I figured she had finished.

"Well, that was oddly specific. Where did you come up with that?"

She grinned now and pointed at the shiny silver-wrapped present sticking out of the guy's backpack on the floor.

"He's also taken every chance he could to touch her. It was obvious he wanted more. She would smile every time he reached his hand across the board," she whispered, as we both laughed now.

I could envision us doing this more together. We had such easy chemistry; so pure and irresistible.

"Alright, you won that one. I like your style. Now it's my turn. You pick the person or couple."

Her eyes sparkled with anticipation paired with an absolutely mischievous grin. What had I started within this woman? She pointed now to a large elderly man sneaking handfuls of sugar packets into his coat pockets.

"Oh, this will be easy. Just watch a pro at work." I winked and looked her right in the eyes, hoping she would not miss my advance. "This man here will be entering a baking contest, and he needs to provide all the necessary ingredients."

"What?" She started to cut me off and I gave her a playful pout. "That makes no sense ... why would—"

"Shh, let the professional continue." I cut *her* off now, and playfully placed a finger over my mouth.

"As I was saying ... he is entering this contest, and part of the rules are you have to provide your own ingredients, but you can't buy anything. You have to secretly get your own ingredients."

As if he heard us, he sheepishly looked our way. Emily put her hand on my forearm, and we both began laughing.

"Kai, stop! I think he heard you!" she softly squealed.

Within moments, the man was stuffing honey packets in his bag when the barista had caught on and began eyeballing his latest grab. Then he tried to shove the half and half bottle under his arm before the barista quickly asked him to stop. He looked horrified that he'd been caught. He threw it back on the table and quickly ran out the door. Emily and I laughed, and the barista joined in.

As I watched Emily laugh so completely unreserved, I wanted to memorize everything about her. The purse of her lips, the pink of her cheeks, the sparkle in her eyes. Her laugh had seemed to become a necessity to me, like the sound I'd been waiting for my entire life and didn't know it. I wanted to reach out and touch the loose curl that had fallen in her face. My heartbeat went fast and hard in my chest … throbbing in all the familiar places. I wanted to make this enthralling woman laugh until I had the vision imprinted in my mind.

She interrupted my musings. "I think with that we need to end our little game, but I will say that you win! That was hilarious!"

I needed to come up with something to spend more time with her, or better yet find out what she was hoping to gain from our meeting this morning. I had my own wishes about what this meeting meant, but then again, I was a single man with a highly active imagination.

We made small talk a little while longer, but as I watched and listened to Emily talk about her frustrations of living through the terrible twos and how she wished she could someday go back to school to study business and such, I couldn't get my conversation with Alex out of my head. He was adamant that Emily knew more than she let on. Even though I'd tried, for what felt like hours the night before, to change his mind.

The thing about Alex was, once he got something in his head, he was determined to be proven right. I needed to focus on the present and enjoy the small amount of time I was able to spend with Emily this afternoon.

"What's on your agenda for the day?" I asked, hoping I could be with her a bit longer.

She was tapping at her bottom lip and looking down at the floor. "Well, not much really. I know it's silly, but after the news this morning I just wanted to see you to go over the details in person." Her pensive look transformed into the most angelic expression. An expression that could make any warm-blooded male go weak in the knees.

"Emily, anything you need to go over, just ask."

"My only question is, what position is your father in, and do you think he *could* uncover more information?"

I had to answer this carefully. Not only because of my father and his security clearance, but for Emily's desire to know as much as possible. "My father is a retired Vet. He has connections that even I don't dare ask about. All I know is that he called in a few favors, and within the hour they had that bit of secret information for him. They have been asked to find out more, but that could take some time. I also know Alex is working all his angles, as well. Emily, you don't need to worry, I have the feeling we will get some answers for you by the end of the week."

One of her hands covered her mouth and with her other hand she grabbed my forearm squeezing it so tight I hoped I hadn't said too much.

"Within the week … the week?" She tried to keep her voice down, but she was so full of emotion. "I *never* thought I would *ever* have answers, but if by the end of the week I do … well, I can't begin to imagine what that's going to feel like! I had almost started to feel comfortable living in limbo for so long, and now this? This feels so real now! But I don't know." Her eyes trailed off as though she were picturing the worst-case scenario. "Am I … am I ready to hear it?"

A small tear fell from her eye, and I instinctively touched her cheek, drying it with my thumb. I then cupped her face with my hand, and she nodded and leaned into my palm, for but a brief moment. A moment was all it took for me to want more. Much more.

Chapter Nineteen

EMILY

Why was I flirting with something that had disaster written all over it? I couldn't help but gravitate towards Kai and his fierce masculinity. He had everything I needed but couldn't have. I knew in the pit of my being I couldn't move forward until I had my answers, yet here I was on the edge of finding those answers.

As Kai wiped my tears gently with his warm thumb, I was reminded how it felt to be cared for. It was enthralling, it was perfectly natural. I was not immune to men looking at me, nor pursuing me despite my situation, but I'd never given any of them a second glance. Kai was the first to make me feel this way after Evan's disappearance, and I was not about to let that go unnoticed, even if it did scare the hell out of me.

"Thank you, Kai. I'll say it again, you just keep on surprising me." His smile now told me things were going to be okay. If I somehow had Kai by my side through this process, no matter the outcome he would at least be a great friend to have around.

"Of course, would you like to go for a walk, maybe clear your head or something?"

It was as if he could read my mind, a walk with Kai sounded incredible.

"Yes, perfect! I know a great trail just around the block." I started for my stuff and headed toward the door when I felt his warm hand grace my lower back as we exited the coffee shop. His hand fell almost as quickly as it was placed, which was disappointing because it felt like heaven resting there.

We made our way to the trail and enjoyed watching the bird's overhead. The blue sky was sprinkled with frothy white clouds that coasted lazily in the gentle breeze. There were very few people on the trail this morning except for a couple joggers running past us, and it was nice having Kai all to myself. We talked about the easy things: Tillie and her spunky personality, his crazy family, and everything in between. There were no lulls in our conversation, and even if there were, it would have still been a beautiful time simply enjoying each other's company.

I looked at my phone, only to notice another hour had already flown by. Kai had noticed me checking the time however, and he appeared slightly nervous.

"I don't want to keep you out all day, so please let me know when you need to go, or better yet just say hey, Kai, 'shut up I have to go'!" He laughed and the smile reached his soft blue eyes. He was doing that thing with his thumbs again, and I smiled as I watched his nervous habit continue.

"I'm okay, it's honestly been great. I don't get much adult conversation these days, so I'm thoroughly enjoying myself."

His smile widened even further than before as his hand reached out towards my face.

"Emily, I hope you know…" and just before he could finish, his phone rang.

Before he even looked at the screen, he answered the phone. I hoped the call that broke whatever moment we had going would not be the phone call to completely shatter my world.

I watched him make a face as he listened to the phone at his ear. "Hey ... yeah, I'm actually with her right now."

There was silence, and I tried to read his expression. "Yeah, I'll ask her ... are you sure?"

His concerned appearance had now turned stoic. "Can Alex meet up with us this afternoon? Seems there's been a new development. He'd like to speak with you in person on this."

I still could not read him, and with every second I became more and more worried this new development was something horrible.

"Yeah, definitely! I'll let my mom know that we need more time today."

As I pulled out my phone to text her, I couldn't help but overhear Kai finish the conversation. He sounded harsh and demanding, a side of him I hadn't yet seen.

"Alex, I want you to promise me this source you have is one hundred percent accurate before we sit down with her and confuse the shit out of her!"

It sounded like Kai was being protective of me, so it didn't bother me that he was speaking his mind to Alex. I put my phone away as soon as my mom texted back that it was fine to stay out and get things situated. Tillie was napping, and the pressure was off that she hadn't completely worn out her grandma.

I kept watching Kai as he had put some distance between us now and was finishing the conversation with Alex. He quickly hung up and shoved it into the pocket of his dark denim jeans.

"Emily, I'm sorry if you heard any of that. Alex has a way of being compulsive, and I wanted to make sure there was complete accuracy behind everything. It looks like he has some pretty solid information. I'd like to drive us now if that's ok?" He looked upset, and I could only imagine what thoughts were going through his head.

I nodded, and we began making our way to his SUV. Kai opened my door, and as I slid into the passenger seat, I couldn't pretend to be laid back with all of this. "Kai, will you just please prepare me a little bit for what I'm about to hear? I've rehearsed bad scenarios a million times over the last three years, but it's never felt as ominous as it does right now." I knew I sounded panicked. But I was completely serious. I needed to know what conversation I was about to have.

"Emily, I don't have all the details, but If you want the truth, from what I gathered over the phone was that you're linked to this whole Alex predicament more than you're letting on." The light in his eyes from before had dimmed significantly. How could he think I had anything to do with Alex? I hadn't even met the senator before yesterday.

"That's insane, Kai, I just met the man yesterday!" I was practically screaming and almost barreled over the middle compartment.

He looked as though he wanted to but could not believe me. "Let's just meet with Alex and see what he's found about this entire situation. I need to wrap my mind around it all before we both get too worked up."

He began to tap his thumbs on the steering wheel and kept his eyes on the road for most of the drive. The drive was quiet, and the air was full of thick tension. I felt on the verge of tears but my anger, however, kept me from doing so. We came to a gated community and pulled onto a circular drive leading to a gorgeous Mediterranean-style home that looked right out of House Beautiful magazine. Of course, this had to be Alex's private estate.

I was nervous getting out of the SUV, and while Kai still looked perturbed, he opened my door for me, and we walked through a marbled front entryway. A wait staff opened the beautifully carved wooden doors and led us into a private meeting room. The large room had a fireplace at one end with plush armchairs arranged nearby... We sat across from each other at a large round table with more plush chairs overlooking a gorgeous private patio visible just beyond the arched leaded windows.

I tried to keep my knees from shaking and looked around for signs of drinking water or something to quench my dry throat. There were pictures on the wall of Alex and Kai. They looked younger in most of them, and in a different situation they would have been fun to browse. Right now, however, I just wished Alex would come and explain what the hell was going on.

Within moments, he stepped into the room wearing a crisp gray suit that seemed as though it had been tailored immaculately to fit his every need, a perfect match for his irritating arrogance. "Hello, Emily, thank you for meeting with me today on such short notice. It was great you two were *already* together."

He gave Kai an interesting look, and Kai rolled his eyes in return. He sat as far away from me as possible. Kai appeared eager now and asked to get the meeting started.

Alex quickly brought out a large black binder and opened it on the table. I was shocked they could uncover this amount of paperwork in such a short time.

As concerned as I was, my curiosity was even greater. "Did you uncover all that overnight?" I asked, as I stood and pointed to the monster-sized pile of papers.

"Yes, it's intriguing, isn't it, what you can uncover when you have power and authority." His eyes were not as kind as Kai's. He was acting smug, and to be honest, it was rather frustrating.

"Yes, it's obvious there were answers this entire time, but I guess I was just not important enough to get them." I scowled sarcastically as I sat back down in my chair and put my face in my hands. I couldn't believe that this entire time the truth was out there, all while I was kept in the dark struggling to keep it together one more day.

Alex came to my side and placed his large hand on my back and gave it a gentle rub. It was cold, and there was no amount of compassion behind the gesture. It was obvious he did not have much practice comforting people in such a way.

"Emily, I'm sorry how I came off, but once you hear what I know, you'll understand why it is I'm acting this way."

I looked up and blotted my eyes with a tissue from the box nearby. I was stronger than this. Nearly three years of nothing. I could handle whatever they were about to throw at me. "Okay, then, what did you find out?"

I leaned over to see Alex pull out his phone as he gathered the binder full of papers. He brought it closer to us and sat down next to me. The documents looked like military reports. Everything from logs to officially stamped records.

Kai positioned himself closer to take a look. Out of all of us in the room, he could probably understand them more than the two of us combined.

Alex shoved the binder toward Kai and then brought up a photo on his phone and placed it on the table in front of me. The photo was a birth certificate. Upon further inspection ... I realized it was Tillie's! As I scanned the image, I couldn't breathe. My heart skipped when I read Alex Greyson's name as the father on the designated line of Tillie's birth certificate!

"What the hell is going on!" I screamed and pushed my chair away from the table. Once on my feet, I kept backing away and wanted to run.

"I'd like to know that as well, Emily," Alex retorted through gritted teeth. His voice was teetering between calm and furious all at once. How political of him.

I looked at Kai, but he wouldn't look me in the eyes. He was glued to the documents in front of him, while I was appalled this could even be happening. Was it a joke? It had to be!

"Alex, you and I both know we've never met before yesterday, let alone slept together! You guys want to know something really insane? I've only slept with one man my entire life and it was my husband so there is absolutely no way you or any other man for that matter could be her father!" I incessantly rambled.

Alex appeared amused at my sudden incomprehensible outburst and gave a smug laugh. "Emily, you can calm down. I don't think I'm the father of your child; I know I've never slept with you." He eyed me up and down and triggered in me a wave of heated anger. "Believe me, you would remember sleeping with me. What I *am* concerned with is how you were able to forge official documents, and almost get away with it ... and for what gain?"

Alex was one of the most arrogant men I had ever encountered. They both looked at me now as if I actually had an answer for this complete insanity.

"I've never once forged a document! Ever! I'm proud to have Evan as the father of my child, and I would *never* take his name off of Tillie's birth certificate!" I narrowed my eyes at both of them and prayed they would finally believe me. Kai couldn't look at me any longer, and there was now a sadness in his eyes. He then looked down and flipped over another document. His eyes instantly widened.

"Alex, I think she's telling the truth." He whispered as he browsed the document further. "This message is in Sanskrit, and it instructs whoever was the recipient of this document to change the birth certificate. It has all of Emily's information and Tillie's. Then down here it has all your info and when to do the change. The change in birth details correlates within the time frame from when you got that cryptic email about needing to pay up or the information would go public."

As he finished reading over the document, he threw it across the table to Alex. Kai looked at Alex, and they both were at a loss for words.

"Can someone please explain to me what the hell all this means?" I cried out. My brain was running a million miles an hour, and I had no clue what to think anymore.

Kai looked at me. I tried to gauge what his puzzled expression meant.

Alex quickly grabbed the papers from the table and began to read.

"Can you be sure that's what this is saying, Kai?" Alex was very open with his aggression. You could feel the tension in the air as his piercing dark eyes stared at me as if calculating my every move and intention. Kai nodded to Alex and they both turned to me and stared.

Kai spoke first. "Emily, we need you to be completely honest from here on out. We have the paper trail right here in front of us. I guess my first question is why target a senator of all people? Did you really think you wouldn't get caught?"

He was looking at me now with profound disappointment. How could the once warm and sensitive man be the same one as the cold and angry one standing in front of me, accusing me of such horrible things? I couldn't find the words to fix this, but I sure as hell had to try.

"I don't even know what you're accusing me of!" I yelled. My emotions were getting the best of me again, and I was so confused how this situation could have turned so quickly. Kai continued looking at me as the angry tears began to form in my eyes. For a brief second, the warmth in his eyes started to return but quickly vanished.

"Emily, what were you thinking? That you could forge the birth certificate and we wouldn't get a DNA test? Or rather, did you think he would just pay you off to keep you quiet and not care about his child? Who are you working with?"

The disgust in Kai's eyes cut deeper than the words coming from his mouth. How could he think I was devious enough to even come up with such an elaborate plan?

"I can't even believe you're asking me these questions! I could never even come up with a plan like this! Shit, Kai, I thought better of you!! Maybe you should take me back to my car right now." I couldn't help but voice my outrage. Mere hours ago, Kai and I were sharing special moments, and he was making me laugh ... something I hadn't done a lot of in the past few years.

Kai shook his head and looked down at the documents again, this time flipping to a couple new ones toward the back of the folder. He pulled out his phone and started doing something that I couldn't quite make out. His eyes grew larger though, and after a few moments, he met my eyes once again.

"When did you get official word that Evan was missing?"

Kai was serious now, and for a second, I had hope again that he would come through with something that would clear everything up. I started with my answer. "It was about three months before Tillie was born, so around May of 2014. The last I heard from him was on a Friday. Everything was normal."

I hesitated with the difficult words coming next that I had tried for too many years to forget. "It was about a week later, that next Thursday, when I heard from his commander that he was officially missing. It was normal not to hear from him for periods of time, but that was the first time I'd heard from his commander. When I first began asking questions, they would give me hope that it was all just a misunderstanding. But as the weeks went by, the answers became fewer and fewer. I begged to speak to everyone, anyone, but by the end of the month they had declared him as an MIA entitlement. Months would go by before they would give me any additional information. Eventually they just stopped returning my calls"

Just as the tears were about to fall, Alex surprised me and came over to put his arms around me. I was shocked that it was Alex consoling me, but I welcomed the gesture just the same. Being held, while the memories rocked me to my core and I was slowly falling apart, felt better than standing there alone.

As I was being held by Alex, I glanced at Kai to see that he was still reading that same document. Worry was written all over his face. I couldn't help but wonder what he was reading. I pulled myself away from Alex, and he gave me a soft smile though it looked a bit forced, but was still kind, nonetheless.

He looked over to Kai and noticed what I had previously. Kai was still focused on the last document in the pile.

"What are you reading, Kai?" Alex seemed worried now and for good reason. This entire situation had to do with him and his affairs, and somehow, my family as well.

Kai looked up finally. His expression was one of deep concern. "You said May of 2014, right?" he asked, looking me right in the eyes with a determined gaze.

"Yes, that's correct. I know because it was three months before Tillie was born."

His face looked ashen, and I was deeply worried about what I might hear next.

"This document states that as of September 2014, he was officially considered a … prisoner of war!"

The moment I heard the words, my entire body fell silent. Sometimes when I lay awake at night, I would assure myself this was all just a bad dream. That someday I would wake up from this horrible nightmare that I called life. I felt as if I were falling back into that very nightmare. My heart pounded so hard I was sure they could hear it. The pulse in my neck pounded like a drum. The walls around me closed in, and suddenly the room went black.

Seconds, that felt like an eternity, had passed, and I came to with Kai at one side and Alex at the other offering me a bottle of imported mineral water. The two men appeared worried, and it was then I realized I was lying on the floor. My upper body ached, and I

112

could feel that I had hit my shoulder on the table or maybe the chair when I fainted. Luckily, Alex was still next to me and must have been able to help me before I did more damage. This was not a dream, and nothing would ever be the same again.

"Emily, I'm so sorry for the way that came out. I should've known better, been better ... are you okay?" Kai had gone back to being the warm and compassionate man I had grown to know and appreciate. His recurring mood changes were enough to make anyone dizzy.

I was sitting in the chair now as I struggled to fit the messy strewn pieces of my life together. "May I see the paper you were reading from? This has to be a mistake; they wouldn't have kept that from me." Kai quickly handed me the paper. I couldn't believe what I was reading. However, in black and white text, clear as day, a report on my Evan and his exact last known whereabouts. Why had this vital information been kept from me?

"I can't understand everything down here at the bottom. It's like in another language. What is this saying?" My hand was shaking as I pointed to the bottom and gave the document back to Kai for him to look it over once again.

He studied the letter for a few moments and quickly got his phone out in a swift fluid motion. His fingers flew across the keyboard and within the minute his phone was ringing. He got to his feet and began pacing as he answered the call.

"Yeah, it's the same case we spoke about yesterday ... well, Alex and his team uncovered more than you were able to retrieve. Can you tell me what all this means? ... Okay, I will send you pictures of the documents pertaining to the official

statement…we don't know that yet, when I find out I'll let you know. In the meantime, do everything in your power to get to the bottom of this … Okay, thanks."

He hung up his phone and was back at my side and put his hand on mine. The gentle Kai had returned, and I was grateful for having him again; however, the whiplash of emotions was making me sick. Alex was at the window now, facing the quiet courtyard outside.

"That was my father on the phone with what he uncovered, and now this. I think there will be more to expose with this, and more discovery for all of us. Emily, I'm not accusing you of anything, and I'm sorry for the way I behaved earlier. But we *must* know, is there anything you can tell us about the letter Alex received regarding the child and the money someone was trying to extort?"

I could feel the tension in the air, and wished I had more answers for them …. for myself. But once again I was in the dark.

"Kai, Alex, I swear to you both that I knew nothing about any of this until you showed up on my doorstep the other day. I wish I did have answers But I'm just as in the dark as the two of you."

Both Kai and Alex looked as if they believed me for the first time that afternoon. Alex stepped closer to Kai and me. "I believe you Emily. From here on out, we're going to get to the bottom of this goddamn mess for the both of us. However, it's clear now, and I think you'll agree … somehow the two of us are tangled up in this web together."

Alex was right. Somehow, and in some way, our two separate lives had been linked together in a search for answers to the most critical questions that we both had.

Chapter Twenty

KAI

As I looked over at Emily, I could not believe the way I had so casually crushed her entire world. I should've known better than to just blurt that out. She trusted me, and I had let her down. In a few short hours my position had done a complete one-eighty. I was afraid there was no recovery from my actions at a time when she so desperately needed someone. I let my anger and mistrust get the best of me. How could I, even for a split second, actually believe Emily had either slept with Alex or was a master con artist? All signs seemed to point to the obvious: Emily was lying to us and trying to receive a large payout. But now after my latest discovery, I can't believe I could have been so arrogant!

So much for my years on the police force. Lesson 101: Don't always believe what you first see. Didn't I know Emily could not be capable of such a devious scheme, yet here I was practically interrogating her? My hand was still resting on hers, and I had no plans to remove it anytime soon. She needed someone and I needed to be near her when she was in such distress that undoubtedly, I had caused.

Alex had a point. How do these two scenarios tie together, especially when these two people have nothing in common? Luckily, my father was helping, and I knew if anyone were able to uncover the truth it'd be him.

"Emily, would you like to get some fresh air?" She hadn't said anything for quite some time, and I was worried. This would be startling news for anyone, let alone someone who'd been lied to for so long. She shook her head, and I didn't press further.

She spoke now with a demoralized tone, and it ripped me open to hear her hurting so.

"Be honest, okay? Does this mean he was captured and held somewhere against his will and most likely tortured to death? I can't … my mind is going a million miles a minute and I need someone to please say something! The silence is seriously killing me!"

She was crying now, and Alex had left the room, likely to find more tissues. I wrapped my arm around her and tried hard to reassure her this time. "Emily, we won't know details until we hear back from our outside sources. But I want to be honest with you. In most cases, not all, but most cases, being classified a prisoner of war leads to nowhere good." I knew she would hate me for saying this, but I had to tell her the truth. I owed her that much.

Alex arrived just in time because Emily was crying so hard the chair was practically shaking. She could hold the heartbreak no longer, and another great sob escaped her. Alex handed her the tissues, and she went through them in no time. My heart was breaking watching this wonderfully confident woman crumble to pieces right before my eyes.

"Would you like me to call your family … anyone?" I asked, grasping for ways to help any way I could. Again, she shook her head then turned to me and buried her face into my chest. Instinctively, I pulled her in and held her there for a few minutes. It felt like a lifetime, holding her as she sobbed. A few minutes had gone by when Emily looked up at me and even through her bloodshot eyes, she was the most beautiful woman I'd ever laid eyes on.

"Thank you for being honest with me, that's all I've ever wanted and never got before now. Deep down I've always had this horrible thought that Evan was not *just* missing … but really gone, but I could never just give up on him. There was always still that sliver of hope."

I had to interrupt. "Emily there still is. This entire scenario doesn't make an ounce of sense. I understand the surrounding evidence is bleak, but I wouldn't give up now, not after all these years." Then I whispered, "Let us find out all there is to know before we reach that road, alright?"

I lightly touched her chin and raised her face so I could look her in the eyes. I gave her my best reassuring smile, wishing for a small glimpse of hope in her eyes for a little bit longer. It was still there, it was faint, but it was definitely there. She was a fighter. "There it is," I whispered.

"I knew you could still see the good, because that's who you are … you are good, Emily. Tillie is so lucky to have you. You know that, right?"

She smiled now, and I was relieved to see it return, even if for a moment. "Thank you, Kai. I knew this day could come. I just thought I'd be more prepared than this." She sighed as she looked down at the tissue she had been twisting into a tight knot. My heart ached seeing her like this.

Alex's phone rang, and he quickly exited the room again. Emily and I were alone once more, and I so much wished it had been under better circumstances. The quiet in the room needed to be filled. I couldn't muster any words to make her feel better but with that look in her eyes, I knew I had to try.

"Emily, I'm so sorry for doubting you, but when I looked at the reports and then the bank information … I couldn't help myself from going there in my head. I know we don't know each other very well, but I absolutely think you are the most amazing woman." I hoped she could see how sincere I was. "I should have listened to my inner voice telling me you could never do something like this."

"Kai, I won't pretend to know what you're thinking, but if I were in your shoes, I'd probably think the same. You're absolutely right, we don't know each other very well. You have no reason to believe me."

She hung her head as if accepting defeat, and I just couldn't be the cause of more sadness on this woman's beautiful face.

"That's exactly it, Emily, I *do* believe you. I know there'll be more to uncover here before we know what's really going on. And I'm convinced you don't have it in you to come up with such a devious plan." She gave me a slight curve of her lips now, and I had hope once again that we were going to be okay.

Alex entered once more and appeared to be needing an audience. We both sat back in our chairs and looked at him as he cleared his throat.

In his domineering way, he commanded the room. "I just received a call that we've found the IP address of the entity that put the order in for the changes to the birth certificate. It matches the one that emailed me! Whatever bastard did this is highly trained, most likely military themselves, because no average Joe would have this type of clearance."

Alex was furious now, as we all were. It was time to call my father again and bring him up to date. I made sure Emily would be okay and excused myself to make my call, gesturing for Alex to follow me into the hallway. I could easily read Alex in most situations and thought he might be on the verge of a breakdown himself. This all seemed to revolve around him, and unfortunately, he was caught in the middle.

We reached an area where Emily couldn't overhear. Alex was not taking the news very well.

"You okay? You don't look very well." He didn't answer and appeared to be calculating his response. When Alex was stressed, the more professional side of him came out and it was increasingly difficult for him to open up. "I've been your friend, for how long Alex? I know when you're shitting me so don't hold back."

His eyes were solemn and the lines on his face seemed more pronounced. "I don't know, Kai, what do you want me to say? This has me thrown for a loop. For months I thought I had a child out there. But wait, never mind, it's all been a lie! But for what gain? To extort money from me? Whoever did this had to have known me. That's what really messes with my head. They knew I'd slept around and how it would be hard for me to pinpoint any one single encounter …. what, am I that shallow that whoever did this thought I would just write it off and not think twice about wanting to be in the kid's life?"

In all my years of standing by his side, I'd never once seen him this emotional. Alex rarely showed emotion, other than maybe excitement on those rare occasions when it was appropriate. He was a calculating and suave businessman. Hell, that's what helped him get into politics in the first place. But when it came to being open and truthful with his feelings, he was as stoic as they came.

"So, are you more upset that someone did this to you, or that it's all a lie and there's probably no child of yours out there?" If Alex was going to be real with me for once, then so was I.

He gave me a look, and I wondered if I had overstepped.

"I don't have an answer to that. It's both, I guess. But what I really hate is that someone out there thought I would just throw money at some woman to shut her up, and that I wouldn't want to know my child."

After all the conversations, after all the years, I honestly thought Alex prided himself in his sexual escapades. I thought it kept him busy and away from the silence that must have been deafening to a boy that grew up in the system, and in and out of foster care. Alex was right though. Whoever did this, knew him. They knew him enough to think that was all there was to him. Whoever did this had made it personal. That was now crystal clear.

"Alex, can you think of any woman, either military or with military knowledge, that you've had a relationship with? I think whoever is behind this *has* actually slept with you."

His eyes widened as if a lightbulb ignited. While he was unwrapping his memories of sleepless nights, I quickly texted my father about my suspicions. As soon as I was done, I decided to text Emily and make sure she was still doing okay.

KAI: *How are you holding up? Want some company?*
EMILY: *I think I am okay at the moment. How much longer do you think we'll be staying here?*
KAI: *We can leave as soon as you say the word. The team can work on essentially everything with you either here or at home. And don't worry, you know I will call you as soon as I hear anything.*
EMILY: *Thank you.*

She was short with me, and I hoped I hadn't become a complete ass in her eyes, and there was still some small chance for me to remain at the very least a friend to her.

KAI: *I'm happy to help, let me wrap things up with Alex and we can head back to your car.*

Emily responded with a thumbs up, and I envisioned the way her bright eyes lit up earlier this morning. There was no doubt in my mind I could ever grow tired of this woman. Though I couldn't help but question where all this was headed. I now believed Emily had no knowledge of Alex's predicament, but no matter where the facts would lead us, she would be crushed either way.

After I looked over the paperwork, the theory that Evan might still be alive was fading by the minute. As always, my dad took his sweet time, and for once I was okay with that. I wanted Emily around as long as possible.

Chapter Twenty-One

EMILY

Sitting alone in the room, unfortunately made my new reality sink in, like a lifeboat full of holes, with no shoreline in sight. Evan was a prisoner of war! Those words had been pulsing in my ears ever since they were first announced. I had always thought there was a bright side to everything, but sometimes there could be no happy ending. There is no moral to the story. You can't always sit back and wait for the good to come around, because sometimes it simply does not come. My new reality, that things don't always work out, hit me to the core. Why did Evan always have to be the hero? He and I both joked that it was his only flaw. A flaw that had saved me a time or two.

I will never forget the first time we met. My old 1999 Galant had broken down on the side of the road, and there wasn't another car in sight. I sat in the driver's seat with the hazard lights flashing. I was so mad at myself for driving with the check engine light on, but I really wanted to get to my friend's concert early. It seemed like hours before any car had driven by.

Turns out it was my lucky day after all when Evan pulled over and offered to help get my car running again. I accepted and remembered feeling like I'd known him forever, as if in some other far away lifetime. I watched as Evan worked on my car. He was meticulous with every action he completed. He was more than fascinating, he had one of those faces that you couldn't soon forget. I knew at that moment I'd dream of him later that night, and possibly more. His towering demeanor and uncombed curls caught my attention almost immediately. He appeared casual with his flint and tinder denim jacket and a pair of dark slacks. His smile was stiff, but the dimple on his left cheek spoke of a deep-rooted kindness.

I couldn't help but feel lucky that it turned out Evan was headed for the same concert that very night. His friend was bartending where my friends were playing. We spent the entire night together. Nothing in the entire crowd that night could tear our eyes off each other. My friend that was meeting up with me later said we were but one flame that once ignited. There was no putting it out. She was my maid of honor at our wedding only a few short years later.

Evan was everything I had wished for in a husband, and then some. It was his kindness that really locked me in. I knew in the deepest part of my being that Evan was truly kind, and nothing could stop him from giving his life for another if it came to that. In fact, it was what I loved about him most. Now the love was replaced with anger. Evan was gone, and what little flicker of hope I had had throughout the day was now steadily being snuffed out. I hated thinking like that, but my gut was telling me to prepare for the worst. What person ever wants to become part of a Gold Star Family? I know I didn't want to. I couldn't!

The door was partly open, but Alex knocked quietly before entering and I slowly turned to face him. He seemed almost as torn up as I was. Our futures that we both once thought of as solid and secure were now being ripped in two.

"Alex, I'm so sorry for this entire problem that's mine alone. You should never have been dragged into it. You're a good man. Are you okay?"

His smile was hesitant, not his usual put-together, cocky smile like one you see on the cover of a romance novel. Was it regret or worry about the future? Or maybe he was just exhausted. "Don't worry about me, I just want to get to the bottom of all this so we can put it behind us. Sure, I'm curious to know the truth, but I'm ready for this drama to be over with. If I am a father, great. If I'm not, well that's great also." He winced as the words escaped his mouth. The words were clearly bitter and untrue.

He had a pained look in his eyes, and I almost felt sorry for the guy. I was sure there could be an actual nice human being behind all those self-righteous walls.

"I hope we hear something soon. You and I both need to if we would like to function like normal again."

He gave me a slight nod and began reading from his phone when Kai burst into the room rubbing the back of his neck. I could tell by his expression that he had something important to say. He cleared his throat as Alex slowly looked up.

"Can I share with you both some more information my father just uncovered? And then I'd like to take Emily back to her car."

We both nodded, and Kai closed the door behind him.

"He and his colleagues have just uncovered where the sender or should I say, hacker is. They have an address, and you won't believe this but it's just a few hours away. Since whoever did this will likely be charged with a military offense, my father called in a few favors, and they're apprehending the person tomorrow afternoon. Emily, if you're up for it, I say we all go and see what they have to say for themselves. It's time for both of you to find out why they chose to target you and Alex, of all people."

I couldn't believe how fast these people could get information and find solutions to what they needed. It seemed as though I was the missing piece in Alex's puzzle, but still I didn't know how I could be tied to all this. I had to go tomorrow.

"I think I can get my mom to watch Tillie. If things are coming out tomorrow, I need to be there. If whoever this is has any information about Evan, I want to hear it straight from the source."

Kai nodded and gave me his confident smile. It was enough to remind me that there was still good in the world despite the darkness creeping in around me.

"That's very admirable of you, Emily; I know this can't be easy on you. But I do have a good feeling about this. My father wouldn't call in any favors unless he knew he was onto something. I can be there every step of the way if you want me to."

Kai's eyes were full of concern, and not just concern for the whole predicament, but for me. I knew he wanted me to feel safe, and if I were being honest with myself, for the first time in a long while, I did feel safe with him.

"I would be more than grateful if you came. I mean, look at me! I'm barely holding on, so I'm going to need all the support I can get. I'm still in shock that you've been able to do all this in a few short days. Be honest with me, how could this have been hidden from me for so long, and yet you can uncover a binder full in a matter of hours?"

Both men nervously looked my way.

"Emily, you have to understand," Kai said. "With the connections we have we're privy to this sort of information. You, being a civilian, would pose a risk in letting these details out. We also may have made some … well… threats." They looked at each other. "Let's just say we had some things to hold over their heads, and we did what we had to."

It felt so good to have these two powerful men in my corner. "Well, what's the game plan for tomorrow? I want to help any way I can." I looked up at Kai and he again gave me the most inviting smile. He came closer and laid his hand on my shoulder and instantly the dark gray clouds in my world seemed less bleak. It felt good to do this for myself, and to have Kai by my side for it.

"Well, I'll arrange for us to arrive as the security team gets there. Hopefully we won't run into any issues that way. It's about a two-hour drive, so the team wants to leave around 5 AM. Emily are you up for that?"

"Five AM? Wow, that *is* early. But yes, I'll find a way to make it work, I need to be a part of this."

Both men nodded, assuring me that they understood my need to be involved in this endeavor. I pulled out my phone and sent a quick text to my mom asking her of her plans for the next day.

The men had a quick conversation before Alex quietly grabbed the thick binder and made his way toward the door. "Emily, thank you for being so understanding. I'm sorry if I came across rudely earlier. I'm hoping tomorrow clears up both our questions. Have a good night." And as quickly as he entered, he was gone. My heart went out for the man, he was noticeably upset.

Kai had kept some of the papers from Alex's binder before he left and was folding them into his back pocket. "You ready to leave?" he asked, as his eyes were solely set on me. I loved the way he watched my every move, almost as if he could read my mind and anticipate my next step.

I nodded as we made our way to the front entrance and let ourselves out. "Do you mind if I make some calls when we're driving?" I asked.

"Yeah, of course. No problem," he answered, as he opened my car door for me. When I went to climb into the large SUV my foot slipped. I felt my entire body falling. Of all times to be clumsy this had to top the list. Before I had a chance to feel the pavement below me, I was wrapped in Kai's arms. He had protected me just in time. I was so caught up in the moment that I couldn't help but stare at his lips as he held me there. I had never felt this divine mixture of desire laced with nervous tension before.

"Good thing you had *me* here, or you would be sporting quite the shiner tomorrow," he smiled, as he continued to hold me in place.

"Thank you, Kai, and not just for catching me. I can't seem to do much of anything lately." My eyes were immersed in his and wanting to feel his lips on mine. We stayed there for a moment staring into each other, and all too soon remembered that we needed to get on the road. As we moved past the moment, I was busy overthinking the way he delicately held me. Was there any way on earth that *he* could be having these heart pounding feelings for *me* with all my heavy baggage?

Now that we were making our way back to the parking lot where I'd left my car, I had several calls to make. First on the list was my mom.

She answered on the first ring. "Hello Emily, is everything okay?" There was worry in her voice, and I knew she was probably bracing herself for the worst. For years I felt she had been preparing herself for me to completely fall apart. But I always knew I needed to stay strong, not only for myself, but for everyone around me. When Evan went missing, everyone treated me like a wounded puppy, a fragile woman falling apart. It wasn't long after that, that I made sure no one could see how messed-up I truly was. Kai had never treated me like I was damaged or broken. He seemed to see me as strong and confident, and I needed to prove him right.

I could hear my dad and Tillie playing in the background. As I filled her in on the newest details, I heard a low sob from the other side of the phone. "Mom, are you okay?" The sound of her laughter had always been my stronghold.

"Yes, Emily, I'll be alright, I just wasn't expecting this to happen so soon. You do what you need to do. You've been let down for too long. As far as tomorrow goes, 5AM is pretty early for Tillie, so why doesn't she stay the night here? This is the perfect excuse for her first grandma sleepover. You gather your thoughts and prepare for tomorrow. I love you so much, honey. I'll be praying for your safety and for this to finally be laid to rest." She sniffed quietly into the phone.

I took in a huge breath of air at her words *laid to rest*. They created a visual I wasn't ready to see. Would we be laying Evan to rest in the near future? I was doing so well, but with the visual of him being lowered into the ground, my heart broke for a second time today. I fought the tears forming in my eyes, but I thought I had fought enough for one day.

"Laid to rest," I whispered. She could hear the cry escape my exhausted body.

"Emily, I am so sorry, that was a poor choice of words. I don't know what I was thinking. Please don't worry about us. Tonight, I want you to just be present and try to relax before such a big day tomorrow."

"Thanks, mom ... for everything. I'll call around bedtime and wish Tillie goodnight. Love you." I hung up and tried to hide the tears. I could feel Kai looking over at me and started to relax just knowing I wasn't alone. Combing through my purse for a tissue I was unable to find one.

Kai reached into his front pocket and quietly handed me some folded-up tissues. As he placed them in my hand, he began to rub small circles into my palm. This small gesture was anything but professional.

"Where did you get these?" I asked, as I blotted my face.

He gave me the softest smile and said, "I took a couple from Alex's office. I thought we might need some on the ride home." He gave me one last smile before he continued to look back at the road. Moments later my face was dry, and I thought, without a doubt I was the lucky one to have met Kai. His presence alone had probably kept me from falling completely apart through this entire day.

"Emily, if there is anything you need, please let me know and I will make it happen."

I knew he would keep his word at all costs. At a time like this, I could not think of anything that would lighten the mood.

Kai smirked again, and this time it was a scheming smile. "You know what? I have an idea that might cheer you up. We're about 20 minutes from your car. Would you mind if I dropped by your house once you get settled? There's something I want to do for you."

His eyes gleamed with excitement, and I was afraid I could never say no to *him*.

"Yeah, that sounds really good, actually. It has been such a weird day; it'll be nice to have someone to talk to." He gave me his all-consuming stare and continued driving.

As we continued on the road, I had to cancel what few orders I had this week and hoped they would all understand. I couldn't afford to lose the customers I had; it had taken me years to get to where I was within my business. I was lucky most of my customers had turned to friends and I was quickly met with words of encouragement and offers to help in any way needed.

If someone had told me a week ago my life would have changed so drastically, and that I would be feeling this way toward practically a stranger, I would not have believed them for a minute. Yet here I am.

Chapter Twenty-Two

KAI

I couldn't wait to surprise Emily with my brilliant idea; there would be no way she would expect this. It was dinner time now, and I was thinking with my stomach. As I made my way back to Emily's, the excitement to see her, if only for a moment, grew and grew. I could see the lights on in her front room, and a faint silhouette of her beautiful figure was outlined behind the curtains. There had to be a way we could move past how we were first introduced

I made my way up her steps and waited to see her expression when she saw what I had grabbed for us. I held the goods up as she opened the door.

As soon as Emily saw what was in my hands, her mouth fell open. "Did you get burgers and milkshakes?" Her voice sounded shaky and unclear.

I hoped I hadn't messed the night up further. So much for doing something nice. "Yeah, I'm sorry if it's too much. I thought it'd be a nice gesture to lighten your spirits this evening. See, I got us shakes to dip the buns in just how you like." I held up the milkshakes and suddenly wished I hadn't thought of this ridiculous idea. This was *her* thing, and it was stupid of me to think she would want to do this again tonight with me. I couldn't read her eyes, but my gut was telling me to abort mission.

"Kai, this is all so sweet. I can't believe you did this." She paused, and her face appeared relaxed once again. "And you said it was disgusting," she then laughed as she sarcastically pursed her lips with a gleam in her eyes.

"Yeah, I did, and it is, but you seem to love it, and I know why you love it. So, I thought that after a day like today, well, I figured this was just what you needed." I handed her the bag and set the milkshakes on the entry table. She smiled, and I saw it again, the happiness this memory brought her.

"I don't know what to say, Kai, this is all so sweet of you. Want to come in and enjoy this *fine delicacy* with me."

I followed her to her kitchen table, watching her every move as she made her way in front of me. She had changed her clothes from earlier, and she was now wearing a pair of black leggings and an old thin college tee. We sat together in her kitchen for what felt like a very brief spell. We talked about our college days, our favorite trips we had taken over the years, places we would like to travel to, our friends and families, and everything in between. It felt so natural with Emily, there was never a pause in our conversation. I felt lucky to have met Emily … my heart continued to race just being in her presence.

There was a silence for the first time all evening, and Emily began to clear the table. As she threw the trash in the trash can, she glanced at the clock on the stove and made a face. "Kai it's almost midnight!

She was in a mild state of shock when she realized the time. I adored how her eyebrows danced across her forehead. She looked even more beautiful when overreacting.

"How could it be this late? Have we really been talking all night?" she questioned me as I laughed at her confusion.

I stood up and moved closer to her. As I reached around to throw my drink away in the trash behind her, my arm slowly brushed her side and I stepped away from her. Her eyes grew large when my fingers lightly grazed her lower back.

"It appears so. I should head out now though, so I can try and get at least an hour sleep before our 5AM departure."

Emily whipped around so quickly that our faces almost touched. I could feel her breath on my neck and tried to keep my composure. I knew I needed to back away now or else I wasn't sure what my hands could be capable of. We both took a step back from each other, but our eye contact continued as neither one of us wanted to lose our gaze. Emily appeared to be stumbling for words.

"You won't get any sleep if you leave right now. Think about it. By the time you get home and settled down, you'll need to get ready to come back here. Why don't you just ... stay in my guest room?"

She was nervous asking me to stay, and I couldn't find it in me to say no to her. I also couldn't help it that the man in me was wishing I were staying for other reasons. I felt like an ass even thinking that this dear woman may or may not find out her missing husband could be dead tomorrow. If that wasn't a mood killer, I didn't know what was. I searched her eyes looking for a thread of doubt. There was none.

"Sure, you're right, I'll take you up on your offer, if it's not too weird for you?" I asked as I continued to look for any sign this was going to be too much.

She shook her head and smiled. "No, I think it will be better this way, makes more sense, and then I won't feel bad having you drive back and forth so much." She gave me an awkward smile.

"I would gladly do it, Emily," I quickly replied, continuing our eye contact.

"I know you would, but I just feel bad, is all. I realize I'm a tag along tomorrow, but I want you to know I'm stronger than you think."

She straightened as she spoke, and again I was admiring all that made her, her.

"I doubt that." I grunted as I began to laugh.

"What is *that* supposed to mean? You don't think I'm strong enough to go tomorrow?"

She looked annoyed now, and I realized she did not get what I was trying to say.

"No, I said I doubt it, because I think you're just about the strongest woman I know. So, you're saying that you're stronger than I think wouldn't make much sense now, would it?" The last thing I wanted to do was insult Emily on a night like this.

"Oh, it's late, sorry … I'm tired."

She smiled, as I noticed a hint of pink touch her cheeks, happy to be the one to place it there.

"Let me get you settled in the guest room. I'll be right back."

While I waited for Emily, I browsed the living room, viewing pictures of Emily and Tillie displayed everywhere on the walls. I admired the way Emily was with her daughter. She had faced so much heartache, yet you would have never known by the smiles on their faces. I wandered down the hall a bit, wrapped up in the scrapbook she had for walls. I stopped at a wedding photo of Emily and Evan. They looked so happy, so eager, so ready for a future that would inevitably be cut short. I couldn't imagine all that Emily endured these last few years.

I startled as Emily popped up next to me and caught me staring.

"You've found Evan, now you can finally put a face to the name." She beamed as she looked at the image of the two of them together. It was evident there was still so much love in her heart for him even after all this time.

"He looks like a great guy, Emily," I whispered, as I brushed my fingers over her soft arm.

"He is ... was ... I don't know how to phrase it anymore."

She caught herself, and I couldn't help but reach out for her again. "Emily, you can't do that to yourself. Keep him alive. In here. No matter what news tomorrow brings."

Without thinking, I had placed my hand right above her heart. I could feel it racing a million beats a second. She was incredibly beautiful, and unfortunately, I was a red-blooded man. I stepped back. "Sorry about that. It's late, and I'm exhausted. I just want you to know that whatever we find out tomorrow, you have my support."

"Thanks, Kai, let me show you where you'll be sleeping."

I followed her as we made our way to a room that looked as though it hadn't been touched in years. It was clean and full of typical bedroom furniture but felt empty.

Emily stumbled with her words again. "This was our *maybe* room. Before Evan was deployed, he swore Tillie was going to be a boy, so he painted this room blue, and we slowly started decorating it. Then, right before he went missing, we found out that Tillie would be a girl. Well, my friends and family knew I was in no place to decorate a baby room, so they kept this room blue and put together a beautiful room for Tillie across the hall."

She looked on the verge of tears again, and I couldn't stand to see her in this state. I was so tired, but seeing her upset made me hurt as well. In the state I was in, I couldn't guarantee I wouldn't try to reach for her and touch her to offer her my comfort.

"I'm sure you gave Tillie a beautiful room, one that Evan would have been proud of. Thanks for sharing so much with me tonight. I know we don't know each other that well, but after everything we've been through already, I feel like I've known you for years. God, I wish I *could* have known you years before. I would have been here sooner, helped you sooner," Why did I have to be so forward with my words? I stumbled back.

"Kai, you've already done more for me than anyone has in the last three years. Did you know that next week is the anniversary of Evan's disappearance? I don't think any of this is a coincidence. I believe in fate. And I believe fate has brought all of us together."

I smiled and agreed. Fate definitely had something to do with this all coming together. We said our goodnights, and I wished I could wrap her up in my arms and hold her next to me.

Trying to get comfortable in the guest bed, I began to worry what the day ahead may bring. Alex needed answers about the possibility of having fathered a child and he needed to know exactly what the person behind these cryptic emails was trying to do. Emily needed to know the truth about Evan and get some kind of closure. And now, I needed to know more details so that I could either prepare to be there for Emily, or possibly reunite her with her missing husband. Either way, this all should end in the morning, and I seriously needed to get some rest. Now, if only I could stop my thoughts of Emily from keeping me wide awake.

Chapter Twenty-Three

EMILY

I'd never had such a hard time falling asleep as I did this night. My mind was spiraling with thoughts of how the day had played out. I could barely comprehend what all had transpired.

To make matters worse, my mind wouldn't let me forget that Kai was just a couple rooms away. I kept thinking I should make sure he had everything he needed. Was I trying to find a reason to see him again? Being a good host *was* necessary, as my mother would say, especially when he had been so helpful to me. I eventually talked myself into checking in on my guest.

I made my way down the hall, and I could see that his light was still on. As I got closer, I could hear him speaking to someone on the phone. He sounded annoyed. His tone was flat, and his words were short. I knew I shouldn't eavesdrop, but I couldn't help that these walls were so very thin.

"No no no stop! We know the situation, but we all want to be there. Dad, you don't understand the urgency, they royally screwed her over… she has not received any answers. I promise I'll talk to her before we get there…yes, she knows the pressure we're under. Well, I guess I'll see you tomorrow then. You really don't need to come. Okay, fine…bye."

I took a step back and praised the Lord above that one issue this old home did not have was creaky floors. As I stood in front of my linen closet, I purposely closed the door extra loud for added effect. I took a few steps to his door and gave a little knock.

"Kai, I saw your light was still on. Is there anything I could get you ... a towel ... some water?"

He quickly opened the door and graced me with his captivating grin.

"Oh, sorry if the light kept you up. Promise I'll pass out as soon as my head hits that pillow. Might take you up on that towel, though. I'd rather shower now than have to wake up even earlier in the morning." He responded as the corner of his mouth twitched.

Great! What was I thinking? Offering Kai a towel? To take a shower? In my home? That was a visual that even for *me* was difficult to pass up.

"Of course, let me grab you one, it's right here." I turned around and pulled a towel from the closet behind me. I don't know what I was thinking inviting him to stay the night. I sure hadn't anticipated this! I showed Kai where all the toiletries were and quickly headed back to my room before I let him see how flustered I had become. Something about his sleepy puppy dog eyes were really making me weak in the knees.

I was back in my room for maybe a minute when I heard my name.

"Emily! Can I get some help in here?"

Help? What could this grown man need help doing? Had he never taken a shower before? I made my way to the spare bathroom and knocked on the door.

"Come in. Your knobs are all jammed. When was the last time this thing was turned on?"

I opened the bathroom door and was greeted with Kai wrapped in just a towel from the waist down. I couldn't help but focus on his tanned skin, was I holding my breath? Actual words could not be formed. My face, I'm sure, said it all. Why had my eyes betrayed me at a time like this? I could not look away, and Kai was made well aware of my desire, and I of his.

I felt horrible for wishing I could just feel him beneath me, dreaming of the way his lips would taste against mine. I envisioned my fingers memorizing the curve of his strong abdomen, how it would feel to smooth my hands over his chest. Time stood still, yet I was brought back to reality when he took a step towards me. His stride was confident, yet aware of how delicate the situation had become.

He looked pleased that I had lost the chance to function in his presence. Kai was now only inches away from me, and I longed for him to reach for me, touch me. We stayed there for a few seconds until he reached up and caressed the side of my waist. He gave it a slight pull, and I was now even closer to him than I had ever been.

In a low raspy voice, Kai began to make me forget how broken I had been for so long.

"Emily, I want to do right by you. I want to be the man you deserve. You're the most incredible woman I've ever met, but I couldn't forgive myself if I let this happen right now."

He searched my face and I admired him for being stronger than I was myself. I knew where he was coming from. I knew he was right. What could I possibly be thinking?

"Yes, of course, I agree. I'm a mess, look at me. Just one look at you and I've made a fool of myself." I began to quickly turn around and wanted to run to my room and never look back at this horrible embarrassing moment.

Kai, however, reached out and would not let me run.

"Emily, listen. That's not what I'm saying at all. You're amazing. Believe me, you're so beautiful I find it difficult to be in your presence. Please believe me when I say I have wanted you the moment I met you."

His striking blue eyes looked at me with such longing, I had no choice but to believe him. After Evan went missing, I never thought I could feel this way again. I never thought another man would find me as desirable as Evan had. Yet here I was completely engulfed in Kai and his touch. Even with his gentle fingers rubbing circles on my shoulder, I wanted to run. This had become too much to bear.

As I began to turn my back, not wanting him to see me cry yet again, he whipped me around and softly claimed my lips with his. I could taste the sweetness of his breath, the passion in his touch. His hands had begun to touch me in places that needed to be brought back to life. His large, warm hands gently brushed my cheek, then made their way to my neck, and finally down my back again. His touch did not scream victory, but instead, desire. His hold had awakened my entire body with a single touch.

There was no denying now the attraction we both felt towards each other. I could not stop myself from deepening the kiss as I arched my body into his. His chest was glorious while shirtless. I was reveling in the feel of his skin under my fingertips, it was everything I had imagined and more. We were there for a short span of time, but it was enough to know this was something we both not only wanted but needed. We gently pulled apart from each other and studied each other's faces. We smiled, and instantly both began to laugh. This was not what either of us had anticipated, yet we so obviously wanted from the very beginning.

"I guess I should say thank you." He laughed, as he scratched his five o'clock shadow that had grown further throughout the night and had made its way across his entire jawline.

"I don't think a thank you begins to cover all that. Let me help with this shower, it's been a while since things have been turned on." I winced as soon as the words left my mouth.

Kai laughed and watched as I messed with the nozzles. "How long since it's been turned on?" he said in a low, gentle growl. Oh, the evil this man possesses! We both knew exactly what he was really referring to.

"Well, that all depends on what we're talking about!" I teased as I continued to mess with the knobs a little more.

Kai stood behind me now, and I could feel his desire. My heart continued to race, the booming was desperate and incessant. With his hands still around my waist as I was bent over trying to fix the shower. I wanted this feeling to never end. It had been so long since I felt wanted, so long since I felt desired. He gently turned me around so that we were facing each other once again. I could feel his muscles tense as our bodies pressed tighter together.

"I'd like to kiss you again, if you'll let me," he whispered in my ear.

I managed to let four simple words escape my mouth. "I would like that." And as if I hadn't already softened to his touch, his hands cupped my face and he kissed me with such passion I felt weak all over. His lips were desperate for mine, and I then buried my face in his neck and kissed him there until I needed air. Kai raised his hand to my hair and pulled the loose strand that was framing my face. He traced his fingers down my jaw and to my neck. He then kissed where his hand had been resting. He looked into my eyes and gave me the most beautiful smile. His eyes were now a deep luminous blue and full of heated need. Kai pulled me closer, and once again I was lost in his arms. I reached up and ran my hands through his short brown locks, messing them up as he pulled his face closer to mine. I stood up on my tiptoes and lightly brushed my lips to his once again. He met me there to deepen the kiss. I could feel him smiling against my lips.

At that moment, the water began to drizzle out of the shower head. The water hitting my face brought me back to reality. I was on the brink of discovering the biggest news of my life, and yet here I was kissing the man set on helping me uncover the truth. It was as if he could see my thoughts spread across my face as I'm pretty sure they were.

"Looks like it's working again. Nothing's broken here." He paused and gave a questioning grin. "What's going on in that beautiful head of yours?" He looked as though he was unsure if he wanted to know the answer or not.

"I'm thinking this could possibly be the most confusing day of my life. But for some odd reason, I'm not so worried about it." I looked up at him, hoping he felt the same. Hoping he felt that even though this entire day was so very complicated, it was also so very right.

He looked back at me with his magnificent blue eyes.

"Emily, I don't want to make you feel anything other than joy. You've already been through enough."

Nothing more needed to be said. We were once again in each other's arms. He leaned down and kissed me with a soft brush of his lips. But I needed more, so I deepened the kiss and parted his lips with my tongue. He grabbed me by the waist and placed me in the shower.

We were both now soaking wet from the shower that finally had chosen to work again. Kai was still in just a towel that hung dangerously low, and I was in my thin cotton pajamas. His fingers slowly traced the hem of my shirt and searched my eyes for any sign to stop. There was none. He gently pulled my blouse off and kissed my shoulder as he threw it to shower floor. My breasts seemed to have begun to fall from my flimsy bralette. Every inch of my neck and chest was then claimed by his mouth. Shock rolled through my body as he placed both hands on my hips and quickly placed me against the shower wall. His hands floated across my breasts, and he slowly placed his lips where his hands once were. I was instantly satisfied when his tongue began teasing my right breast, the sensation of his newly grown beard brought me to my toes.

Everything about this moment drew me closer to him. I was close enough now to feel his desire as I reached up to run my hands across his chest once more. His muscles were solid, and I wanted to appreciate every inch of this magnificent man.

We stood there appreciating each other for what felt like hours, my lips felt bruised from the work I was putting them through. The water started to lose its heat, and my body began to slowly tremble.

"Emily, you're shivering! Let's get out." His tone was soft and concerned. I had no plans of removing myself from his arms; I was happy here, and my body needed to cooperate.

"Not yet, I don't want this to end," I mouthed in between kisses to his jaw.

I stood on my tiptoes and tried to reach his lips again. He leaned down and assisted in my desire for more. The next thing I knew, I was being picked up, and my legs were now wrapped around his hard, secure body. I could feel the towel somehow still wrapped around his waist, it was drenched, and I secretly wished it would fall off. With one hand on my ass, he then used his other free hand to turn the water off and we made our way to my bedroom.

My bedroom … the bedroom I last shared with Evan. The memories, and all that surrounded Evan and his disappearance came crashing down like a tidal wave. I was now short of breath and searching for the words that had previously escaped. I could not do this … not now …not yet.

As we continued towards my room, I pressed my hands against Kai's chest and gently pushed myself from his hold. "I'm Sorry Kai, I can't do this right now … not here."

He looked confused, but then as if he were reading my mind, his eyes became tender with understanding as he scanned the room behind me.

"Emily, I really don't want to rush this, and I want this to be something we both have fond memories of … very fond memories."

His smile made my heart skip, and I felt as though I could walk on air. "I would like that. Would you mind just staying in here with me?" I selfishly forgot how great it felt to have someone near me.

He had no response other than grabbing a long tee hanging from my closet and handing it to me. After I slipped it on, I swiftly removed my wet leggings and stood there in only a t-shirt. Even though the shirt was large enough to hide the rest of me, Kai's eyes were solidly on me and my body standing before him. As I was getting undressed, it appeared Kai had removed his soaked towel and continued to wrap the bed sheet around himself. Once finished, he silently reached for me and pulled me close to him onto the bed. With his large warm hands and strong arms, he wrapped me up in him. I press closer, wishing if I just sink into him a bit more, broken Emily might just disappear, at least for a little while.

Chapter Twenty-Four

KAI

I couldn't help but pull her tighter to my chest to make her know that my intentions were only to *be there* for her and nothing more. I had a dozen things I wanted to whisper in her ear as we lay next to each other but none of them seemed appropriate or even necessary. Emily was everything I looked for in a woman but never thought I'd find.

With Emily nestled beside me, I began to memorize her curves and how perfectly they fit in mine. I could feel her breathing, which had calmed to a low hum, and her hair, still wet from our shower, caressing my shoulder. Instinctively, I kissed her shoulder that was pressing into my chest.

I realized as I was holding Emily, that I was wrapped in a damn sheet. Being this close and feeling her beautiful body pressing up against me in all the right places reminded me that I needed to get some clothes on and fast.

I gently moved to the edge of the bed and made sure not to lose the sheet in the shuffle, which was a miracle in itself that it had stayed on this long.

"I'm going to put some clothes on. I'll see you in the morning. Would you like me to wake you up?" I whispered to Emily as she quickly turned over onto her stomach and looked at me with her tired, heavy eyes.

"Can you stay in here tonight?" She asked with a look of reluctance.

There was no way I could say no to her, certainly not now, not ever. In a few short days I had become completely intoxicated by this woman and the feelings she induced in me. "Is that really what you want, Emily?" I replied.

"Yes, it feels so good having you here. I'm so exhausted I'll probably be asleep by the time you come back, but I would really like to have someone here tonight."

She scooted to the middle of the bed and looked absolutely tantalizing sitting there in her thin cotton t-shirt, her wide eyes were practically begging me, and who was I to say no?

"Then of course I'll stay here. I'll be right back." I bent to kiss her forehead and made my way to the guest room. As I finished getting dressed, I checked my phone one more time, and set an alarm for two hours. My adrenaline from the past few hours was not going to help me fall asleep much before that alarm sounded. I couldn't help but feel excited to lay next to Emily for the next couple hours, even knowing it would lead nowhere good.

When I returned to Emily's room wearing only my boxers, she was fighting sleep worse than a child. Her long, dark lashes shadowed her half-opened eyes but grew wide when I entered the bedroom and slid in next to her wrapping my arms around her once again. I would take things slowly for her and go at whatever pace she was comfortable with. Tonight, there was nothing happening other than holding this wonderful woman I was lucky enough to meet.

I thought she had fallen asleep when I heard a low sob. For a second, I thought it was nothing more than the sound of her beginning to drift off. But when I heard another sniffle, it was clear she was crying.

"Emily, are you okay?"

She turned facing me and shifted a bit in my arms while her sobs softened in my chest.

"Hey, look at me," I whispered. It broke me to see her so upset.

"I'm embarrassed, you're exhausted, and I've asked you to stay in here. And now I'm keeping you up with my incessant crying,"

"I wasn't going to be able to sleep anyway if it makes you feel any better. Now how 'bout you tell me why you're really crying." Her brow was scrunched up and I could tell there was more she hadn't said.

"Kai, I'm not really sure how I should say this so forgive me if I don't make any sense at all. When I'm with you, I forget who I am, even what I've been through ... you know. Of course, you know what I'm going through and everything. I just can't fathom having feelings again for someone so soon after just having met. I haven't been this close to another man since ..."

She trailed off and I knew her next word. Evan was all around us, our situation, how we met. Hell, even his picture was on the nightstand looking at me.

"I know perfectly well what you mean, Emily, and you know what? That's a hundred percent okay. We both know how strange everything is. We both know it's way too soon."

She quickly replied. "You feel the same?" She studied me for my response.

"Of course, I do. How could I not?" I laughed and smiled at her, relieved that she returned the laugh.

"Oh, Kai, I wish I could just move on, but I can't until things are settled. It just doesn't feel right. The what ifs far outweigh any logical thinking. I know the odds are not in his favor. I was told to give it a year after he went missing and then it would be time for me to move on. It just never felt right." She paused as she refined her next expression.

"That is ... until now. This is the closest I've felt to doing so. It's like I'm struggling to let his memory rest. Breaks my heart even thinking like this."

She breathed deep then yawned and closed her eyes. She was the most breathtaking woman I had ever seen. Her honesty was what made me respect her even more than I already had.

"I want to be here in any capacity you need me to be. If you want me here ... great. I'm here as long as you would like. If you want me to leave, I can be out before you finish the sentence, if that's what you want. I won't rush you into anything. I'm here to help you find what you need. I'm here for you, Emily, and nothing more. No hidden agendas here."

Emily lowered herself onto my lips and I deepened the kiss as I wrapped my arms around her curvy body. I guess that answered my question. She wanted me to stay, and I was more than happy to do so.

Chapter Twenty-Five

EMILY

Kai made me feel as though I could say anything, and he would willingly accept me, flaws and all. I could never grow tired of the way he held me the rest of the night and kept me feeling safe for the first time in years. His kisses were deliberate and full of passion. The heat of his body felt like I'd come home. Throughout the night … well, the short time we were able to attempt sleep, I could feel his kisses down my neck, on my shoulder, and in my hair.

Lying with Kai was amazing and yet incredibly confusing. I loved having him next to me, but I knew I was acting selfishly. I also hated the fact that I'd asked him to stay in a moment of weakness. Kai deserved better. He deserved a complete package. Someone he didn't have to worry might fall apart at any moment. He needed someone that was baggage free, and I knew better than anyone my baggage was over the carry-on limit.

It was still dark when I heard the alarm on his phone. A soft melody that made him stir. Grabbing the phone, he silenced the alarm then turned to face me. Once again, I was staring into his all-consuming blue eyes. Kai smiled and without thinking I leaned down and tasted his full warm lips. He immediately intensified the kiss, and again I was wrapped in his arms feeling his warm body pressed against mine.

"We should get dressed," Kai whispered in between kisses.

Talk about a contradiction! He was saying we should get dressed, but his lips and body were saying something entirely different.

As much as I wanted to spend the day exactly where I was, kissing Kai, I knew how important today was. I had to get up and go find my answers. Today was the day I had been waiting years for.

"If you want to take that shower you never got to take, I'll go make us some coffee," I said as I began making my way off the bed. As I sat on the edge of the bed, Kai came up behind me and softly kissed my shoulder. His warm lips lingered there for a few moments, and I treasured the sincerity of his unspoken words.

"That's a great idea. I think I'm going to need a cold shower," he agreed.

I quickly turned around to see his laugh making adorable lines form around his eyes. I laughed with him, enjoying the sarcasm. Without warning, Kai stood up and was stripped free of his clothes … all of his clothes! I was shocked at his confidence. However, he did have a lot to be confident of. He made his way to the master bath, and as much as I knew I should look away, I couldn't take my eyes off him. He was absolutely a work of art. I stood frozen in my room, unable to move, unable to function. He must have felt my stare because he looked back at me before he stepped into the shower.

"I'm sorry, I'll go make that coffee now," I blurted, embarrassed he'd caught me staring.

"Emily, I don't mind. You can look all you want."

He boyishly smirked and gave me a wink before he closed the shower door. My eyes were still on him when the shower door shut.

Someone should've slapped me, so I'd come back to reality and prepare myself for the severity of this day and all it meant. I was but steps away from discovering what actually happened to Evan and finally having the chance to move forward one way or the other. Would Kai be a part of my moving forward? Would my situation end up being too much for him to handle? Would I become a lost cause? What if Evan was still alive? Would he still want me, even though I had now spent the night with another man?

The questions whirled inside my head like a category five hurricane. I knew I would be a nervous wreck the rest of the day. Nothing coffee can't fix, right?

Chapter Twenty-Six

KAI

Well, that was fun! Getting Emily all riled up and flustered was now my new favorite pastime. I didn't think ahead before I started taking my clothes off, but once I saw her staring, I knew I needed to go all in or nothing. Sleeping with Emily was the most exhilarating experience, feeling her curves against my body all night long, breathing in her scent when she moved closer to me. I needed more than the time I was given, I knew of the severity that today had for her, but I also knew I needed Emily in my life and would stand by her no matter what we found. As I finished drying and getting dressed in my day-old clothes, I smelled coffee in the air and was eager to get on the road.

Emily was at her kitchen table and appeared to be lost in thought. With all that she was going through, I hoped my being there hadn't made the situation more difficult. As I entered, she looked up at me with her beautiful smile.

"I poured you a cup, but I didn't know how you liked it." She smiled as she handed me my steaming cup.

"I'm good with just a splash of milk, nothing fancy for me," I said, pouring a dash into my cup. As I brought it to my lips, I felt my body wake. I checked the time, and we only had a few more minutes before we needed to get a move on.

I took a seat next to Emily and could tell she was still lost in thought. She was tapping her fingers on the table, and I gently placed my hand on top of hers. She instantly looked energized at our sudden touch. "I know today is a big day for you Emily. You just let me know what you need, and when you need it, and I'll do whatever it takes to make today easier for you."

She smiled and shook her head. "Kai, you've already done everything you could. You've been amazing without even trying." She placed her other hand on top of mine and gave it a squeeze.

"Oh, believe me, I'm trying. I'm trying really hard." I laughed, trying to ease the intensity of the day ahead.

While we sat, she wanted to know the rundown of the day's agenda. As she warmed our coffee, my phone rang, and rolled my eyes when I saw that it was Alex.

"Good morning, Senator," I facetiously answered.

"Why the hell do you sound so chipper this morning? You better be on your way over there!"

"No, I'm not on the road yet. Emily and I are getting ready to leave right now," I answered, picturing Alex's smug grin.

"You're with her already? Did you stay the night there?" I didn't have to report anything to Alex; it was none of his business what I was doing with Emily. I knew what his obnoxious tone implied, and I hated the fact that his mind went *there* when it involved Emily and me.

"Yeah, this way was easier. Was there a reason you were calling?" I asked as he began to laugh on the other end.

"Um, yeah … wow someone's defensive. I was just calling to make sure you were up and getting on the road. But it sounds like you're already doing just fine. So, I'll see you two soon." He chuckled and the call ended.

I could have given him a punch to the gut. I knew what he was thinking and hated that he thought I would take advantage of Emily, especially at a time like this.

I instantly pocketed my phone. "Emily, we should get on the road now. It's a couple of hours away."

She nodded and made her way to the living room to grab her sweater and oversized purse. As we got in my car, I saw her pull out her phone to send a quick text. She must have seen me glance her way.

"I thought I should give my mom a quick update based on the details you gave me this morning. I've never been away from Tillie this long ... it feels strange."

"I can only imagine, but I think it's for the best. She's probably a lot safer with her grandma for the day."

Emily's eyes widened at my bold statement. "Do you think this person's dangerous?" she asked, with a nervousness in her voice.

"Not necessarily, but I wouldn't think it'd be a safe place to bring a two-year-old."

She nodded as if she understood. "Of course, that makes sense. But what do you think we'll even find when we get there?"

"Well, what we do know is, whoever we're meeting with today is the one behind the email sent to Alex and is likely the same person who changed the birth certificate. They're obviously trying to link the two of you together. I'm hoping that whatever their reason was, it will also lead us to answers about Evan." How I wished I had *all* the answers to help this amazing woman.

"That's the best-case scenario though. Couldn't this person just be some nut job messing with people for fun?" She lowered her head and let out a heavy sigh.

"Not exactly, this person must have some pretty high clearance, as well as military knowledge. The systems they were able to hack into are incredibly tight. My dad mentioned that this person must have had quite the training with a military background, so that's why you'll see several military police there today. I don't think they're going to ambush the place, but I wouldn't be surprised if it's a bit intense at first. Alex has our team on it as well. But because the systems this person hacked into were military documents, it's become a high priority case."

I didn't want to scare Emily, I just wanted her to be prepared for what was about to happen. She sat in silence as she took the information in. Without a word she reached over and grabbed my hand and held it in hers. It was strange and natural for us to be touching like this, for her hand to be resting with mine. This small comforting act felt like we needed each other's presence more than we dared to admit. We drove for the next hour with our hands interlocked.

We talked about memories she and Tillie had made over the years, as well as our favorite bands we listened to as kids. Our conversations were so easy and full. I'd never experienced this sort of instant chemistry with a woman before. Fortunately, Emily seemed to share our instantaneous connection, as well. No matter what it was that brought us together, I was happy it had happened all the same.

I glanced at my navigation and saw that ETA was in ten and pressed my Bluetooth to update the team. "One moment, let me call the team and tell them we're about ten minutes away. I don't want to arrive in the wrong area and ruin the whole operation."

She nodded as I pressed send and within seconds Alex answered.

"Hey, you almost here?" There was a slight pang of fear in his voice, and I could tell he was nervous.

"Yeah, we're about ten minutes away. You okay, man?" I didn't want to make him uncomfortable. Yes, I was arriving with

Emily, but he had to know I was there for him and his protection above all else.

"Of course. I want to catch this son of a bitch. I'm just waiting to get the green light to interrogate this mother—"

"Yeah, yeah, yeah, we all are Alex, just stay put. Who's all there?" I interrupted him because Emily looked uncomfortable with the direction Alex was taking the conversation.

"Well, your dad's here, apparently, he is fronting the whole operation. He put some calls in, and it appears this hacker, or whatever, has done some other things in the past and this was turning out to be their sloppiest work. His men are pretty happy we caught on to them when we did. Just because I know your dad won't say it, he's really proud of you for catching onto that message you decoded. I overheard him talking to some of the officers and he was talking you up big time."

That was a shock. My father was a man of few words, but when he did speak, you'd definitely want to listen. I couldn't believe he was going to be there today, and we would actually be working together on something this high profile. I couldn't let Emily see how nervous I'd become for this new turn of events. Working with my father brought back all my insecurities of never being good enough in his eyes.

"Thanks for the update, Alex, but I won't hold my breath. We're just a couple blocks away, so can you ask around where Emily should go first? I want her in a secure place before we make initial contact."

"Yeah, of course. I'll ask around. We set up a small white tent around the corner from the home. Don't go directly to the house, or you'll blow this whole thing up."

Emily's eyes widened.

"Okay, Alex, wrong choice of words there huh, yeah, I'll pull in near the tent. Go ask around and I'll text you when we get there." I hung up the phone and reached over to hold Emily's hand. When it was safely in mine once again, she smiled up at me and then planted a soft kiss on my cheek. For several minutes there was a new silence between us. We both knew all too well how important the next few hours were going to be.

As we approached the street where we needed to park, I spotted the white tent and pulled in nearby. I sent a quick text to Alex. Waiting for his reply, I looked at Emily. She was nervous and had every right to be. Hell, as a cop, I'd been in similar situations before, and even I was nervous for today's sequence of events. I think Emily had been so good at hiding her insecurities, I almost didn't catch the fear in her eyes. She looked at me, and then quickly looked out the window toward the group beginning to form near the front of our car.

"Hey, could you look at me for a moment?" I whispered, as she slowly complied.

"I'm not sure how to feel or act right now, Kai." She sighed as she stared into my eyes. A sight that continued to make me weak.

"I'm going to make sure today goes as smoothly as possible for you, Emily, okay? You have my word on it. If we don't get you answers today, you know I won't stop until we have them."

"I appreciate that, Kai. I actually believe I might get some answers today." She looked over my shoulder. "Oh look, here comes Alex!"

She pointed to my side of the vehicle, and I rolled my window down. Alex looked like he hadn't slept in days but appeared as though he just downed ten energy drinks to cure his lack of sleep. However, he was still Alex and his charm and determination settled perfectly on his face.

"We have everything ready, but your dad was waiting for your arrival before making initial contact. They have a safe place ready for Emily and me. After you assess the situation, we'll join you for the questioning."

Emily looked at both me and Alex. "Take me to where I need to go. Let's get things started." She was full of determination and if she was fearful, she was hiding it well.

Alex nodded and we all went directly to the tent. Once inside, it was as if we had stepped foot into police headquarters. There were two rows of tables filled with computers and tracking devices. There must have been over a dozen people in the tent, each one meticulously doing their designated task.

Emily's eyes widened and she appeared overwhelmed. I drew her close to my side and felt her body shiver as I pulled her closer.

"Don't worry, this is all just protocol. Honestly, I'm sure my dad is doing this for show. He's all for the theatrics." I laughed trying to make light of the situation. That was until I heard my father's low growl behind me.

"Theatrics, huh?" he scowled abruptly as I turned quickly to face him. "You know I'm doing this as a favor to you. The least you can do is say thank you!" He grumbled.

"You and I both know as soon as you discovered the subject's ties, you jumped at the opportunity to solve another case. But thanks for setting this up so quickly, it was rather … unexpected."

He looked at me as though he was at a loss for words. "I take it this is the missing soldier's wife?" He nodded at Emily, and then rested his eyes on our close proximity.

Knowing my father, he would have an opinion on my behavior concerning Emily. I didn't care what he might eventually say because Emily was important to me, and I wouldn't let his opinion damage things for us.

"Yes, this is Emily, Emily, this is my father, Chris Taylor."

They quickly shook hands and looked each other over. Emily stepped back to my side, and I had the urge to guard her from my father's coldness. He, no doubt, already had his opinions.

"We were told to meet here for a safe place to wait," I said as I tried to break the silence. He was still eyeing Emily, and for the first time I thought I saw a thread of sadness in his hard stare. Maybe I was wrong about him.

"Yes, it's nice to meet you. Follow me, we've arranged everything. You don't need to worry darling. Like my son said, I have a way of doing things more on the dramatic side." He was smiling now.

In all my life I had never seen my father act this way, let alone to a complete stranger. Normally, he waited for people to prove themselves to him. His Texan roots must have been pushing through because I'd definitely never heard him call anyone *darling* before.

"Dad, she needs to be involved in everything, even if she stays in here for a good part of the operation, she needs to be involved. It's because of her we even found this—"

"She'll be involved. We have a headset and everything for her to be in your ear. And by the way, our subject goes by the name of Matt Stone," he added. "Does that name ring any bells for you?" he asked as we both looked at Emily.

Emily looked down at the ground with a cold stare, all the color had drained from her face. She wouldn't make eye contact with

159

either of us, yet I couldn't look away. A tear fell from her eyes, and I knew the name meant something to her.

She didn't look up, and her voice was shaky as she began, "Matt Stone was Evan's best friend in his squadron. They w…were stationed together before he went missing. Is he here, is he involved somehow … is he alive?" Her face went stoic as tears pooled in her eyes.

My father, looking concerned as well, answered her. "Yes, he's alive. We think he's the one behind all this." He was no longer warm and comforting. "Emily, did you know anything at all? Have you had any contact with this individual?"

I wanted to protect her from his harsh calculating tone, but Emily had no need for my protection. She was bold in her response. It was evident she had had enough with the accusations. "I have had absolutely no contact with Matt! His family *has* presumed him dead. He went missing around the same time as Evan!"

Emily had every right to be angry. Her face said it all. "Where is he? I want to see him! He must have a good reason for all this." She looked around as if she wanted to find a way out of the tent. Here again, someone was accusing her of taking part in this scheme and she would not let it pass this time.

My father stepped between us. "We can't have a civilian involved in this until we get clearance. Now that we know you know him, let us make sure he's not a threat, and then we will bring you in. Does that sound good?" It surprised me that my father was being understanding and actually helpful again.

Emily appeared pleased with his response as she settled into my side. "Yeah, I can do that. Can I have a moment alone with your son please?" He nodded, and he and Alex went to the entrance of the tent.

We took a seat and I put her hands in mine. She looked up at me, and I could see she was a million miles from me. The urge to hold her was overwhelming. Instead, I looked her in the eyes and tried to assure her the only way I knew how.

"Emily, we're almost there; you're getting your answers. We have no idea how the rest of the day will pan out, but you know I'll be here through it all." I prayed that what I was saying was going to help.

"I know. Thank you, Kai. Please take it easy in there. If it *is* Matt, he was always such a nice guy, a little strange at times, but always so sweet."

"Strange, as in how?" I asked, needing her to clarify what she meant.

Emily hesitated briefly and said, "Strange, as in always wanted in on every conversation. He idolized Evan. He was a bit younger than Evan, but he was so smart that he made it to the top faster than most. I remember when they told me they were both missing. I didn't give it a second thought. Matt was like Evan's shadow … they were best friends. So, it made sense for them to be together when they…"

She was beginning to ramble, so I took her in my arms and held her there for a moment. I could feel her struggling not to cry into my chest.

"I'm so sorry, Kai. This is just all becoming so real again. Go ahead and get this thing started, the quicker you go in, the quicker we can all get answers." I nodded and helped wipe her tears.

My father was pretending not to be watching us, but I knew better. I stood up and grabbed Emily's headset. I gently placed it on for her and smoothed out the hair around her face. They had a laptop waiting for her, ready with my father's body cam footage. I positioned my earpiece and bent to give Emily a kiss on the forehead before making my way to the exit.

Alex came and stood behind Emily. I was glad she wouldn't be alone. He gave me a quick nod. Alex may be a pain in my ass most days, but he was also my best friend, and I knew she was in good hands.

I joined my father and we met up with the rest of the team. I recognized a few of the men who were assigned to make initial contact. We were all aware of the gravity of the next few minutes. Once we got the okay, we knocked on the door. Here goes nothing.

Chapter Twenty-Seven

KAI

Three times we knocked on the door. No answer. I really didn't want this to become a hostile situation. Now that we knew of his relationship to Evan and Emily, I hoped he would be cooperative and accommodating.

My father wasn't so hopeful. He was detached and ready for a fight. This time he pounded on the door and yelled. "Matthew Stone, we have you surrounded! Open the door, or we will force entry!"

His shouting blared through my earpiece. We heard some shuffling inside, and we were now on high alert. People don't respond well to being ambushed ... go figure. Slowly, the door began to open.

"I'm not armed, I promise. Please don't shoot!" His voice was strained and sounded utterly terrified. I had my men lower their weapons hoping to gain his trust. As I took a step towards the door, I signaled for my father to keep his weapon drawn.

"Matt, can I call you Matt?"

He made eye contact with me through the door and gave a sheepish nod. The guy looked petrified.

"Okay Matt, we had our men lower their weapons, but we have to keep ours drawn until we can secure your home and make sure you're no threat. Do you think you can allow us to do that?"

He gave another nod and opened the door further. Once it was wide open, he stood in the doorway, and we immediately sensed he was not an immediate threat. Matthew Stone was missing his left leg and could barely stand with his crutch as a support. There was absolutely no room for him to hold a weapon.

There were six of us that entered the home. I began to pat him down. Once he was cleared, the other men searched the house, and within minutes they gave us the green light.

Matt was looking me over and took a seat at his cluttered computer desk. One of the team read him his rights, and we all took a seat in his small, dark living room.

"What's this all about, anyway?" he asked.

My father and I looked at each other debating who should approach the question.

I spoke first. "We have reason to believe you made threats to the senator, Alex Greyson. Is this correct?"

Matt began to look around the room and as he stared at the void where his leg should have been, he appeared defeated. "Well, it appears I've lost my touch. What gave me away?"

My father began to stir, and I could tell he wanted to play hard ball. We obviously had two completely different interrogation tactics. I continued, "Matt, I need you to be completely transparent with me. Are you saying you are the one behind the email?"

He nodded and slowly rubbed his hand down his face. "Yes, but you have to know I never wanted to hurt anyone, I know what I was doing was wrong, but…" He couldn't finish his sentence.

My father who was growing more impatient beside me interjected, "Do you have any idea the wasted manpower we've had to exhaust over these issues? I don't care what your story is. You're one of our own! You knew what the consequences of your actions would be. You knew better than to do something like this."

I glared at my father for speaking out of place. This was *my* interrogation, and he was ruining the rapport I was trying to gain. I raised my hand to silence him though I knew I'd hear about it later. I looked back to Matt and got his attention.

"Excuse him, but we're all on edge here. Matt, we know about your involvement with Emily Decker and changing her child's birth certificate. Would you care to enlighten us on how that has anything to do with the senator?"

Matt was clearly taken aback not expecting me to know of the birth certificate, or Emily, for that matter. His face went ashen. He swallowed hard and then asked, "Before we get into everything, I have to ask … does Emily know about me?"

He looked so desperate I truly felt sorry for the guy. "Yes, she knows everything, and she is just as confused about all of this as the rest of us. We cannot figure how the two of them … the senator and Emily, could be linked together. I wasn't going to tell you just yet, but Emily is here. And she needs answers, Matt."

Matt's eyes sprung open. "Emily's here?" he sheepishly asked as he looked down at his missing limb. I read worry and regret in his eyes.

"Yes, and we were going to let her join us once the timing was right. She also knows it was you behind everything, and she has already informed us about your friendship with Evan. There's no room for any more lies, Matt. We're here now, and we need you to explain everything from the beginning."

Matt nodded his head and made a quick turn to his right. At his sudden movement the team instinctively drew their weapons, and Matt raised his hands.

"Damn, I'm just grabbing a notebook from my desk. No need for the guns."

The soldier in him was coming out, and I sensed he was losing the fear he had earlier.

They lowered their weapons as Matt grabbed a worn notebook from the bottom drawer of his desk. "This will explain everything. Can Emily join us? I have so much I've wanted to say to her… but I just wasn't allowed to."

What could he mean by *not allowed*? There was definitely more to the story.

My father was making a call. I waited at the door, and within minutes Emily and Alex were standing in front of me eager to enter.

Alex came in with his arm around Emily, and in a different setting, I would have wanted him to step away from her. Emily's eyes were reddened as though she had been crying, and I knew he had been consoling her. Even through her tears, Emily was incredibly brave. Her confidence was radiating now more than ever. I knew she was determined, and nothing could stand in her way. I moved between the two of them and placed my hand on her lower back. Alex took the hint and stepped aside.

"I'm ready to see him. Lead the way," she demanded.

"He's right this way." She followed me into the living room, and once they made eye contact, Matt broke down. It was a strange sight to see a strong man fall apart like that.

Emily kept her distance and sat next to me on the couch opposite Matt. She was incredibly at ease, holding back tears of her own.

Once she started to address Matt, I could see her struggling for control.

"Matt, we thought you were dead! Do you know I cried with your mother when the news came out? I only recently found out more information on Evan. What the hell is going on?"

Emily was shaking beside me, and I wished I could hold her and take her in my arms. I sensed her confidence was now hanging by a thread.

Matt finally gained some composure and opened the notebook. He looked at Emily and cleared his throat. "Emily, what I'm about to tell you won't be easy. I have everything that happened here in this notebook. I have answers for all of you right here." He then looked to Alex. "I even have answers for you. I'm sorry I had to involve you, but there is a reason you were brought into this. It had to happen, whether I wanted it to or not. It's what they wanted."

Emily's shaking continued, and without giving it a thought I put my arm around her. "Matt, as you can see, you need to elaborate on what that all means. Emily has waited too long for this conversation. And as far as Mr. Greyson is concerned, we all need a clear explanation."

Matt nodded and began to flip through his worn notebook. "Like I said, what I'm about to share with you won't be easy to hear.

I'm sorry to everyone involved, especially you, Emily. I always wished I would never have to tell you this."

And with that said, Matt began to read from his notebook.

Chapter Twenty-Eight

MATT'S NOTEBOOK

So, today's the day, we're about to do another search. Catherine has been missing for 3 days now and things are not looking good for her. Evan and I arranged for a team of 5 soldiers to accompany us, but captain keeps pushing the departure time back. We have a good idea where she could be held, but we don't want to take any chances. I know Evan feels as if he's to blame, and it's killing him that we haven't located her yet. I wouldn't be surprised if he goes off on his own... not that I would let him. We made a pact to stick together through hell and back. He knows I'd give my life to save his. No one understood me and my past. No one seems to care like Evan - he always wants to do what's right. I, on the other hand, don't mind bending the rules to get shit done. Evan grew up in a good family, mine... not so much.

Catherine was always there to mother us, and now she was going to be a real mother to some lucky kid. Sucks that she got pregnant by some asshole though that doesn't even bother to check in on her. I wish I had a phone number to call the dick. Apparently, he is some hot shot with plans to run for senator. Catherine knew his reputation beforehand, and I wasn't about to ruin her happiness. She's happy for the kid and doesn't plan on ever letting the guy know... her choice. She says he wouldn't even remember her. Who in their right mind could forget Catherine ... I have no idea.

We have to find her. Evan's taking it extra hard because he's about to be a father in a couple months too. We're hoping to get him home in time, but he hasn't heard back yet on a date. Emily and Evan are serious marriage goals. Seriously, the two of them are perfect for each other. I don't think I'll ever find someone to love me like that. Such is life. I'm trying to sleep, but I can't. I'm worried about Catherine. I know the reputation around these parts. Why did she go out all alone? What could've possibly piqued her interest enough, that she went by herself and without any protection?

Evan's tossing in the bunk beside me. I know he's not asleep. Neither of us can sleep knowing Catherine is out there all alone... I've got drills in the morning, so I'm about to try to sleep. Out.

Evan has a plan. If captain pushes the search party back one more time, we're going out on our own. A few of the guys said they would come too, but we're not sure we want to include them in case this ends badly. Shit... I hope it doesn't end badly. More news later - we have a meeting with the captain in 20.

Looks like they couldn't care less about Catherine- seems they think she went AWOL. We all know that's a bunch of bullshit. She would never leave. And if she did, she would've told us, she wouldn't have left everything. Something doesn't make sense here. Evan and I are going to leave tonight to find her. Two more guys have agreed to join, and we have a plan in motion, but no clue if we're going to be able to stick to it. Evan hates that I hacked the captain's login, but from there I was able to find the last ping from her radio. Ever since Tuesday night it hasn't been accessed or turned on. Evan seemed to know the area and is confident we can do this successfully. He knows he doesn't have to talk me into anything, I'm coming. Evan called Emily but didn't want to mention the plan. He knows she would freak and try to talk him out of things. Poor guy looked downright sick when he had to lie to her. They're still talking, and I can hear Emily mentioning name ideas with Evan. So far, they both like the name Tillie- seems cute.

Evan will be a great father...I can't wait for things to get figured out so we can all just move past this. Catherine will have to name her kid after one of us after all this drama she's putting us through.

169

We're heading out in about 20. Waiting for the guards to make the night switch. I'm a bit nervous, but with Evan so confident I know I shouldn't worry. Oorah!

■■■

I looked up from the notebook to make eye contact with Emily. It was so strange seeing her in the flesh. I never thought I would see her again, or anyone from that time in my life, for that matter. She had tears in her eyes, but from years of experience she remained calm and determined for answers. I believed she knew what was about to be read, but from someone that lived through it, you wouldn't want to have the memories attached to these pages. I knew what I was about to read and the hurt these next few pages held. I never wanted anyone to know what happened. I had worked years on trying to keep it from her ears. I couldn't hide them any longer. My silence wasn't doing any favors for anyone,

Emily stared at me and started screaming. "Is that it? Matt what happened to Evan? I know there has to be more than that!"

"I don't think you should hear this Emily, it's dark … I never wanted anyone to read this. I've worked so hard to keep my promise."

My eyes fell back to my missing leg, and I couldn't fathom the pain she must be in. For the first time, I felt as though maybe I shouldn't have kept it hidden. Maybe I should've told her the truth from the very beginning.

"Okay, I'll read the rest, but I have to warn you that I wrote this as it was happening in real time. I wrote whenever I could, as it was the only way we could remember everything."

Emily straightened up and slowly nodded her head. "I'm ready. I've waited long enough to know the truth, Matt." She was right. Things *had* been hidden for too long.

Uncovered

It was time to let the truth be told.

■■■

We've been captured.

Catherine is here too. In bad shape.

Evan knew the way alright, only issue was Catherine was taken to this holding cell, or whatever you want to call this dump.

No idea where we are now- we had been traveling all night. Luckily, they searched my backpack for electronics, but didn't care about a flimsy notebook.

Evan looks worried.

Catherine's not looking good. We're all being held together in a small room. We tried to help her as much as possible, but they roughed her up pretty good. We don't have the right supplies to do much.

This is worst case scenario.

Only hope we have now is that the two guys that were with us got away before we could. Hopefully, they make it back to base and will send help soon. That is if they haven't been found and killed.

It's been two days. Catherine is barely speaking now.

Evan and I are worried she won't make it.

We have officially run out of food and water.

Catherine was able to tell us what she went out for that Tuesday night. Prenatal vitamins?

We don't believe her, but who am I to argue with a dying woman?

I'm trying not to be upset with her.

Catherine is bleeding pretty bad.

Evan thinks she's losing the baby- her body isn't strong enough to fight.

The scumbags outside this room don't give a shit and won't even listen to us.

I almost lost my notebook. I've been hiding it in my pants behind my back.

They threw us some scraps today like we were dogs, one water bottle for the three of us.

We gave most of it to Catherine. She's not doing good.

She's lost a lot of blood.

Catherine's gone. I fell asleep for maybe an hour when I heard the screaming. It was dark, I don't know if it was Catherine, or Evan or the guards, but the cries were enough to wake the dead. The guards- they dragged her body out of the room as if she were a pile of trash.

I will not let them get away with this. Her blood is on their hands.

Now that Catherine is gone, they seem to be moving on to us.

They grabbed Evan about 10 minutes ago, and by the sound of things- they're doing their worst.

I've tried getting out of this room. But I just can't.

I can't help Evan.

Evan came back around dawn. I could barely recognize him.

The second they threw him down to the ground I could hear his ribs crack.

His lip is nearly pulled off of his face, and the smell of gasoline is pungent on his clothes. These idiots don't know what they have done.

I will kill each and every one of them.

Last night was quiet.

Evan's hurt. I'm no doctor, but the blood coming from his head doesn't look good.

They threw us more scraps tonight and again one water bottle.

I gave it all to Evan- he needs it more than me.

Uncovered

I know I'm next.

Two more days have gone by. They haven't done or said a thing to either of us.
Evan looks as though he may just pull through after all this.
He is strong.
He made me promise to take care of Emily and the baby.
I told him I'll do no such thing- he'll be around to do it himself.
I may have gotten a smile out of him.
But if I did, it didn't last.

It was finally my turn.
My turn for a good whack.
I must be lucky. I only look half as bad as Evan.
Can't write more- my hand is probably broken and my whole-body hurts.

Evan talked more today- he sounds horrible.
We are beginning to lose hope that the other two made it back to base.
I'm worried Evan isn't doing good. The gash on his head looks infected.
When the guards threw us our scraps, they noticed too.
Please come ...someone come soon.

Evan is worse.
Don't know what to do.
The guards have been weird.
I'm scared.

Evan hasn't been speaking, but he asked me to write something.
I didn't want to let him, letting him do so accepts defeat.
We will not give up hope.

But he insisted, and I have no clue what's going to happen from here.

Dear Emily,

I love you so very much. You are my world. If the time comes for Matt to give this to you, please know I had to help. Raise Tillie to be as strong-willed and compassionate as you, I know you will be the best mother. Our child is lucky to have you. I'm lucky to have you. I'm so sorry. Please forgive me if things end badly, my only wish is to return to you. I'm sorry I'm such an idiot. My whole heart belongs to you Emily. Forever.

Love, Evan

I couldn't help but read what Evan wrote. I knew where his mind had been the last couple days. I just hoped he still had some hope.
Hope is dying- just like the both of us.

The gash on Evan's head looks worse today.
We have to get out of here soon.

The guards have been whispering a lot today.
No clue what's being said.
But it can't be good.

Uncovered

From what I gathered something is happening tonight.
I can't make out what more they are saying.
God help us.

■ ■

Three months have gone by since I've had the guts to open this notebook and go through those last few days. I wish I could say we were saved. I wish I could say it was all just a nightmare, but that was not the case. That was not the case at all. For three months I've had the time to process what happened those last few hours. I am writing this now so that our story will not be forgotten.

The night I heard the guards speaking came and went. I thought we were in the clear. We both did.
I never told Evan what I heard- I didn't want him to worry more than he already was. He looked to be healing and they had let him be for a few days. We both were woken late one night to shouting- shouting in a language neither of us understood. They pulled Evan and me up to our feet and dragged us to an open field a couple feet from the entrance of the building where we were being held. I could taste the blood in my mouth as they hit me in the jaw with a large wooden bat. I couldn't understand why they would hit me and not Evan. They had been picking on him more than me from the beginning. Maybe it was just my turn. Two men who looked younger than me handcuffed us to a rundown soft-top jeep. Once they were done, they walked away and were no longer visible.
For the first time in days, we felt the fresh air.

I remember the moon was bright that night. There was enough light around us that I finally got a good look at Evan. I wasn't able to see the full extent of his injuries in the dark room where we were held. I was worried about him. He looked at me and gave me an attempt of a smile.

175

"You look like shit too, buddy, don't give me that look."

He still had a way of making me laugh in the shittiest of times. I think for a moment, that we both thought they were really going to just leave us there. This was the end of things, and we would eventually be found soon. They had done their bit, and we were of no use to them anymore. The whole time we were there they never once asked us a single thing- they just wanted to beat the shit out of us, and they did a damn fine job.

A couple hours went by, and the sun was starting to rise. My arms were going numb and from time to time I would nudge Evan with my shoulder to keep him alert. He looked like hell.

I don't know if it was minutes or hours, but a group of men came barreling over to us in a dilapidated truck about to burst at the seams. There were no doors and no top, just six men piled in. The dust whirled around us, and I could feel it grinding in my teeth.

They approached us and started shouting in another language. I'd been overseas long enough to catch on to some of what they were saying, and from what I gathered, they were not just going to let us go. This was not the end we had hoped for.

One of the men, who I assumed was the leader, walked over and took one look at the two of us and laughed. He spit on me, and I saw red. Two of the men began to grab Evan and unlock his handcuffs. I had a horrible feeling and wished I could've known what I know now.

The leader pulled out a gun and waved it in our faces. Evan's eyes were wide open now and for the first time in days, one of them spoke in English.

"Get up." the man screamed in Evan's face and pushed him to his feet.

I tried to move, but the cuffs were too tight. Once Evan was stumbling to his feet the man hit him over the head with the gun, and Evan fell to his feet once again.

"I said, get up," he screamed again while laughing to his friends. Evan tried to get up but just couldn't, he staggered and fell at the man's feet. The man

began to kick him, and I tried with every ounce of my strength to get free and stop

more from happening. They all began to laugh at me. I didn't give a shit- I would

keep trying. The soldier that could speak English looked at me.

"Don't worry you'll get your turn." The evil in his eyes still makes me

sick to my stomach.

Two of the men from the group pulled Evan to his knees, and for a moment it felt

like the world stopped. It finally dawned on me what was happening. Without

missing a beat, Evan knew it too. It took all his strength, but Evan lifted his head

and screamed over to me.

"Don't let Emily know how it ended." His voice was hoarse, and I shook

my head… I could not make that promise… this wasn't happening.

The men were speaking to each other and finally screamed over at me,

"What the hell was that?"

I had no clue what they were talking about. "Evan, look at me!" I was

desperate for him to not give up hope. "This isn't the end." The rest happened so

fast, that I'm still trying to piece it all together- I finally feel I have it ready to be

written.

I was watching Evan when suddenly, bullets flew by from behind me, a bullet hit

one of the men from in the group, and they all started to panic. The one that spoke

English began screaming to the others to leave. For a second, I thought we were

saved. The leader, or who I assumed to be the leader, grabbed Evan from the

shoulder and pulled him up. Looked at me in the eyes and back at Evan. Evan

never showed fear to the man. As he began to raise his weapon to Evans's head, I

screamed.

"I promise!" and with not a second to spare the man shot Evan in the

head. Evan fell instantly to the ground. As soon as I saw Evan falling, I felt

someone unhooking my cuffs. I was free. I was free to kill the man that just killed

my best friend. I turned to see my platoon coming in behind me. The guy that

177

uncuffed me handed me a gun and screamed, "Get Evan!" He didn't even have time to finish his words before I was already rushing over. Once I was by Evan's side, I realized he was still trying to hold on. He was shaking rapidly, and blood was pooling in and around his mouth. I grabbed his shoulder- I had never seen that much blood- at least not from someone that survived. My clothes were immediately drenched in Evans's blood, and I knew there was no way he could survive this. His eyes never stopped looking up at me and as quickly as I had gotten to his side, he stopped shaking, and I knew he was gone. At that moment I remembered my hands- there was a gun in one of them- and I had plans.

I raised the gun and found the leader who had shot Evan. I shot him three times in the face before he had a chance to blink. I could taste his blood on my lips.

I knelt down to Evan and knew he was gone. I closed his eyes and scanned the area to see that the rest of the men in the group were already dead from the ambush. I picked up Evan's battered body and lifted him over my shoulders. I couldn't even think of my injuries- the only thing I knew that moment was to get us back to camp. I carried Evan over to one of the choppers that had landed a couple hundred feet away.

How could they have been so close but still no help? I couldn't care less if I made it or not, but Evan had people that cared about him. I was alone again…Evan was all I had. Everyone hustled back to the chopper, and we made our way back to base. As I sat there with Evan's body lying in my arms, I knew I would do anything and everything in my power to keep Evan's last plea.

Emily will never know the truth.

Chapter Twenty-Nine

EMILY

Breathe! Just Breathe! My head pounded and my mind was numb. The words Matt read pierced like a knife to the chest, and now that he had finished, there was now no way to remove it. I wasn't sure if I could hold it together much longer. The truth was worse than anything I had ever imagined. Over the years I never let myself really think of all the possibilities. I held on to the hope that Evan was still alive. My worst nightmare could not come close to the chilling reality.

"Can I see the note?" I managed to whisper. I was desperately clinging to the one item I may have left of Evan. Upon hearing myself, I was startled by how defeated I sounded. I needed to be strong for Tillie, for our families. God … do I even tell them everything?

Matt carefully tore the page from the notebook and handed it to Kai. Kai placed it in my shaking hands. I saw Evans's handwriting and held it close to my chest. No matter how hard I tried to be strong, my tears began. A small shrieking sob escaped my throat, and my body folded to its knees. Suddenly, I felt strong arms around me. Matt was by my side in moments, and although I knew he was only trying to do what Evan wanted, I was angry at him. I couldn't believe he had all this knowledge with him this whole time!

"Matt, how could you keep this from me? Do you have any idea what it's done to me … done to our families?" I was crying so hard now that I could not stop shaking.

Matt's eyes were full of tears. "Emily, I wanted to tell you for so long, but I…I just couldn't let him down again!"

Evan had asked of Matt the impossible, and of course Matt would keep his word. It would go against his character if he didn't. Matt felt the blame for Evan's death, but that was just not the case. Not by a long shot.

"Matt, we both know you'd never let him down. He could always count on you for everything, right down to his last breath." Matt squeezed me tighter. No words were needed. We both lost the most important person to us that day.

I had more questions for Matt. "Your family thinks you're dead," I whispered into his arms.

He loosened his hold on me. "Great, let them. I mean nothing to them," he answered.

"That's just not true, they were completely devastated." Matt had a cold stare as he pulled further away. "They never gave up hope you were alive." I whispered hoping he understood the severity of his lies.

He shrugged and shook his head. "I'll reach out when the time is right; I'm not ready yet!" he demanded. He looked over my shoulder as he pulled away.

It wasn't my place to push his decisions any further. "Matt, is that the whole story? Why were you declared missing if you obviously got back to the base?"

Matt rubbed his large hand over his face and through his black curls. He still had that same boyish charm from when I last saw him, but now I could see he appeared distant and cold as he gazed down at his missing limb.

"I went back," he stated flatly.

All eyes in the room went wide open. "You did what? Why?" I shouted. After everything they had been through, did he have a death wish?

"Yeah, I went back. I told you I promised I would kill every last one of them. And I keep my word."

I shook my head. Evan would be devastated to see how stone-cold Matt had become. "Matt, what did you do? Is that how you lost your leg?" I asked bluntly, needing to hear the rest of the story.

Matt took his seat across from me again and rubbed the area where his thigh ended right below the knee.

"Yeah, that's when I lost my leg. See, when we got back to base, I couldn't get the goddam flashbacks to go away. I knew I needed to go back and finish what I promised I'd do. It took about two weeks to recoup and be well enough to get back there. I didn't care if I died trying. I knew I'd be dead to the rest of the world anyway."

Kai interrupted him. "Excuse me, but with two weeks to heal, how on earth did you manage to stop the military from contacting Emily?"

Matt's eyes went cold and distant. "I hated keeping it from her, but everyone knew Evan's last plea, and I made them swear to take it to the grave. Legally, however, they had to inform Emily, so I hacked the system and intercepted every letter, every call, everything that had to do with Evan. In every sense of the word, to them and the national database Evan was declared missing in action and nothing more. They eventually stopped after I changed all her information. Once that was taken care of, Emily had given birth. That was when they found out about Evan's next of kin … Tillie. I needed Evan to not be the father, or else they would be able to track down Emily once again and continue contacting her. Cue dickhead senator over here."

Alex rolled his eyes and stormed out of the room. The door slammed behind him, as everyone in the room jumped from the commotion. He lost something that day too. Catherine was pregnant with his child, and although I never met her, I had spoken with her over the phone a few times, and she seemed like a kind woman.

"Matt, you can't be serious," I said.

"Every word," he stated coldly.

"Tillie is proudly Evan's child, and I would never take that away from him. Evan would be heartbroken! I don't think that's what he had in mind when asking you for such a favor. But why the money … where does that come into play?"

My words had truth and he knew it. Matt was hunched over and gave me a long, pained look before breaking eye contact. "Since Evan was officially declared missing in action according to the military files, you would never receive the benefits and I knew Evan would want you two provided for. Since Catherine was pregnant with the senator's child, we all knew he wouldn't want anything to do with any of it anyway! Catherine knew it, but I figured he would pay whatever he could to get the situation cleared. Now that he was senator, even better. *The* Alex Greyson would not want this type of scandal right at the beginning of his term."

Kai shook his head. "That's where you're wrong! From the moment Alex found out he had a child out there, he's been searching. You, Catherine, everyone … you were all wrong. Alex wanted to know this child. That's where your plan failed … hell, that's how we found you!" Kai shouted to Matt as he checked his anger.

Matt looked confused and defeated. "I had no idea he'd care, I honestly thought he would pay it off without batting an eye. Catherine was so sure." Matt was shaking his head now and a stream of tears finally escaped his eyes. "I just wanted to help everyone. That's all I've ever wanted. I should have been the one to die, not those two. They were good people. I'm the piece of shit that can't even keep a promise."

His dark hands covered his face, and I went to sit next to him. It was my turn to console. Matt cried loud deep sobs, and I joined him.

When I was able to continue, I looked at him. "Matt, you did what you felt you had to do. I don't think you're a piece of shit, I think you're brave and you're strong. I don't know what else happened after you went back, but if you're here now, then you must have done what you promised to do."

Matt wiped his face with his t-shirt and looked at me with dull eyes. "When I got back to the location where we had been held, I wasn't alone. I made some of Evan's close friends come too. They wanted to help but didn't think we should go back. I talked them into it. Luckily, when we got there, the same group of idiots were still there, except this time they had two new prisoners. We saved them, and I killed every single one of the scumbags that tortured us. I let them plead for their lives, then gave them hope I wouldn't kill them. But in the end, they knew what this was about.

"Before I was able to kill the last one in the group, he threw me a grenade. He knew he was about to die anyway, so he tried to kill me as well." He buried his face in his hands with his elbows resting on his knees and continued. "My buddies were able to save me along with the two prisoners. Once we got back to base, I thought our captain would finish the job, he was so angry. I was basically dead to him. He didn't give a shit what happened to me. Then, once I was healed enough and could get around, I left. They assumed I killed myself. I didn't care what they thought, I might as well be dead."

I squeezed Matt's shoulders and shook my head. "You will never understand how much it hurt not knowing this. I was upset about you as well."

Matt's eyes opened and he held me close. "I'm so sorry for everything, Emily," he whispered. He looked around the room at Kai and the other officers. "I guess this is when you cuff me and make the arrest."

Kai shifted on the couch and cleared his throat. He appeared to be affected by all this, as well. "Honestly, I don't think a holding cell is the best place for you. If you'll accept it, I'd like to get you in to see a doctor. And before you go on thinking it's because I think you're crazy, don't. It's because I think it's your best shot at moving forward and getting past all of this. I think you've been through hell, and now that we have the full story, I can see this isn't some cut and dry case. I'll talk with Alex, but I'm sure I can get him to drop the charges."

Kai looked over to his father who was already shaking his head. "Captain, what do you say?"

His father continued to shake his head. "It's your call, I'll follow your lead on this."

Kai looked surprised that his father was submitting to his lead. At that moment, I felt so lucky to have Kai on my side, on Matt's side.

Matt looked down, and to my disbelief he agreed. "Yeah, I think it's time this is settled once and for all, I'll do whatever you think is best. I'm sick of running." He reached for the journal laying on the coffee table and handed it to me gently. "If you want it, I think you should have this. It's not my story to hold onto any longer. His family … your family, you all deserve to know the truth. Evan was a hero and should be remembered as one. I can't continue to keep that from him."

Uncovered

I took the notebook and gave Matt a strong hug as I heard a door open and saw Alex standing in the doorway.

Matt looked over at Alex and said, "I owe you an apology too, I had no right to assume the worst. Whether you knew it at the time or not, you lost something that day, as well, and I'm sorry for keeping that from you. I should've never dragged you into this."

Alex looked coldly at Matt. He had every reason to be upset. He was hurting too. "I'm glad you've agreed to get some help. I won't be pressing charges." He said his piece and walked out of the room.

The sadness in Alex's eyes had been excruciating to see, I felt it too. We all lost something. Whether it was a loved one, truth, or hope, hearts were shattered in this room today.

Chapter Thirty

KAI

Matt and Emily talked for a few more moments alone before we took Matt to the hospital where the team had arranged for him to be admitted. I couldn't believe how this all ended, how he meticulously thought of every detail. A piece of me thought he could've gotten away with this if he really wanted to. But to a certain extent, I believe he wanted to be caught. This was too much of a burden for one man to sustain. Best friend or not, this had been eating him alive.

I hadn't had any time to speak with Emily after she learned about Evan. I kept rehearsing in my head what to say but didn't think there was much anyone could say to help her process the news she received today.

Emily gave Matt a long hug, and it looked as though they were both crying as they separated. Matt was helped into an SUV, and I radioed the driver to let me know when they had him checked in safely.

Emily was making her way over to me, and I felt myself get tense. When she got close enough that we were almost touching, I wanted to close the gap and hold her in my arms. "Emily…" I sighed as I searched her eyes. I needed to know what I could do to help. What I could do to ease the pain.

She just looked up at me too exhausted to cry. "Kai, I need to get back home. I need to be with my family. I have so many phone calls to make."

I placed my arms around her. I couldn't let her stand there alone. She had to know what torture it put me through to watch her devastation unfold. "Of course, the car is ready. It's right this way. Let me walk you over and I'll go return my equipment."

The once persistent and confident Emily was now somewhere else, and in her place was a defeated and dejected woman I hardly recognized. My heart was breaking for her. I closed the door after she got situated in her seat then made my way to the tent. The entire team looked the same. It was as though we all lost something that day. The story Matt told was hopeless on all fronts.

I'm sure my father had heard similar stories in all his time in the military, yet even *he* looked defeated. "I'm taking Emily back home; I'll give you a call later tonight once things have settled. Do you need anything from me?" I asked him, as I set my equipment on the desk before him.

He eventually looked at me and shook his head. "I'm proud of the way you handled yourself in there. This type of story isn't something I've come across, and I don't know if I would've been as understanding as you." There was a small pause, and he let out a large breath of air. "But you know what? You made a good call. This Matt fellow needs help, and we are all prepared to help him."

I was speechless. My father had never even come close to words like that before. "Thanks, that means a lot coming from you," was all I managed in return.

He then patted me on the shoulder and shook my hand. It was a strange moment that I didn't have the time to dissect. "Go on, get her home. She's just had probably the worst day of her life."

I nodded, knowing full well how terrible this day had been for her. Making my way back to the car, I hoped that I could find the best words to say to Emily. When I got in the driver seat, I saw that she had her phone out and was staring at an empty message screen. "Would you like me to help with anything?" I asked, hoping she would want to talk.

She continued to stare at her phone. "I'm trying to figure out where to go from here. Do I call his parents, and do I tell them everything? Do they need to know every single detail? And where is his body? Who do I even call about setting up a funeral … oh my god … I need to plan a funeral!"

Everything she was thinking came to a halt with her last words. Her eyes once again filled with tears. Her hands went to her face to hide deep sorrowful sobs. I put one arm around her and rubbed her back. At the time, it was all I knew to do.

"Emily, you're not alone. Your family will be with you for every decision you need to make. As of now, my advice would be to use this car ride as a time to process what you've just learned. Leave the legalities to me. I'll contact the right people to get his … remains."

Her sobs grew louder. "Kai, I can't…"

She couldn't finish the sentence and just wept for the next half hour. My hand never left hers for the next few hours. Every once in a while, I would get a slight squeeze, and I would squeeze it back. From time to time, I would rub my thumb up and down her small hand. It was the best thing I could come up with. After a while I had noticed that Emily had dozed off, and I hated being the one to wake her.

"We're about fifteen minutes from town. Would you like me to take you straight home, or your parents' place?" I waited for her to finally answer.

"Actually, yes, please drop me off at my parents. Tillie is there, and I just want to stay the night there. Make a right up here."

The next few minutes I followed Emily's directions wishing I somehow had more time with her. My mind was racing when I realized this could be one of the last times I might see her. Where would we go from here?

Emily woke me from my thoughts. "It's the blue house right up here on the corner," she whispered as her voice was full of defeat.

We pulled up to the house and parked in the driveway. I knew I wouldn't be going inside with Emily, but I wished to be the one she could turn to…to be there for her the rest of the night. I wanted to hold her till she fell asleep again. I wanted to comfort and hold her as she told her family about Evan.

Emily looked over at me with teary eyes. "Thank you, Kai… for everything today. I know I couldn't have done any of this without you. You'll let me know when you have more information about…" She trailed off and I didn't need her to finish to know her request.

"Yeah, of course, you don't need to worry about anything. I've got it all handled. You go be with your family, let them be there for you through all this, and remember it's okay to not be so tough all the time."

She nodded and opened the car door. I couldn't let her leave like this. I jumped from my seat and met her at the passenger side. "Emily, I haven't had a chance to do this yet, but I really need to." I leaned down and folded her in my arms for the first time that evening. "I'm so sorry about how today went. I wish I could take this pain away."

Instead of deepening our embrace, she pushed me away. The sadness that was once in her eyes was replaced now with annoyance. "Kai, I have to go inside. This isn't the right time. Please just let me know when you hear anything."

And just like that she walked away from me and into the house.

What had I just done?

Chapter Thirty-One

EMILY

As I was walking up the steps to my parents' house, I knew I should be thinking about how I would share the news with my family, but my mind was replaying the hurt look in Kai's eyes when I pushed him away. It felt incredible to be in his arms again, maybe too good. Yet I literally pushed him away. I couldn't let myself have these feelings for him, especially not now.

Fear overwhelmed me as I got closer to my parent's front door. What would the future hold? There seemed to be no greater pain that one can experience on this earth than losing the one you thought you were going to spend forever with. I can still remember Evan coming down our front steps in his military uniform all arranged to leave; it was surreal thinking those were now the last memories I would have of him. I hugged him with all the passion I could muster, and I wished I would never have to let go. But I did have to let go, I had to watch him board that plane, and I had to watch him be taken from me forever.

When my doorbell rang almost three years ago, I knew something was wrong. It was 4 in the afternoon, and I was alone. Waiting for my friend to come over to make mommy-to-be mocktails. I opened the door to three men in uniform. This was something I had imagined many times before, always thinking of the worst-case scenario, my thoughts hadn't done this particular nightmare justice. My mind made up excuses. I was pretty sure I thought of every excuse as to why they could be there. Every other reason in the world seemed to make more sense than what was being said at that moment. Missing. Missing in Action. More questions formed. It had been weeks since I'd spoken to Evan, it wasn't terribly uncommon for days, sometimes weeks to go by in between contact. But we always found a way to connect no matter what. I was sure I would hear from him any day now. I waited, waited for the phone to ring, waited for a new email to come. Nothing ever came. Before today, finding out Evan was missing was the lowest point of my life, but then that turned into years of not knowing. But now … now I know the truth, and that is what made today the worst day of my life.

Without realizing where my feet were taking me, I was already inside my parents' home. My mom quickly turned around as I shut the door. "Oh! You scared me, Emily! Tillie's already in bed. She loved her bath tonight. Let me show you some pictures. She did this hilarious thing with–"

"Mom, I'm sorry, but where's dad?" I had to stop her. I couldn't do this with her right now.

The excitement in her face vanished, and her eyes grew wide. "I'll go get him. I think he's upstairs … Emily, is everything okay?"

Her concern brought tears to my eyes once again. "Just please go get Dad," was all I managed to say.

She ran up the stairs, and within moments they were both sitting next to me on their oversized couch. Once I'd composed myself, I began telling them the entire story. Where to begin? I pulled the notebook from my purse and handed it to my mother. Over the next few hours, we all cried as we memorized the contents of Evan's last few days.

My family always had ideas as to what could have happened to Evan, but I don't think any of us thought we'd ever really get to the truth. And now that we did, we wished we hadn't. Knowing the truth held much more pain than living in the dark.

It was almost midnight when I finally rested my head on a pillow. Even with all the stress of riding the day's emotional rollercoaster as well as being enormously sleep deprived, I couldn't stop my thoughts about what would come tomorrow as I would have to tell Evan's parents the truth. Luckily, I would have my parents for that conversation, and my mother promised to help, if not to say it all for me.

The next few days were a blur. I was grateful to have my parents with me. I was grateful Tillie was so young and nothing much really changed for her. However, someday, I would have to tell her what happened to her father, but I was grateful that day was far in the future, and I wouldn't have to face it just now. I had temporarily closed up shop for my business, I was sure to take a hit from my recent time away. Baking now seemed meaningless and my body was numb to the distraction baking used to bring. There was no way to distract myself anymore.

Today was the first day all week that I had not woken up crying. I looked at my phone for the millionth time hoping Kai may have had news for me. We were so close to finalizing the details for his funeral, all we needed now was the details of when his remains would finally make their way to us. Evan's parents were flying in later this afternoon, and I hoped to have good news for them when they arrived.

My mom peeked her head into my room and softly smiled. "Good morning, Sunshine, Tillie's awake. I thought I'd let you know I have breakfast ready for everyone."

I had been staying at my parents' house since Kai dropped me off. I couldn't go back to my own house; I couldn't be there alone just yet. Now that I knew Evan was truly gone and would never step foot in our home again, I couldn't face being in that old home any longer, the house that was supposed to be *ours* together.

I could remember the day we bought the house together. We'd just found out I was pregnant. Everything seemed so perfect. We were young and in love, yet little did we know, he would be deployed in only a few short months, and that would be the end to our love story. Rather, more like a short story in a romance magazine. Over before it had started.

The last few days had my emotions bouncing all over the place. One moment I'd be filled with grief, then the next, my anger would be arduous and nearly suffocating. I found myself cheering that Matt went back and killed them all for taking Evan from us. I would rest there for a brief moment, but I knew I couldn't let myself linger on that path again. The moment those thoughts crept in I'd remind myself of Evan's authentic goodness. Evan wouldn't want me to live my life tainted with animosity.

And then as if on cue, my phone began sounding and I jumped from the startling ringtone. I don't want to talk to anyone now. Over the last few days, friends had slowly heard some version of the truth revolving around Evan and his disappearance. And quite frankly, I wasn't going to be the one to answer their morbid questions. But as I glanced at the screen, about to ignore the call, it read Kai Taylor.

I hadn't spoken to him since the night he dropped me off. There were a couple times I had composed a text and was about to press send, but I would then delete the text all together. The only thing I needed to focus on was Evan and my family. Kai was a distraction that would only cause more confusion. Yet, what was this feeling in the pit of my stomach at seeing his name flash across my screen? Without giving it another thought, I pressed Accept Call

"Hello," I answered, nervous to hear his voice on the other end.

"Emily, do you have a moment to chat?" he asked. He sounded nervous as well. In the past, Kai sounded confident and ready to swoop in and save the day, but today, it was evident he was holding back. My actions had undoubtedly hurt him and his confidence.

"Yes, definitely. Did you get a hold of that contact you mentioned?" My voice was shaky, dammit.

"Yeah, that's actually why I was calling. I spoke with a friend of my fathers. They had no idea what Matt had done. They're taking care of everything, and his remains should be here in two days," he stated directly.

"Oh, wow. So soon." After a brief moment of silence, I whispered, "Thank you, Kai, for everything … I …" I struggled for the words to properly thank him.

"Emily, of course. I told you I would do anything for you … to help you. I just—"

"How is Alex doing?" I interrupted.

He paused. "He's doing okay. He's taking it like I thought he would. Pretending it doesn't affect him, but I know he's hurting. He'll process this whole thing in his own way. He always does. How are you?" he asked.

I could tell he was nervous to ask me that after the way I treated him the other night. "Probably the same as Alex. Just need to process things my own way. Haven't slept at my house all week, but I know eventually I need to go back there … Evan's parents are flying in today."

"Well, that should be good. Do you need anything?" he asked.

I began to wish I could see his face as he asked the question. "No, I'm okay, but thank you. Since I have you on the phone, I wanted to let you know we're having a memorial. Obviously, it'll look a lot different than any normal funeral, but we want to do something. Some of Catherine's family will be there too, and I wanted to invite you and Alex … if you wanted to come, that is."

I had to invite them even though it felt strange doing so. After everything they did for me, it was the right thing to do. And no matter how Alex was processing things, he had every right to be there and mourn his loss too.

"Of course, I'll be there. I can't speak for Alex, but I think he'll want to go as well."

"Great, I have one last question for you."

"Anything," he quickly responded to me.

"What's going to happen with Matt?" I asked. I had been worried about him all week, and since I wasn't family, the hospital wouldn't release any information.

"Well, I recently spoke with his doctors, and last I heard, it's still up in the air at this stage. Why?"

"Well, my family and Evan's were hoping to see him and let him be there for the memorial."

"Oh, I see. Well, with everything that's come to light, Emily, he's most likely looking at doing some time. I know his intentions were good, but he broke the law."

"Yeah of course. Forget I even asked. We understand." I knew how much Evan would want his best friend there, and he deserved to have those that loved him attend his memorial.

"But Emily … I'll try my best to get him there."

"Kai, you don't have to do that. I know what he did was wrong."

"No, no, I want to help. And you're right, he should be there."

"Thanks, Kai. If you're able to speak to him, could you ask about his family ... and if we should invite them to the memorial?"

"Of course, I can ask. Let me work on a few more things at my end, and I'll let you know when everything has ... arrived." His voice sounded warm. "It was great to talk to you again."

"That sounds good ... okay I'll talk to you later." I was about to say goodbye, but I had to get something off my chest. "Kai, it's great to hear your voice again. I look forward to hearing from you soon."

"Emily?" he asked with a deep husky resonance.

"Yes?" I countered.

"I've missed you."

"I've missed you too Kai. Talk to you soon." I smiled as I said his name. He always seemed to have a way of making me forget my heartache ... almost. Because as soon as I hung up, the ache inside of me had returned as freely as it had left.

Chapter Thirty-Two

KAI

I'll admit, I was thrilled she answered the phone as every nerve in my body was telling me she would not. I thought my forwardness the other night would bite me in the ass, but the way she said my name, I knew she was thrilled I'd called. Now, I just needed to find a way for them to let Matt attend the memorial. The last I'd checked they were not planning on letting him out any time soon. I wanted to do this for Emily, but first I needed to send the woman flowers. It was long overdue. Since hearing her voice, I knew I needed to do something to bring a smile to her face, even if I wouldn't be there to see it.

I made a few calls ordering flowers, calling Matt's doctor, and arranging the pickup of Evan's remains. After several calls to the hospital, it was clear that I needed to speak to Matt's doctors in person.

When I arrived at the Information Desk, I was wishing I could do more for Matt, but I knew he would be dealing with his own personal demons. I knew friends that had returned from overseas, and they just didn't know how to move forward once back home. Flashbacks from the battlefield were daily struggles for most of them. For Matt's sake, I sure wished this stay at the hospital would be the right start for him moving forward with life again.

I spoke with the woman at the front desk and told her the urgency of the situation. I wasn't leaving her desk until she knew it was imperative that I spoke to his doctor today. There was no chance I was leaving here without the green light. After a few minutes waiting in the lobby in their uncomfortable chairs, the front desk attendant looked my way.

She was clearly annoyed but motioned for me to follow her. "Mr. Taylor, the doctor will see you now."

The doctor had a rather large stack of papers in front of him, and he didn't look happy to see me. "Hello, Mr. Taylor … I hear you're making quite the fuss."

"Please call me Kai. Mr. Taylor is my father." I laughed as I sat across the desk from him.

The doctor nodded with a slight smile on his tired face. "Okay, Kai, what can I do for you?"

"Well, as I mentioned to your receptionist, I understand your patient Matthew Stone is under your care. I don't know if you've had time yet to meet with him and understand his situation. But his best friend's funeral is in a couple days, and the family of the deceased would really like him to be there, if possible."

The doctor quickly opened a file with Matt's name on it. "I *have* met with Matt. I see here you are on his paperwork as an emergency contact. Are you two related?" he asked.

"No, there's no relation. I'm just the officer to be contacted. As of now, he has declined to have his family notified on his status."

The doctor nodded and began to scribble something on Matt's folder. "Okay, well, since you're on the paperwork, I take it you're inclined to be notified of Matt's progress. Matt's fully aware of his actions, and I don't see any problem with him being able to attend the funeral, that is if he's under your watch. He must return here after the service."

"Yes, of course. We'll have a whole team there to keep him in custody."

"Good, because even though Matt's aware and understands his situation, he's a very disturbed young man. The things he's had to see and endure. He needs to continue with our services. Has he mentioned a notebook to you?" the doctor questioned.

"Yes, it was a written account of what happened to him and the others. I saw it myself."

The doctor's eyes widened. "You saw it?"

"Yes, I witnessed him reading it myself. He left the notebook with the deceased soldier's wife. Why?"

"I just assumed he was meaning he had this notebook figuratively. During his intake, I noticed signs of PTSD, which would be completely understandable in his case. I will tell you though, that after my last discussion with Matt, the notebook probably doesn't begin to cover the trauma these men suffered. Matt should have come here years ago. We really could've helped him before things escalated the way they did."

The doctor seemed to genuinely care for his patients, and I was relieved that Matt was in good hands. I said to the doctor, "I can't imagine what these men went through. Matt's been pretending to be dead for the last few years and never speaking a word of it to anyone until now … I don't doubt that he's suffered from it."

"I believe you're correct. It's been difficult for him, but he's accepting the help, and that's the first step. Would you like to see him now?" the doctor asked.

"Sure, I think that's a good idea. I can let him know about the funeral arrangements … unless you think that's too much for him right now."

"No, I think that should be okay. I'm on call tonight, so if he'd like to talk about it later, I'll be here."

I nodded, relieved that Matt had a great doctor on his side. We shook hands, and the doctor called for the attendant to take me to a meeting area in the hospital.

I sat waiting for Matt, thinking how I would phrase things. I was wondering about his state of mind when I looked up to see Matt coming towards me. I could already see a difference in his bearing. He looked in much better spirits than the last time I saw him. I stood up and went to pull his chair for him.

"Don't even think about it. I've gone this long doing things for myself. Sure as hell don't need help now." he playfully grumbled.

I took the hint and sat back down. "Alright, forget I ever tried. Won't happen again," I smiled. "You look good, Matt," I said, as he lowered himself into the open chair across the small table.

"Thanks, I honestly feel better too." He responded as he positioned his crutches on the back of his chair. "Guess what?"

"What's that?"

"They fitted me for a prosthetic leg the other day, and it looks like I might be getting to throw these crutches away for good," he said with a smirk.

It was the first time I saw a glimmer of hope on his face. "Good for you, man, you deserve it! When do they think you'll get it?" I asked, hoping he would have it before Evan's memorial.

"They said sometime in the next few days. Apparently, the grenade that took my leg was considerate and cut it off at an easier place for a fitted prosthetic." He laughed at the face I made.

I shifted in my seat and got to some of Emily's concerns. "Matt, I spoke with Emily this morning, and the family would love for you to attend the memorial for Evan. They mentioned that some of Catherine's family might even attend. They know your stance on your family, so they haven't reached out … but should we do that?" I asked, watching for his response.

"Well, you see, I want to go for Evan and Catherine, but my family drama needs to be left for another day. I don't want to start that right now; I need more time."

He stared me in the eyes, and I couldn't argue with the man. His candid expression said it all. Leave it! "Yeah, we can do that. I'll let Emily know you want to be there. I already spoke with your doctor, and he thinks it would be good for you."

Matt nodded his head and ran his hand over his face and then through his dark curls that almost completely covered his forehead. "Great, since you're here, I'd like to ask you a few things about Alex."

With my interest now piqued, I cocked my head to the side. "Um, yeah? What would you like to know?" I asked.

"Well, Catherine mentioned he was very … how do I say it … busy in the sheets. Does he even remember her?" he asked, as I shook my head.

"You're not wrong in your assumption, but he does remember her. In fact, when you first sent that email, that was the first name he had me look into. Once we found out she had passed, we moved on and didn't give it a second thought."

Matt looked confused. "I honestly thought I was helping everyone. Well, no, I take that back. I didn't think I was helping Alex, but I didn't care. From what Catherine had said, he wouldn't have wanted anything to do with her and the child … he'd likely just throw money her way and go on about his life." He paused for a moment, and you could see he was troubled by his past decisions. "I'd like to apologize to him if possible. I want him to know I'm not an evil person."

I knew Alex honestly wanted to move forward from this. "I think that can be arranged since he'll be at the memorial, as well."

"Great, thanks for everything Kai." He paused just then and asked, "Hey, before you leave, there's something I have to ask. Are you and Emily a thing?"

I was unable to hide my shock from his direct question. I didn't have an answer for him. I'd been wondering the exact same thing all week. He continued to stare at me until I gave him an answer. "No, we're not a ... thing. She's processing everything that's transpired over the last few weeks, and I've just been lucky to help her discover the truth about everything." There, that sounded good, right? That should be enough to stop him from wanting to hurt me.

"Your face said it all, Kai. You and I both know Emily's a wonderful woman. Something Evan and I talked about those last few days was her moving on someday. He hoped she would find someone to love her, someone to protect her and Tillie. I think after everything, you're a surprisingly good candidate for the role. Evan's been gone for almost three years. She should find happiness again."

"Matt, you've known all along that Evan was gone, but to Emily ... she feels like it just happened. It's a lot for her to process at the moment. I'll be there for her in whatever capacity she wants me to be, but it's completely up to her." Matt has to know how much his deceptions had truly impacted Emily's healing.

"Spoken like a man that truly respects a woman. Evan would've like you ..." He stopped mid-sentence with a smile that quickly faded. "I know what I did was wrong, Kai. There were so many days I wanted to pick up the phone and call her ... but all I could do was see Evan dying in my arms and hear his last words that were burned in my brain. I did what I thought I needed to, but now all I see is the pain I caused."

He shook his head and looked me in the eyes. "Thank you for taking this case upon yourself to figure out. It needed to be done. Emily needed you to come into her life."

Hearing Matt's words made me smile, hoping she might possibly feel the same. But I had doubts of late about her feelings for me. "Matt, I'm glad you told me this. Things could have gone one of two ways … and I'm glad you're so accepting. You're one of the good guy's Matt … don't let yourself think differently. I have to get going now, but I'll check back in once I get more info on the memorial. I'm glad you're going, and I know Emily will be too!" I shook his hand and as I stood to leave, I thought of how this tiny gesture would bring a small bit of happiness to Emily during this time.

Matt nodded. "Thanks for stopping by. Hey, the next time you see me, hopefully I'll have two feet on solid ground again."

"Definitely!" I agreed.

I had a few more errands to make, but decided I should … well, more like, I *wanted* to, call Emily and let her know the latest news on Matt. I would be lying if I said I wasn't hoping that my getting Matt to come would bring her some new appreciation of me. I pulled out my phone and quickly dialed Emily's number.

Chapter Thirty-Three

EMILY

It felt strange to be back in my house once again, but I knew I needed to get the house ready for my in-laws' arrival. I had just finished getting dressed and was ready to head to the airport when my cell phone rang. It was Kai. For some reason, I forced myself to hide my excitement of getting two calls from him in one day. I debated answering, but I couldn't deny the feelings I got when I heard the sound of his soothingly deep voice.

"Hello?" I answered.

"Hey, you, I promise I'll text anything new from here on out, but I had something important that I needed to tell you. I just left the hospital and saw Matt."

I gasped, expecting bad news. "Oh no, is everything okay, is he okay?" I frantically asked.

"Yeah, he's doing good actually. Better than the last time we saw him. I wanted to let you know I spoke with his doctor, and Matt will be able to attend the memorial. His doctor thinks it'll be good for him."

My breathing relaxed. "Thank you, Kai, I don't know what strings you had to pull to let him attend, but I'm so grateful. What about his family … were you able to ask him?"

"Yeah, I did ask, and he's just not ready for that right now … he wants the day to be about Evan and Catherine."

I let out a large sigh. I knew it was a long shot, but I was hopeful. "Okay, I understand. It's probably for the better. There's so much going on over here, my in-laws will be arriving in the next hour, and I haven't seen them in over a year. It's always been so hard to see them. Don't get me wrong, they're great people. It's just the distance and the hurt we associate with seeing one another. But hopefully this weekend will help with all that." I stopped myself, again, I was saying too much. "Sorry, Kai, here I am rambling again."

"No, please, get it off your chest. I am here for you. Is there anything I can do to help you?" he asked, his voice was full of concern. It was refreshing to know someone cared enough to help.

"No, you've done enough ... just a second. There's someone at my door."

From the window I could see that it was a delivery woman with a large bouquet of beautiful flowers. As she handed the flowers to me, I had to set the phone down to take them from her. I put the arrangement on my entry table near the door and read the card.

Emily, I hope these flowers will brighten up your day.
Every time a new flower blooms, please know I will be thinking of you.
Thank you for the gift of knowing you!
-Kai

I shoved the note in my back pocket and put the phone back to my ear. "Did you send me flowers?" I jokingly asked.

"I did. I take it they just arrived?"

"Yeah, they did. They're beautiful Kai! You really didn't have to do this." By some miracle, I was all smiles.

"Actually, I did. I do wish I were there to see your face, though. But you, Emily, definitely deserve flowers."

His warm laugh completed the visual I had of him answering me.

"Kai, these are … they are wonderful. Thank you!" I couldn't stop smiling.

"Of course, so again can I do anything?"

I wished there was something I needed him to do, something that could keep me talking to him. Over the last week, I realized just how much I missed seeing him and spending those quiet intimate moments with him.

"No, I'm just heading to the airport now. Wait, actually yes, you *can* do something." I hesitated to ask, but the desire to see him wasn't going to go away.

"Anything," he replied, his voice husky and intense.

"My in-laws are bound to have a hundred and ten questions. Would you be able to be on standby in case it gets to be too much, and I need an escape?" I let out a small sigh, hoping he wouldn't notice my pathetic attempt at another excuse to talk to him.

"No need to say more. If you need me, just text and I'll come up with something."

"You're the best. Thank you. I should go now, though. I don't want to be stuck in traffic. Talk to you later … Bye Kai!"

"Goodbye Emily." He replied with a raw and deep tone reaching me in places I couldn't say aloud. We both hung up our phones, and I stood in my entryway looking at the gorgeous vase full of pink peonies interspersed with white rosebuds and unopened tulips of some kind. I was smiling like a crazy teenager. I sure hoped I would get the chance to see him later. It had been over a week, and I needed those captivating blues to be staring into mine once again.

The last few hours after I had picked up my in-laws and answered my fair share of questions, enough for a lifetime, and even though they had already been told every bit of information I had, as predicted, they assumed I magically knew more.

Tillie was happy to see her grandparents, though, and it made me happy they always put effort into being so involved in her life. They absolutely loved her and always told her fun stories involving Evan and his childhood. Tillie only knew from pictures what her daddy looked like; it was a sad reality that she never had the chance to meet him, and now she never would.

Being back in what was supposed to be my and Evans' space, now even the walls seemed to sense how empty it was. I was thankful that my in-laws insisted on putting Tillie down for her nap. For the first time all morning there was some silence in the home.

Once they both returned to the living room I blurted out, "I think I may sell the house."

Both of their eyes widened. "Why?" Evan's mother Denise asked.

"I always felt this house was for me and Evan to grow in. It's too big for just me and Tillie, and now that we know ..." I paused as I took in a deep breath.

My father-in-law shook his head and looked me in the eyes. "You and Evan loved this house. He wanted Tillie raised in this house."

"Yes, you're right. We did, but it's just time. We now know Evan won't be coming back, and the sooner we accept that, the sooner we can grieve his loss and cherish his memory. I've been stuck in some strange version of hell waiting for answers, and now, I finally have them. I'm sorry, if you can't understand that I cannot live in this house any longer."

I knew I was being dramatic, but I needed them to understand all the pain it caused me to stay in this home without Evan.

They both nodded. Denise began to speak. "Of course, we can understand. We both have a hard time even looking at his picture some days. We'll back you up with whatever you decide, Emily."

"Thank you," I said with a smile. I wanted to be happy that they were going to back me up with my decision, but the look on their faces said they weren't perfectly okay with this. For the time being, I would accept the fact that they were at least going to try.

Over the next hour or so they caught me up on their latest travels, and what they planned to do when my father-in-law retired next year. That was when it dawned on me. *What do I call them now that Evan is truly gone, and I am a widow? I am a widow! At the age of twenty-nine I'm a widow.*

Okay, I think it's about time I text Kai. I need some air. My in-laws … or whatever I was to now call them, began to start preparing a late lunch. I pulled out my phone and found Kai's name.

EMILY- *Still free?*

KAI- *Definitely*

EMILY- *Great because I think I need some fresh air.*

KAI- *What do you have in mind?*

EMILY- *Want to meet me at Elm Street Park, at the entrance … say 30 minutes?*

KAI- *I'll be there. See you soon.*

EMILY- *Thanks Kai!*

KAI- *Of course, so do I need to fake a phone call or are you okay to go?*

EMILY- *I should be good, my 'in-laws' probably want a break from me right now. I just need to make sure they are cool with watching Tillie.*

KAI- *You could bring her with you if you want.*

EMILY- *I could, but I think they would want the extra time with her.*

KAI- *Yeah, of course.*

EMILY- *Okay, I just spoke with them; they are happy to watch her. They're going to walk down to the creek near our house. See ya!*

KAI- *Great.*

As I got ready to leave the house, I was glad my in-laws were here to spend time with Tillie. I wondered if Evan's passing would change the dynamic of our relationship. Tillie was still their granddaughter, that would never change. I pushed the anxious feelings creeping back into my head away for the hundredth time that day. Like everyone who was tangled up in this web of deceit, I had no clue what the future looked like. Take it day by day, as my mother would say ... and that was exactly what I would be doing. Right now, however, I was getting ready to see Kai, and I couldn't stop my excitement and feel normal again even if for a few brief moments. I looked at myself in the mirror for a long time. Had the news of Evan's passing made me look different? I felt as though I looked ten years older and a hundred times more tired. No matter what I put on, I looked strange. I settled on a floral summer dress that hit right above my knees that perfectly matched my blonde curls.

Looking in the mirror again, I felt like I was playing dress-up with the newest Barbie collection. "And here we have Tired Widow Barbie," I whispered as I looked at myself. This is the best it's going to get without raising any red flags with my in-laws. I had told them I was going to a floral shop to pick out flowers for the funeral. It wasn't completely untrue; I was going to pick out flowers ... just not at a floral shop. It was Evan's and my secret flower picking spot. It would be the perfect place to see Kai and collect flowers for Evans's memorial.

Chapter Thirty-Four

KAI

I pulled up to the park entrance, and as I looked around, I realized Emily hadn't yet arrived. I scrolled through my phone for the first time all day. Social media was never my thing, but I occasionally browsed it for mindless enjoyment. Today, I felt the urge to find Emily's page, and a couple of clicks later I finally found her. Her page was filled with pictures of her and Tillie. It looked like they did a lot together. I couldn't imagine doing everything alone. Raising a child seemed hard enough ... doing it alone, thinking your missing husband may or may not return someday was a whole new level of difficulty.

There was this one picture of just Emily that especially caught my eye... she looked so unbelievably beautiful. She was sitting with her coffee in hands at her table in the kitchen looking out towards the street. The photo was a bit blurry, but it added a special sort of effect. She was wearing pink cotton shorts and a gray tank top. You could see all of her wonderful curves. She was absolutely breathtaking. I couldn't help but wonder what was going through her mind in this particular photo.

I tried to tap on the description, but accidentally *liked* it instead. Well, there goes my pride ... she's definitely going to know I was stalking her page. The photo I liked was from a year ago, and I would've had to scroll down awhile to get to it. Yeah, social media was definitely not my thing. Since I liked the photo, both figuratively and now literally ... I decided it would be less creepy if I just requested to be friends with her. As soon as I hit the request button, a tap on my window made me jump.

"Oh my gosh, you're jumpy. I'm sorry I scared you," Emily laughed.

I, on the other hand, was mortified for the second time in five minutes. I opened my door and stepped out of my car. I was stunned that she was able to approach my car without me noticing. "You're too quiet. I didn't even hear your car pull up."

"The beauty of a hybrid," she laughed as she pointed to her small sedan parked beside mine.

Her smile continued to drive me wild; I couldn't believe I'd been in her presence for a whole minute and hadn't yet touched her. It took every ounce of stamina to stop from reaching out and holding her close. "So, why are we meeting here?" I asked, hoping I could keep myself from slipping up and reaching for her.

A small smile formed on her near perfect lips once again. "I wanted to meet here because it was a special place for me at one point in time. There are some really great flowers right this way that I wanted to scope out and later pick for the memorial."

She then reached in her bag to read her phone. "Sorry, just one second. My phone keeps going off, and I want to make sure it's not my in-laws." Within seconds of looking at her phone she began to laugh. "Were you stalking me, Mr. Taylor?"

Oh, great Lord above, why did she have to say my name in that tone? This woman is doing things to me I cannot put into words. "I swear it was an accident, it was a great photo and I just wanted to read the description." I laughed as I tried to hide my embarrassment.

"So, you liked the picture?" she winked, holding back a laugh as she took a step closer to me.

213

I had to answer truthfully. For it was the best photo of her I had seen. "I did ... I do." I replied, as our faces were nearly touching. I was now officially a love-struck thirteen-year-old in middle school.

"You know I only posted this photo because Tillie took it. She was so proud of herself for taking a picture of mommy and I thought it was kind of cute."

She shrugged her shoulders; it was the sexiest thing. When her shoulders were raised, her dress lifted higher up her legs, and of course I couldn't help but notice. "Seems like you have a future photographer. It's a great photo of you. It makes me wonder what you were thinking in it." I replied as I played with the tip of her shoulder strap.

She stared directly into my eyes. "Actually, I do remember what I was thinking in it. It was Tillie's second birthday, and if I'm being honest, I had been crying all morning. I ended up letting Tillie play with my phone to distract her while I got myself together. She then took that picture." She continued to stare at the photo on the screen.

"It's a great photo, Emily. It shows a strong woman that's always doing her best for her family." I replied as I continued to play with the strap of her dress.

She looked up and smiled at me. "Thank you, Kai, that's sweet of you. it's difficult, but I do try ... for Tillie." She replied with less of a smile.

There was a pause as she looked around the park. "Follow me, I want to show you this amazing field of flowers. I haven't been in years, but it's always been a favorite place of mine."

I followed Emily as we made our way along a narrow path. There was a row of trees, and in between two weeping willows a

214

clearing. I looked at Emily and saw a look of panic develop on her face. "Is everything okay?" I asked.

"They're gone! The flowers! They're all gone … this was our thing! I needed them for the memorial. They have to be here! I must be in the wrong spot!"

Emily was frantic and ran ahead looking all around. She was surrounded by tall weeds, but it was not a large park, so the odds that these flowers were somewhere else nearby were slim.

"What kind of flowers are we looking for?" I asked, desperately hoping I could help her find whatever it was she was looking for.

"It wasn't just one type of flower, it was hundreds. This whole field is always filled with wildflowers this time of year. I can't believe they are gone! Everything is gone, why is this happening?"

And then it hit me; she was not just upset about flowers. I sensed it had to do with Evan as well. "Maybe we can drive around and find some in another park?" I asked.

Emily looked at me like I had just given her a gut punch. "This was the spot, Kai. I can't just go to another field and hope for flowers. It doesn't work like that! This was the field … this was *our* field … and they're all gone … everything is *gone* and they're not coming back … gone … he's gone, and *he's* never coming back"

She breathed the last words so silently I almost didn't hear her. She fell to her knees in the dry open field and began to weep. I slowly walked over to her and sat next to her on the ground and quietly tightened my arms around her trembling body. "Just let it out, there is no wrong way to process everything that's happened over the last few weeks." As we both sat in that open field, I held her in my arms for several moments and let her feel her loss. It wasn't about flowers; it was about the loss of love. The hurt and pain that lingered was unbearable, and often suffocating.

A few minutes had passed, and the sun was dipping below the tree line. Emily slowly looked up at me. "Can we go sit in your car for a bit? There's no reason to be here anymore," she asked with a note of defeat.

I nodded and helped her to her feet. When we got into my SUV, I turned on the heater to warm our chilled bodies. I looked over at her and wished I could zap the pain away.

"Kai, can I ask you something?" She looked at me now with a wide, open expression. The tears had all dried, but she now had a look of desire swimming in her eyes.

"Of course, ask me anything."

My interest was at an all-time high. I was nervous as to where this conversation was headed. She looked down to the hem of her dress and played with a loose piece of thread. As I waited for her to ask whatever it was that she needed to ask, she instead moved her hand over the middle console and onto my thigh. Before I had time to react, her mouth was on mine.

I didn't have one iota of strength in that moment to deny her of this. Her kiss was as if she had something to say, but not with words. I relaxed into the kiss and slid my fingers into her hair. I grabbed a handful and tried to keep the moan from escaping my body. In an instant, I was lost in her lips and our bodies were pressed together, but the damn console was once again separating us.

She put both her arms around my neck and tried to pull me closer. I gave in to her tugging and was almost completely over the console on top of her. She moved her lips to my neck and kissed my scruff. The sensation of her wet lips on my neck nearly drove me wild.

Although there was still a console jamming into my thighs, all I could feel were her soft curves pressed against my body. As the kiss deepened, I felt her body relax, as if all the pain she had buried deep over the years was slowly releasing.

I couldn't help but hold her close, having Emily in my arms kissing me was the most wonderful feeling I'd ever had. I then slipped my hand into her hair and began to rub her neck with my thumb. I kissed her long and hard, lightly stroking her tongue with mine. My lips slowly brushed hers once again, and as I slid my tongue across her lips her moan was my reward. The need emanating from her drove me to grind my hips to hers, and she moaned once more while she pulled me closer. I leaned down and kissed her, a soft brush of my lips was now wet with hers. Emily was the one to deepen the kiss once more, her full lips parted, and I was immediately allowed entry.

I don't know if I'd ever felt so conflicted in my life. Every inch of my body was screaming to continue the kiss, and the rational part of me was saying Emily was working through some really difficult things, and this wasn't the best time for this to be happening.

Her hands had begun to touch my chest, and they were discovering every groove and curve of my body. What kind of guy would stop this from progressing? A good one, that's who. I slowly backed away from Emily and leaned back towards the driver window.

"As much as I completely love what's happening right now, I feel we might need to pump the brakes a bit. You don't know what your kisses are doing to me, and those hands … they are making things extremely hard … I mean difficult. They are making things extremely difficult," I corrected myself. "I just don't think right now is the best time for this. I want to do things the right way, and that's not what is happening right now. You've got a lot going on, and I don't want you to look back and wish things had happened differently."

Her eyes went from heated desire to a heated anger in mere seconds. I went to touch her cheek and she backed away from me. "Are you serious, Kai?"

Without giving me time to answer, she began to make a break for it and started to open her car door. "Emily, you have to understand where I'm coming from." I pleaded, hoping she would hear me out and stop trying to leave me like this.

"Actually, I don't have to do anything. What happened to *there's no wrong way to process everything that has happened?*" she yelled.

It wouldn't take a rocket scientist to understand I had messed up and must have done the wrong thing. I just wanted to be a good guy for her. "And that's true, but I just don't think whatever was happening here would've made you feel any better tomorrow. Maybe for tonight … at the moment. But come tomorrow …" I trailed off. I couldn't finish the sentence. There were no perfect words for this difficult situation we found ourselves in.

"Yeah, tomorrow. Tomorrow Evan will still be dead, and I'll still be all alone. Yeah, you're right, Kai. Tomorrow I will still be a lonely widow with a dead husband. I'm well aware of what tomorrow brings, so sue me for wanting some ounce of happiness tonight. Sorry, but I don't need this right now."

She gave me one last look as she slammed the door shut. It was enough to rip my heart to shreds. I watched her drive away, and for the first time I could ever remember I felt tears in my eyes.

Chapter Thirty-Five

EMILY

Kai had snapped me out of my need to be desired quicker than it had started, and once again it was a lonely place to be. And now, he made me feel awful in the process. I knew he was right, but that didn't make the sting of rejection hurt any less. I knew it was too soon to have these feelings. What awful person would try this sort of thing days after they learn of their husband's death? Luckily, there was not a car in sight as I slammed on my brakes. I pulled into the parking lot of an empty strip mall and buried my face in my hands. I screamed so loud, thankful there were no cars nearby. I don't know how long I sat there but I cried the entire time, for what felt like hours. Where do I go from here? I felt so completely broken. I had no idea how to fix what I had just done. No idea how to live my life with the answers I've been given to my deepest, darkest questions...

Just then my phone vibrated, and I saw a text from Kai flash across the screen.

KAI- *Emily, please know how badly I wanted tonight to happen... believe me... how I've wanted this. I know this is nothing compared to what you are feeling ...but when I lost my mom, I turned to things that later on I wished I hadn't. I don't want to be the cause of something you wish hadn't happened. I want to be the one to make you happy. I couldn't live with myself if I hurt you. I want to be there when the time is right. I will wait, I am prepared to wait, I know we have something special. You are my something special, Emily.*

If only he knew how long I'd waited to have these feelings for someone again. How I wondered if it was even possible to find something like this for a second time in this precious life. Without ever fully knowing Evan was gone, there was always a small voice in my head telling me he was never coming back. The light his spirit had made in this world had flickered out long ago. My other half was gone, and deep down, for years I knew he was no longer walking this earth. Matt had given me the final closure I needed to open a new chapter in my life. Kai said he was prepared to wait, but I doubt he wanted a widow with a young child that would never be completely over her heartbreak. I knew in my heart it would be better to cut things off now, before I was completely crushed once again. I read the beautiful words in his text one more time and wrote a quick reply.

EMILY- *I think it's best if you don't come to the memorial. It will be better for everyone involved. Can you send me Alex's number?*
Thanx.

I cried as I wrote the entire text. My phone had puddles of tears forming around the screen. It broke me to tell him not to come to the memorial, but I knew I needed to cut things off sooner than later. Just as I would tell Tillie: Better to rip the Band-Aid off as quickly as possible … it would hurt less in the long run. Maybe Kai was right. I was looking for a distraction from my pain, and now it was time I focused on my family and the memorial. My phone vibrated too quickly with his response.

KAI- *If that's what you think is best … 949-555-0954.*
I'll let him know you'll be contacting him.

Nothing more. No begging me to change my mind, no hopes for this to just blow over. The pain in my chest was getting stronger, and I was beginning to regret my decision. I knew that I had to focus on the memorial and get things settled. The feelings for Kai were too much to think about right now, and I needed to focus on this chapter of my life happening in current time before I got too far ahead of myself. I pulled myself together and left the abandoned strip mall parking lot.

Over the next few days, I practically lived on my phone. Whether it was phone calls to vendors, phone chats with family and friends, or texts from my friends making sure I was doing okay, I would do anything to stay busy. The memorial was tomorrow, and I had yet to hear from Kai about anything. I knew I pushed him away, but I thought I would at least hear *something* from him.

As the phone rang in my hands, my heart skipped a beat, but the name on the screen read ALEX. I answered the phone.

"Hello?"

"Hey, Emily. It's Alex Greyson," he answered smoothly.

"Hey, Alex. What can I do for you? Did you get the itinerary I sent your assistant?" I asked.

"That's actually why I'm calling. She just gave it to me. I just got word that Matt will be arriving about ten minutes before it starts … is that okay?" he asked, his voice almost shaky and out of breath.

"Yeah, that's perfect… is everything okay, Alex?"

"Um, yeah … but can I ask you something?"

"Of course, what is it?" I asked, hoping I would have an answer for him.

221

"Well, it's actually something I'd like to talk about in person. Would you have a free hour this evening? If not, I understand." His voice was shaky and not at all like the strong and commanding Alex Greyson I had met a few weeks back.

I gathered my thoughts and knew I had an hour to spare. "Yeah, I can get away for an hour. Is everything okay?" I asked.

"Truthfully, no. I'm really struggling with all of this, and I have a ton of questions. Obviously, you don't have the answers, but you're the closest person I know who may understand what I'm feeling right now," he stammered as he gathered his thoughts. "It would really mean a lot to me." The silent plea in his voice was bordering heartbreak.

"Unfortunately, I understand better than you can imagine. Let me talk to my mom about watching Tillie, and I will text you back. Does that work for you?" I asked, nervous to be alone with Alex. I was never nervous around Kai, everything felt so natural and as it should. With Alex, I was anxious and fearful I would do or say the wrong thing.

"Yes, that's perfect, I'll be waiting. We can meet near you to make things easier. I know of a place not far from your house," he offered.

I found myself with a smile across my lips. It was nice to know Alex had a thoughtful bone in his body. "Okay, that helps. I'll text you when I have …" Before I had a chance to finish my thought, or to say goodbye, Alex had hung up the phone. And just like that, he was back to being the Alex I'd known before.

"Bye to you too, Alex." I murmured under my breath as I walked to the living room where my parents were playing with Tillie.

"Would you two mind staying with Tillie as I go meet Alex for an hour?"

My mom's eyes grew wide. "You're going to see Senator Alex Greyson?" she asked, her entire face filled with curiosity.

I laughed. It felt good to laugh again. "Yes, Mother. *The Alex Greyson*. And if you're lucky, you may catch a glimpse of him tomorrow at the memorial."

"If only I were young again," she sighed as she looked over to my dad who was rolling his eyes at her fangirl obsession.

My dad looked at me with a worried expression. "We will watch Tillie for you, Honey, but please don't get caught up in something with that man. I may be old, but I've seen the tabloids."

My mom rolled her eyes. "You can't believe everything you read. I happen to think our wonderful daughter has great taste in character, and she can do what she pleases." She looked my way and raised her eyebrows. "Is there something we should know about between the two of you? I know you mentioned his connection to Catherine and the mix-up with Tillie's birth certificate, but I didn't know there was possibly *more* to the situation."

"There is nothing going on between the two of us. Don't get me wrong. I see the appeal, but there could never be anything more than friendship between us." I was quick to answer, and my parents both looked at each other and then back over to me.

"What are you not saying, Emily?" my dad asked.

"What do you mean?" I asked.

"You're doing that thing you did when you were little, where you would tell the truth but hide something behind it."

I grew nervous, remembering that my parents knew me better than anyone, I knew I couldn't hide from them any longer. "You two and your interrogation tactics! Don't worry about me, I have … things to figure out, but everything in due time." I nodded, hoping I came across as confident as I thought I sounded. Maybe saying it aloud would help my worried thoughts.

My mother looked at me with her trademark stare. "I'm just worried about you, Emily—"

"Mom, please stop. I have so much to deal with. Can I just go see a friend without you thinking there is more to it than what it is?"

She nodded her head and looked over to my dad. He gave her *the look* and picked up where she left off. "We support you, Honey, with whatever you choose to do. Go see your *friend*. We'll be here with Tillie for as long as you need."

I smiled. "Thanks, Dad ... and Mom, I know you mean well, but is this really the best time to be playing matchmaker ... really ... the night before Evan's funeral?" I saw the hurt in her eyes and wished I hadn't accused her.

"I wasn't playing matchmaker, Emily. Before you interrupted me, I was going to say I know how you are. You tend to push people away when you need them most. Don't let that continue to happen with these new friends of yours."

"New friends as in plural? What do you—?"

"Call it a mother's intuition, Emily. Now go on and go see your *friend*."

She emphasized the word friend, and I rolled my eyes. "Thank you, guys, I'll be back in an hour or so." I kissed Tillie goodbye and waved to my parents as I walked out the door.

As I stepped down my dingy stairs, it dawned on me that from here on out it was my chore alone to fix all the broken pieces of this old house. Another thing I had subconsciously been hoping and anticipating that Evan could still help me with someday. That hope was now gone.

I pulled out my phone and texted Alex my availability. He quickly responded with an address to meet him. It was right in my neighborhood a few blocks away. When I arrived at the little Italian restaurant, I realized I had no clue what car to search for. I stepped into the restaurant hoping to find him waiting for me inside, but that was not Alex's M.O. so I asked the hostess, and she got a table ready for me and my plus-one.

Before I had time to question myself and why I was even meeting Alex there, a flash in the corner of my eye from the media cameras nearly blinded me. Alex came hurling in with a bodyguard at his side. It was as though time stopped, and now Alex had casually approached my table. He was wearing a tailored royal-blue suit with expensive tan leather loafers. His sunglasses were on, and his hair styled to perfection. In another setting, I would be head over heels for the man. He was absolutely and devastatingly handsome. Every woman … possibly even every man … wanted Alex Greyson. Alex knew he had a special charm, and one hundred percent of the time he used it for his advantage. He stood next to my table towering over me. His presence instantly commanded my attention.

"Oh Hon, we can't sit here in the front of the restaurant, we'll be blinded before we get our drinks. Follow me to the back of the restaurant, but don't get up for a few minutes, I'll have the hostess escort you back."

And before I had a chance to respond, he was walking away. Casually strolling to the back of the restaurant like he owned the place, and maybe he did.

After a few minutes passed and the last of the reporters outside had left, I was more than happy not to be plastered all over the media with Alex. My mind wandered as I sat waiting for the hostess to approach my table. I could see the headlines now ... 'Homely Woman 'seen with Senator Alex Greyson. What Could He See in Her?' I slumped into my chair and wished I hadn't come. This was the last thing I needed today.

"Would you follow me, Miss?" An attractive curvy woman appeared beside me. I stood and followed her to the back of the restaurant and to a dimly lit intimate setting where the one single window was covered in heavy brocade.

Alex sure knew how to command a room. The moment I saw him with his top two buttons open and his sunglasses now removed. I was awestruck in his presence. He was leaning back into a large half-circle booth with both thick arms stretched over the top, so the only way to sit at the table would be right beside him.

"Come, sit. This is my favorite spot in this place." He gave the seat a gentle pat. "I promise, I don't bite, Emily ... well, most of the time." He chuckled at his own joke.

I, on the other hand, was mortified and nervous as hell. I made my way into the booth and sat directly next to him. Alex gave me his celebrity status grin and flagged the waitress to our table. "Emily, would you like a glass of wine, or possibly something stronger to drink? I'm sure we could both use a drink ... or two."

He looked at me as the waitress handed me a menu. A drink sounded nice. "Actually, yes, that sounds good. I'll have a glass of... champagne."

Alex's eyes widened. "Champagne? I wasn't aware we were celebrating. We'll take a bottle of your best champagne, please." he said to the waitress as she gave him an inviting smile. He barely noticed her, as he was still looking at me and watching my every move like a predator stalking his prey. Again, in any other setting, it would have been attractive as hell.

"So, champagne? Dare I ask why?" He smiled as he asked. "There's no reason, really. I just haven't had any in, well ... years, and what can I say ... I like the bubbles." I laughed and sounded like such a child.

"Alex nodded his head and continued to stare into my eyes. He then slid closer to me with his shoulders curled towards me, and before things got too uncomfortable, as they slowly were becoming, I decided it was time to find out why he had to talk to me in person.

"So, why did we need to meet in person? Is everything okay?"

Alex sat up straight and regained his stoic distant expression. "Yes, I have a few questions regarding the memorial tomorrow and things revolving around ... Catherine." He said her name as though it hurt. There was sadness buried deep behind his piercing eyes, and you could almost feel the tension radiating from his body.

"What would you like to know?" I asked.

"Will Catherine's family be there?" He slowly let all the words escape. I could hear his breathing intensify. It was strange to hear insecurity in this strong man's husky voice.

I needed to answer him truthfully. "Yes, they'll be attending. It's just a memorial though, so there won't be a burial. I don't know if they told you or not, but Catherine was never recovered."

There was a long pause on both our ends as we stared at each other. I broke the silence. "Her family has been given all the official information. They're aware you might be coming tomorrow and that you may have questions. They want to meet you, Alex."

He cleared his throat and hesitated. "Do they? Or do they think I would have just thrown money at her to keep her quiet?" His voice was strained as though he was still angry.

My answer was quick, and I spoke the truth. "Not at all. I'll let her family tell you everything. I know you will appreciate speaking with them tomorrow. They're going to love you Alex, you're a good person."

He let out a deep sigh, and I sensed his relief. I placed a hand on his forearm and gave it a small squeeze. He looked at me with a candid expression, and for the first time all evening, I felt as though I might be seeing the *real* Alex Greyson.

The waitress came with our bottle and poured us each a glass. We lifted our glasses and clinked them together. As I raised the glass to my lips, from the corner of my eye I saw Alex watching me. I noticed he finished his glass in one swift gulp.

"That's not how you drink champagne, you know. It's supposed to be savored."

He set his glass down and looked me in the eyes again. "What if I am savoring something else here tonight?"

The self-obsessed and not-at-all charming Alex was back. I rolled my eyes. How could he even think I would go for something like that? "Smooth, Alex. But really … about tomorrow …"

He cut me off and as he placed his hand over mine, the warmth his hand radiated was nothing short of compelling. "Emily, how are you doing? Can I help with anything for tomorrow?" he asked, quickly changing the direction of the conversation.

"No, I think we have everything covered. I have a small army to back me up." I laughed and took a longer sip of my champagne.

"Perfect, well, just let me know if you need anything." His eyes were now searching me, as if on a hunt. "Emily there was something else I wanted to ask."

To break this strange scenario, I reached across the table and filled our glasses again. I hesitated. Had Kai told him of our argument, and he was trying to help his best friend now? "Yeah, what is it?" I asked, cautiously sipping my champagne.

"Kai mentioned to me last night that Matt wanted to say something during the service. He wanted me to ask you if it was too late to let him say a few words."

The second I heard Kai's name; my heart sank. I hated that he didn't feel he could ask me himself, that he had to have Alex ask for him. "Of course, we can make that happen." I gave him a reassuring nod as I quickly answered.

He seemed happy with my response and took a large sip of his drink. "Great, I'll let the team know."

I thought for a moment that I was free from having a conversation about Kai. That all changed once Alex cleared his throat.

"So, what's going on with the two of you?"

I nearly choked on my drink at his audacity. I was definitely feeling the champagne now, and I tried to get my words to catch up to my thoughts. "With who?" I asked, hoping I could get out of having this discussion.

Alex laughed. "Emily, you know very well who I'm talking about," he playfully stated. He brought his glass to his lips, took a long swig, and licked his lips as he finished his glass.

I couldn't stop my eyes from watching his tongue slip in and out of his mouth. "I'm sorry. I have no idea who you're referring to." I replied, as I pretended to look over the menu.

Alex shook his head. "So, you wouldn't mind that there's a picture of us having dinner together and my hands strangely placed on yours?" he said as he pulled out his phone to show me a picture.

"What? Who took this? There's no one around us!" I shrieked as I scanned the room.

"Probably one of the wait staff, but who cares right?" He laughed again as he continued to scroll on his phone. "You know I could send this to my team and have them find out who posted this, and it can be removed in seconds if you just answer my question," he said as his eyebrows playfully raised in my direction.

"Fine, I'll answer your question, but only because that's a horrible and misleading photo. I assume you're speaking of Kai. Am I right?" I asked as I rolled my eyes in his face.

"Ding, ding, ding! We have a winner!" he continued looking at me as he began typing a message on his phone.

"Well, what do you want to know?" I asked.

"Is there something going on between the two of you?"

"I don't know how to answer that," I replied. If I was honest with myself, I had no idea *what* was going on between the two of us. I wish things had happened differently, but I was sorely aware I had pushed Kai away, and sadly the damage had already been done.

Alex didn't appear happy with my answer. "Kai's my best friend. I'd like to say I know him better than anyone. After I spoke with him this morning, it was pretty obvious something had happened between the two of you, and it wasn't good."

"Well, I think Kai is an amazing man, and he has truly helped me more than I can ever put into words. If it weren't for him, I don't think we'd have the answers we have now."

Alex shook his head. "Honestly, Emily, we'd still be at square one if it weren't for him. The fact that he called his father and asked him for help really says a lot about how he must feel about you." He motioned for the waitress, and she quickly rushed to his side. "Can we get some appetizers, please? All of the chef's favorites, and that will be it."

The waitress began to bat her eyes at him, and then asked. "Is there anything else I can do for you?"

"No, that should be it … no, wait. There *is* one more thing. You can delete the photo you took of us earlier. I don't want to have to have the restaurant fire you for breaking my confidentiality agreement."

His powerful tone radiated from his body. The waitress nodded her head as she quickly reached for her phone and showed him, she had deleted the post. She walked away like a scolded puppy as she slowly retreated to the kitchen.

"Sorry about that. Picture has been deleted. So, where were we?"

"You humiliated that girl, Alex," I stated as I took in the entire scene. It was obvious the man had no intentions of sugar coating the situation.

"The photo needed to be deleted as soon as possible, and I got it done. She should have known better." Alex retorted as he poured us another glass.

"I'm sure it could have been handled differently." I shrugged, as I finished my thought. "What did you mean when you said the fact that Kai reached out to his dad?" Alex took another drink, and I continued to sip mine. I told myself I needed to cool it with the champagne if I was going to be driving home later.

"Kai and his dad have always had a *difficult* relationship. His dad never wanted him to quit the police force and work with me. He saw it as petty work, a glorified bodyguard, if you will." Alex shook his head. "I have a bodyguard, and it's not Kai. Kai is the head of operations for a senator. It's obviously not some petty work, but his father has never understood our dynamic, and he's definitely never understood me. When Kai sets his sights on something, don't even bother getting in his way. Hence, my need to ask if there was something between the two of you. I don't stand a chance if Kai and you are involved." He eyed me up and down as he drank me in.

I laughed. Did he really think he ever stood a chance, even if Kai was not involved? "Alex, you and I both know I am a couple, if not a hundred, miles from the type of girl you are normally seen with," I laughed, as I looked over to meet his fixated eyes.

"Emily, are you serious? Do you really think that?" he asked with a serious tone.

I nodded, unsure how to answer his question.

"You are evidently oblivious to the effect you have on men. You are absolutely captivating, Emily," Alex whispered as his hand found its way to mine.

Without a moment to process where this conversation was heading, I almost laughed as I responded. "Captivating? Really, Alex? How many women have you used that one on?"

"It's not a line, Emily. You and I have both been given this horrible news that can, could and should break us. Yet here we are. Our tragic situations have brought us closer together. We only have each other to keep ourselves going." He then began to slide even closer towards me in the booth and gave me a sly grin.

I instinctively backed away. "Alex, I don't know what you think you see, but yes, I am broken. I'm so broken that the thought of you using our situation as a play makes me sick. I can sympathize with you, really, I can. Having all your hopes and dreams shattered in one single moment, believe me … I know that feeling all too well. But you see, I have Tillie, and *that* is what keeps me going. That is what keeps me from being completely broken day in and day out." I found myself practically yelling in his face.

He paused for a moment as he collected his thoughts. "Forgive me Emily. You're right, I don't have a child! At least not anymore … I might have, but that was taken from me," he pleaded, as his eyes were filled with regret. "I have no excuse to try and make these kinds of statements. *Especially* when I know how Kai feels."

Once those words were said, I drank the rest of my third glass. Alex reached for the almost empty bottle of champagne. "Are you going to be able to drive after drinking all this?" he asked as he poured me another glass.

"What do you know about Kai and me?" I quickly asked as I finished my liquid courage, and before I talked myself out of asking it.

"I know enough to know he's hurt by not being able to go to the memorial tomorrow," he blankly responded.

Our waitress came with four plates of assorted appetizers, each looking more delicious than the next. As soon as the plates were set on the table, the waitress left with her head still held low.

Alex caught me looking and laughed as he placed a piece of bread in his mouth. "Don't worry about her, I'll find some way to make it up to her." I shot him a glare as he gave me a wink. "And I will *sincerely* apologize," he laughed as I scoured the wide array of food before me.

"I feel awful about Kai, but you don't know the entire story," I was finally able to say while placing a piece of I-don't-know-what in my mouth. It was the most decadent food I'd ever had, like some form of puff pastry with a garlic scallop, and my mouth was still watering from the taste.

"You're right. I don't know the whole story, but I don't need to know it all to know Kai would be the best person to have around tomorrow. If you think of him as even a friend, let me tell you from experience … he's the best one there is. He's got me through some tough shit in the past."

Before I was able to answer, we were both startled to hear the door to our private room slam open. The waitress was standing there after being pushed to the side.

"I'm sorry Mr. Greyson, I tried telling him this was a private meeting, but he wouldn't listen."

My eyes widened as they were met with Kai's piercing stare. His face was washed with a tormented expression, and something deeper flashed below the surface.

He quickly looked away and shot a glare at Alex. "What the hell, Alex? A private meeting?" he asked as he made his way to our table. I couldn't begin to imagine how this must have looked.

Chapter Thirty-Six

KAI

What the hell had Alex done? In my attempt at getting my mind off of Emily, I'd been trying to make myself busy the last couple of days. Apparently, I'd made myself too busy. Seeing Alex cozied up with Emily made me want to throw a punch at his pretty boy face. Emily's cheeks were rosy, and I could see her half empty glass of champagne sitting in front of her. She wouldn't make eye contact with me now, and I couldn't help wondering what her intentions with Alex truly were.

"What the hell, Alex?" was all I managed to mutter.

"Well, hello to you too, Kai, nice to see you. Please join us while the food is still warm." Alex shifted in his seat as if I were honestly going to join them.

"I'm not here to stay," I replied. Emily was looking at me again and I felt she wanted to say something to me.

"I am curious though, how did you know where I was?" Alex asked as he smugly looked at his phone.

"I'm the head of operations, Alex. Do you really think you can do anything without me finding out?" My voice was embarrassingly loud.

Alex smiled, and it felt like a punch to the gut. Had Alex known I would soon find out and wanted me to see him with Emily? Was this his sick way of thinking he could lay claim to Emily as if she were a prize to be bought? This had to be the lowest he had ever stooped.

"Well, now that you've arrived, maybe you can escort Miss Emily back home. It seems she's had a bit too much to drink, and I don't want to have any *more* accidents linked to me."

There was an unspoken pain behind his cruel words.

"Wow, thanks Alex. That won't be necessary. I can drive myself home," Emily countered with a clear annoyance in her tone. She drank what was left in her glass and began to grab her purse and started to slide out of the booth. At her first step, her foot suddenly got caught in the strap of her purse, and within moments Emily was in my arms once again. She would have fallen right on top of the table had I not caught her.

"Are you okay?" I asked, worried she may have twisted her ankle.

Her complexion turned a brighter shade of pink, and it nearly took my breath away.
"I'm fine, you can let me go Kai," she squeaked just barely loud enough for me to hear. The pink of her cheeks still remained.

"I think that gives us all the answers we need. Emily as your senator, I *command* you to let Kai take you home." Alex laughed as he grabbed the champagne bottle and gave it a chug. As the bottle emptied, he motioned to the waitress to come closer. "Can you be a doll and get me something stronger? Pick your favorite ... I'm planning on sharing it with you," he whispered to the waitress as he gave her a wink.

"Alex, the moment I start thinking you have a soul, I am reminded you clearly do not," Emily stammered as she straightened herself and rubbed her head. "And Kai, I'm not far from here; I'll be fine, don't worry about me."

I took a step closer to her so that we were nearly touching, I spoke quietly enough for just Emily to hear. "Emily, that's all I've been doing these past couple days, is worrying about you. Can I please take you home? I'll drive your car and uber back. I can't let you drink and drive. I'm a former cop, remember?" I hoped and prayed she would say yes. I needed to speak to her if only for a minute.

"Okay, but only because I can't deal with all this right now," she whispered.

I turned to look at Alex and realized he had already been given his new bottle. He had the bottle to his lips, and the amber liquid jostled in his hands. He then waved to both Emily and me as we began to make our way out the door.

"Goodbye, Miss Emily. I do hope you had a splendid evening," he yelled in our direction. We could both hear the condescending tone in his voice.

"Yeah, thanks Alex. You should slow down if you're planning on showing up tomorrow," she stated coldly.

He smiled his playboy grin. "Oh, don't worry about me. I've dealt with worse, and look at me ... I'm in the top ten hottest bachelors." And with that he brought the bottle back up to his lips.

"Come on, Emily, we should leave." I motioned, hoping to get out of there before Emily had to see any more.

"Is he going to be okay?" she asked as we shut the door behind us.

I shook my head as we began to make our way towards the exit. "Unfortunately, this isn't unusual for Alex. This is how he copes with things. It will last for a few days, and then he'll go back to being composed and rigid once again. His bodyguard is here. He won't let anything bad happen to him, and we know how to stop him when he gets to a certain limit." Emily nodded her head as she understood, and we continued walking to her car.

Once we made our way to her small blue sedan, I was reminded of how small it was. Driving her small sedan would be difficult with my much larger frame. As we both began to get situated in our seats, my knees were quickly beginning to contort.

Emily let a laugh escape as she saw my knees squished to the wheel. "There's a lever on the side of the chair that will let you back it up a bit," she smiled as she watched me stumble. "Here, let me show you," she said as she reached across my lap and began fumbling with the buttons on the side of the seat.

My heart raced as the warmth from her arm crept across my lap.

Emily must have realized her close proximity and pulled away right as the seat backed up. "I'm sorry, too much champagne ... I'm so weird," she whispered as she twirled a loose curl with her finger.

"Emily don't apologize. You're not weird ... What was weird was finding out from my security team that you were on a date with Alex. I know it's not my place to ask, but Alex? Really?"

Her eyes shot right to mine. "This was absolutely not a date, Kai! Why does everyone think that? If I were going to go on any sort of date, it would NOT be with Alex, it would be with y–"

She stopped mid-sentence, but it was too late, I knew what she was about to say. "With who Emily?" I teased as I shifted my body toward hers.

"Come on, Kai. I know you heard me. YOU, it would be with you." She looked over to me with wide eyes as she continued to play with that loose strand of hair. "Alex wanted to talk about Catherine and her parents coming to the memorial tomorrow. I think he's more upset about it than he's letting on."

"Of course, he is. The guy never lets his real emotions come out. He always has a front. But, enough about Alex. I've been beating myself up the last few days thinking I ruined any chance at something with you. Have I?" I asked, hoping she would not gut me twice in a matter of days.

She paused for a moment, as she gave my question some thought.

"No, Kai, you haven't. But you're right. I just have so much going on, not only physically, but emotionally right now. I don't want to hinder you. It's not fair."

"I'm a big boy. I can decide for myself what's fair or not, Emily." I laughed and started the car.

She smiled yet shook her head. "I know you're a big boy, believe me … I know. I just don't know how this could or should all play out for us," she said as I began driving to her house.

"Then let's not plan anything. Let's just let things happen as they happen."

Emily looked over to me and a slight smile formed on her perfectly shaped lips. "Okay, let's let things just happen as they happen. I like that." She looked at the road ahead and realized we were driving. "How do you know how to get to my house?"

"I had to stalk you, remember?" We both chuckled, and slowly Emily's hand made its way to mine on the center console. It felt wonderful having her hand in mine once again. The few short days in her absence had been difficult.

Emily was right, the restaurant was close to her house, and within a few minutes we were already parked in her driveway. "I'll probably just walk back to the restaurant. You weren't kidding when you said you lived so close."

"Yeah, but I'm glad we had this time together. Kai, thank you." She smiled as she stepped out of the car.

I followed her to her front steps. "I'm sorry for assuming things tonight with Alex. He has some not so nice habits when it comes to women, and I couldn't let him take advantage of you."

"No need to apologize. I caught on real quick how Alex operates. That's not my style anyway. I'm kind of into someone else," Emily said as she inched closer to my face. I could still smell the alcohol on her breath, sweet and tangy.

This time around I didn't let any thoughts cloud my judgment, and I closed the gap between us. With our lips pressed together, she intensified the kiss and pulled me in. I grabbed her waist as she leaned into me. We both smiled as we slowly pulled apart from each other.

"Now this is how every meeting should end... but I should head inside before someone sees us. I don't want to have to explain anything just yet." She stumbled with her words, and I was glad I drove her home.

I smiled, knowing this evening could have ended completely different. "Of course, I'm going to walk back to the restaurant. Bye, Emily, as always, it was amazing seeing you." I cupped her face for one last kiss.

She began walking up the stairs, and I couldn't help but watch her as she entered the house. Once she reached the last step, and was now on her front porch, she turned to look at me one last time. I was grateful for the small amount of light the streetlamps provided, for it was just enough to illuminate her delicate face, and it was then I was able to catch a glimpse of her bewitching smile. And that was it, I was long gone. I was Emily's once again.

While on my way back to the restaurant, I made a quick call to Brannon, Alex's bodyguard for the evening.

"Hey, Boss, what's up?" Brannon asked in his deep broody tone.

"Just dropped Emily off, and I'm walking back to the restaurant. How is Alex doing? Should I be worried?" I asked, afraid to hear what I knew was coming.

"You don't need to worry, it's my night. I got this covered."

"You're not answering my question, Brannon. How's he doing?"

Brannon hesitated, "Let's just say it's not *how* he's doing, but *what* he's doing?" he quickly mumbled with a low chuckle.

"Wait, what are you saying?" I thought I knew the answer, but now I wasn't sure.

"Alex is planning on taking that pretty little waitress that was making eyes at him all night home. We're just about to leave the restaurant now. They finished the bottle of jack together, and now he wants me to take them back to his place."

I let out a huge sigh. This was leading nowhere good. "Let me talk to him before you guys leave. You think you can stall him for another five or ten?" I asked, quickening my pace.

Chapter Thirty-Seven

EMILY

Every time I'm with Kai, my worries seem to dissolve into the air, and I can breathe again. I exhaled as I kicked off my shoes in the foyer and entered the living room. A scent of garlic drifted my way. My mother was graciously cooking a giant lasagna for the entire family that was staying at my once-empty home. It was nice to have all the extra rooms when family came to town, but other than that, my home felt empty with its missing pieces, a painful reminder of our loss.

Entering the kitchen, I saw my mother at the stove. "Oh, Emily, you're back! I just finished making dinner. Could you grab the plates? They're in the second cupboard on the right."

My eyes shot open. "Mom, I know where I keep my plates … this is my house, remember?"

She laughed. "Of course, Emily, it's just a mother's habit. I have to admit, I'm going to hate it when you sell this place. It's such a lovely home," she whined as she pulled the lasagna from the oven and placed it on a hot pad.

I had to agree, this home *was* beautiful … or could be, if I had made all the upgrades we'd talked about. "Oh, you mean the missing floorboards and chipped paint? Yeah, it's a beauty all right."

My mother rolled her eyes. "You know, you could have been updating this home all these years, right?"

"Wow, Mom, what a great idea! Why didn't I think of that?" My reply was full of sarcasm. I could still feel the champagne's lasting effects and began to set the plates on the table. Lasagna sounded rather good, actually.

"You know what I mean, Emily. I know you don't want to hear this, but you've had your entire life on pause for the last few years. Think about what this house could be for you and Tillie now that you have the chance to move forward again."

She smiled; I knew her heart was in the right place. "I know, Mom, but that's the thing. I am ready to move forward, and this home just keeps bringing me back to the past. My broken and sad past." I fought the tears from falling.

"Oh, Honey, you can mourn the loss and still move forward at the same time. Think about how happy Evan was buying this home. He wanted you guys in this home before he left for deployment for a reason. He knew it was a great home for his family. Even though Evan is physically gone from this world, his spirit lives on, in not only our hearts, but through Tillie." She placed an arm around me and gave me a tight squeeze.

"Tillie doesn't need these four walls to keep Evan's spirit alive but thank you for saying that." Just then, Tillie ran up to me and tugged at my leg. Over the last few days, I'd been so busy planning the memorial that I had little cuddle time with my favorite person on this earth.

"Mommy! Mommy, you're back! You say my name?" she squealed.

"Well, yes, I did. Mommy and Grandma are talking about our house. Do you like this house, or do you want a *new* house? Wouldn't that be fun? We could pick out a new house!"

Tillie shook her head and began to throw her famous toddler fit. "No, no, no! My house ... dolly loves my house. I like my bedroom. Please, no, no, Mommy!"

I was shocked she was so attached to this old fixer upper, who knew? "Honey, we wouldn't be moving today. It would be months from now."

Tillie still continued to shake her head. "No! No move, Mommy," she continued to howl and throw her fit.

"Okay, honey, no need to get upset. We won't move for a long time, okay?" I said, in my soothing voice that always seemed to calm her down.

"Yay! I love you, Mommy."

Tillie's sweet words, and looking at her just then, reminded me how blessed I was with my own wonderful memory of Evan and his sweet smile. She looked so much like him, that sometimes I would catch myself just staring at her.

Denise came up from behind me and rubbed my back as I hugged Tillie. "Evan's two-thirds," she whispered as she continued to rub my back.

What did she just say? I turned around to face her and gave her a questioning look. Tillie was getting antsy to play again so I let her down as she ran to her toys in the playroom.

"You know that's what he called you two, right?"

I shook my head; I'd never heard him call us that.

"The moment he found out you were having a baby. He said he knew you two were going to be inseparable ... especially with him deployed and all. It would just be the two of you, and he was the third."

I was completely confused. "I don't quite understand. Two-thirds? Why leave the empty space? Where is the missing one-third? I swear, sometimes he never made any sense at all, did he?" I shook my head. The anger I had pent up all evening started to spill all over the kitchen table. "On the topic of things just not making any sense, why did he have to play savior and go find Catherine …" I continued crying.

My mother-in-law stepped closer to me. "Catherine was all alone and pregnant. You know how Evan was, he couldn't just let her go missing."

I couldn't hold back my anger and the champagne wasn't helping. I started screaming. "I was all alone and pregnant … his wife! I was all alone and pregnant, and he left to go overseas … and he … and he died!" All the anger I had compartmentalized for years was now spilling out at my poor mother-in-law.

She flinched at my words, and I instantly regretted saying them. The look on her face was one I never wanted to see, let alone be the one who caused it. I quickly checked myself. "I'm sorry, Denise. That wasn't aimed at you," I continued to cry.

"Emily, it's okay, dear. I've asked myself the same thing. I was so mad at him when your parents told us the full story. I couldn't believe he would risk everything, but that's just who Evan was. Ever since he was little, he had to save everyone … everything. I can remember having to pull over whenever the poor kid saw something that had been hit on the side of the road. He just had to help."

I nodded my head; I knew she was right. In fact, I loved that about him. His heart had always been full of compassion. "I know you're right, but it doesn't make it hurt any less. He was my everything," I cried.

Both my mother and mother-in-law stood on either side of me wrapping their arms around me in a giant embrace. I looked at them and gave them each a tight hug. I drew in a deep breath with my nose and told myself inwardly that I had cried enough for one day. A weight lifted when I voiced my anger in front of the people who loved me. Instead of holding everything inside, it was liberating.

After a few moments passed, my mother rallied the family around the dinner table, and we all shared our memories of Evan. We shared the funny moments, the silly memories, the happy days, and of course, the sad times as well.

Evans's spirit was alive in this home, and that night I knew I couldn't sell this home. This home filled with small conversations from two families coming together was too special to leave behind. It was once again full of life. It had been lacking for too long. All this home needed was love. I just needed to be reminded that it was out there.

As we cleared the table and the evening was winding down, I retreated with my little sleepyhead to tuck her in for the night. Once I had finished getting Tillie to sleep, I made my way to the living room where my family was now finishing up for the evening. I collapsed into my plush wingback chair and stared at my phone still on the coffee table. I reached for it to see if I had any notifications. When it lit up, all I could see were three texts from Kai.

.

KAI- *I forgot to ask, I know you said you think it's best if I don't go to the memorial tomorrow, but I have to be honest and say I think that's the worst idea you've ever had. I want to be there for not only Alex, but I need to be there for you.*
KAI- *By the way I already miss you.*
KAI-*I loved seeing you tonight, you always find a way to make me smile.*

My heart skipped a beat. No matter how I'd tried initially to push him away, he still wanted to be there for me. Even if it would be difficult to see him tomorrow and not actually *be with him*. I couldn't be the cause of him not being there for Alex. Tomorrow would be a rough day for Alex, and I knew as well as anyone how comforting Kai's presence was.

EMILY- *Please come tomorrow, you should be there. Tonight, was just what I needed.*
I miss you too.

I hoped he would respond before I fell asleep, but I could barely keep my eyes open. Tomorrow will be one of the most difficult days of my life. After staring at my phone for twenty minutes, I finally went to bed and fell asleep with it still in my hand.

Chapter Thirty-Eight

KAI

I arrived at the restaurant, and into the private room to see Alex obnoxiously groping the waitress. She looked to be enjoying herself, and poor Brannon was stuck in the cross hairs waiting to leave through the back exit.

"Hey, Boss. Glad you're back, Alex really wants to get outta here. Think you can handle him while I pull the car around back?"

"Yeah, I'll be fine, go get the car. I only need a minute." I quickly responded.

Brannon nodded and exited through the back door.

"Alex, can I interrupt and speak to you alone, please?" I asked, hearing a low moan escape from the waitress as Alex kissed her neck.

"Well, since you're the reason I'm getting this fine piece, I think I can spare a moment or two. Give me a second, babe. How about you go grab your things … you're coming home with me," Alex muttered. The waitress gave him one last kiss, giggled, and ran out the side door.

"So, Alex … what the hell was tonight all about?" I asked, hoping his alcohol buzz would break down some walls of defense and he would answer me truthfully.

"Oh, it wasn't obvious?" he grinned. "You two needed a push and I was the asshole to do it. From you moping around the past few days and Emily obviously immune to my apparent charm, I knew you two needed the help."

I couldn't believe he thought I needed his help. "I can deal with this on my own, Alex. You have your own shit to deal with, so don't go creating more drama by playing games!" I was angry that Alex brought Emily into his ridiculous mind games.

"Kai, you and I both know you needed me. Just say thank you and let me take the girl home. Erin, I think it was … who knows … maybe she'll have a name tag and I can pretend to remember," he laughed as he began making his way out of the private room.

I knew he would have a hell of a hangover tomorrow. "Alex, you need to be there tomorrow. I know you don't want to be there, but you should."

"I'll be there, Kai. No need to worry about me, I'm good. I am *real* good. I'll see you tomorrow." The waitress was waiting for him at the back door, and Alex swaggered his way toward her, trying not to stumble.

I waved to Brannon, got in my car and headed home. The rest of the evening was spent getting things lined up for Matt to attend the memorial the next day. Matt's doctor wasn't too happy that I wouldn't be personally escorting him to the memorial anymore, but I eased his worries by showing him the fat stack of security papers for Alex to be in charge. He seemed satisfied, but I still tried to come up with a way to be there.

It was late by the time I finally looked at my phone and realized I'd forgotten to ask Emily about the memorial. After tonight, I hoped she had changed her mind about me attending. I sent her a text and then two more and waited restlessly for her response.

I would be lying if I said I wasn't upset about not going. But I respected Emily enough to follow her wishes. The way our night ended though, I felt as if the tide may have turned in my favor.

I plugged my phone in my charger, set an alarm for an early wake-up call, and began my nightly routine. After showering, I plopped onto my bed, thinking of how I could try and show up tomorrow without causing an issue. A few days ago, Alex had mentioned his desire for me to be there but once I gave him the short version of why Emily had asked me not to come, he understood.

His response was annoying as hell. He tried to hold his laughter in but failed. Typical Alex, laughing at the worst times. He knew I'd never been one to fall for a woman so quickly. In fact, throughout our whole friendship, I'd only had two relationships. I didn't date around and when I did date … it had to be serious.

I didn't have time for flings unlike Alex who made time for a fling or two each week. I could never understand how he could be so detached from the women he dated. As head of his security, I had to witness a few too many broken hearts when the early mornings came. With any luck tomorrow would be closure for him so he could move forward, and maybe stop acting like an asshole. I sure hoped no press had gotten wind of any of this.

I was fading fast and couldn't reach my phone without getting up, so I made a mental note to contact his publicist in the morning to fill her in. For now, I was exhausted and couldn't stay awake a moment longer.

In the morning my alarm continued to blare in my ear. I squinted at the sun shining through my blinds and jumped out of bed to silence my phone First thing I saw was a text from Emily.

EMILY- *Please come tomorrow, you should be there. Tonight, was just what I needed.*
I miss you too.

When had she sent this text? Last night at 10:45? Great! Right around the time I took my shower. Which meant I could have seen this before I went to bed. I really needed to get better about checking my phone. If I'd seen this, I could've saved myself some time by scheming up ways to attend the memorial. After days of holding my breath, the words on my phone gave me new wind and I texted back as fast as my fingers could type.

KAI- *Good Morning, Beautiful! Say no more, you couldn't keep me away.*

I thought it was time to talk to Alex and let him know I'd be attending the memorial so he wouldn't have to think about the extra security for Matt.

He answered quicker than anticipated, his voice raspy and dull. "Hello."

"Alex?" He didn't sound like his normal cocky self.

"Yeah, what's up?" he answered through a yawn.

"Are you just waking up?" There was no way, the put together senator, was just now waking up. Even on his craziest nights he found a way to wake up early and hit the gym. One thing you could always count on Alex for was his consistency.

"Yeah, so what? I can sleep in whenever I want, Kai," he growled.

"Yeah, sure man, but it's just weird since you have a pretty eventful day ahead of you. You're usually up before the sun."

"Correct, so why are you calling?" Now he was annoyed.

"I was calling to let you know that I'm going to the memorial today. I can take care of Matt and … you okay, Alex?" I wondered if he had forgotten most of the night before.

"Yeah, man. Just drank too much last night and slept in. Don't worry about me. I'm glad you're going now. So, it's all cool with Emily?

I was surprised he cared enough to ask. "Yeah, she texted me. You need anything? Want to drive with me? I can pick you up."

There was a short silence. "Yeah, that'll work. Pick Matt up first and then swing by here. That should give me enough time."

"Okay, I'll let Security know, and they can meet us there. Sure, you don't need anything before I pick you up?" I hesitated to ask.

"Kai, I'm fine. Just do your job and I'll be good, okay? See you later."

There was no doubt that there was some hostility in his tone, and I knew him well enough to know he must have drunk a hell of a lot to sleep through his workout. Alex and I rarely snapped at each other, so I was fired-up about going to the memorial for more reasons than one.

I rushed around my apartment trying to stay on time. I settled on a dark navy-blue suit with a wine-colored tie. I made sure my hair wasn't in my face and no toothpaste on my fresh suit then bolted for the door.

Driving to pick up Matt, I put my phone on speaker and called Alex's publicist, Trisha. After explaining the long story of the past week's insanity, we finalized details and had a statement ready for when Alex gave the green light.

By the time my call to Trisha had ended, I had arrived at the hospital. Matt was ready to go, and I almost didn't recognize him dressed up and standing tall.

"Look at you, man! You clean up nice!" I smiled.

"Notice I'm taller than you now, buddy?" His grin was ear to ear.

Wow! How had I not noticed he was standing on two feet, no crutches, just a cane now.

"Wow, yes! Matt, you look great! Let's see the bionic leg!"

He pulled his pant leg up to show off his new addition. The new light in his eyes had been missing before. "It looks great! Really happy for you. Let's get you signed out, and we can get on the road."

Once we got settled in the car, I let him know I would be joining him and Alex today after all.

"That's good, I didn't think Alex wanted to be watching over me anyway." Matt snickered.

"Well, can you blame him after what you said about him?" I said laughing.

"No, but that was before ..." He looked out the window and shuffled in his seat. "I know a lot of what I wrote was pretty harsh. I was unbelievably angry and well ... alone."

"Well, I think today will be a good fresh start for you. I think there'll be a lot of people there that really care about you and want you to regain your life. You'll see."

He nodded and gave me a quick side grin. "You're right, Kai. Guess I just need to accept how things happened and move on with my life."

I knew he was doing better, but these scars were deeper than any of us could ever imagine. I gave him a nod. Some things were better left unsaid. "Matt we're making a pit stop before we get to the venue, we're picking up Alex first."

"Oh great, my biggest fan," he said with a laugh.

"He knows we're all going together, and I think he's put things behind him. My advice is that you should do the same. He's a good guy. This thing with Catherine has done something to him so be easy on him. He lost a future he never knew he wanted the moment he heard the truth about Catherine."

Matt nodded, seeming to understand how much the severity of his actions had had on everyone involved. "Got it, boss. I have no issues with Alex Greyson."

"Good, because this is his house right up here." I turned onto Alex's circular driveway as Matt let out a huge sigh.

"Of course, this is his place. What is he, a prince?" He laughed at his own comment.

I shook my head. "Be nice, Matt." I grabbed my phone and texted Alex that we had arrived. When the front door opened, Alex came down the steps in typical Alex Greyson style, dressed more for the Academy Awards than for a memorial.

Matt shook his head. "I promise I'll be nice, but this man is ridiculous. What does he think this is, a fashion show?"

"What can I say? Alex likes the finer things." I hid my laugh as Alex opened the back passenger door. He was still solemn, but I noted a slight shift in his stance from the night before. Alex had always been good at keeping things buried so to speak, but if there was an audience, he gave them a show.

"Well, look what the cat dragged in," Matt joked.

Alex didn't smile. "Nice to see you too, Matt. I almost didn't recognize you all cleaned up."

"Ha-ha, very funny. You probably wouldn't recognize me now that I can stand on my own two feet again," he said as he tapped on his metal prosthetic.

Alex looked over the seat and peered down at Matt's new addition. "Oh shit, good for you, man. I'm honestly happy for you." He gave Matt a pat on the shoulder and leaned back in his seat. "So, what's the game plan for today?" he asked, looking at me.

It was standard procedure to go over details before a public appearance, but today didn't concern him. Today was about Emily, Catherine, Matt, and most importantly, Evan. "The memorial will begin around 11:30, and from what I gather, it's going to be pretty casual. There won't be a burial, but his ashes will be present at the reception site." I glanced at Matt as his eyes grew large.

"Evan's here? But how did they …" he trailed off, unable to finish his question.

"My dad pulled a few favors, and they rushed the request. Were you not aware they had his remains?"

Matt shook his head. "No, I thought my buddy Trevor would keep them as we'd promised, but I'm happy they'll be with Emily … he should be with Emily."

"You knew where the remains were this whole time?" I wanted to be angry, but I remembered Matt had his reasons and it wasn't the time to start a scene.

"Yeah, Trevor was one of the guys that helped rescue us. He also felt responsible for Evan's death. He thought that if he'd just been a few minutes earlier, Evan could still be alive. Out of guilt, I talked him into holding onto his remains. He was there to hear Evan's last plea … we all wanted to keep his wishes. Does he know about the memorial today?"

I nodded. "Yeah, when we figured out who had them, he was informed where they were headed and was told about the recent turn of events."

Matt shook his head and looked concerned. "Is Trevor in trouble?"

"No, we made sure there were no charges filed. I don't know if he's going to be there today or not, but he knows about it."

Matt nodded and the car was silent for a few minutes.

"Am I supposed to say anything today?" Alex asked, as he stared out the window.

"No, why would you be saying anything?" I questioned.

"I don't know what's expected of me. I don't even know why I'm going. I spent one weekend with Catherine. I'm sure her parents don't want to see the reason their daughter is gone … I'm just an insult being there."

Alex was growing more annoyed by the second. I hadn't seen him this upset in a long time. I watched him in the rearview as he shoved his face in his hands and slowly dragged his fingers through his hair, loosening some strands from their perfect placement. Those loose strands were a sure sign something was off with him.

Before I had a chance to speak, Matt surprised me. "Alex, you can't think like that. Believe me, if anyone has experience holding onto guilt, or whatever you have pent up inside, it's not going to get you anywhere good. That's for sure!" Matt had shifted his body and was leaning against the window looking directly at Alex now.

"You aren't responsible for Catherine's actions. She knew what she was doing. She knew going out alone was dangerous. She was ordered not to for good reason, and she took it upon herself to do it anyway. You, Greyson, have nothing to feel guilty or responsible for. You hear me, senator?"

They stared at each other in silence.

"I hear you Matt, but you do know everything you just said can be directed right back at *you*, right?" he stated plainly.

Matt nodded and shrugged. "Touché, my brother, touché. I'm working on it."

"Great, we'll work on it together."

I looked in my rearview mirror again and saw a slow smile form on Alex for the first time that morning. Maybe these two were not as different as they thought. Matt was a good guy beneath all his shortcomings and regrets, and Alex could use more friends like that in his life.

As we pulled up to the venue, I realized this was a bigger event than I'd thought. There was a solid mix of both soldiers and civilians in attendance. I scanned the crowd. "Evan must have had a lot of people that cared about him. Looks like he made friends with the entire town."

Matt laughed. "You got that right. Everyone loved Evan. There wasn't a place he could go and not make friends."

It was nice seeing him happy even if it was short-lived. "Well, I promised your doctor I would stick with you the entire day. So, lead the way," I motioned as we made our way into the crowd.

Matt scanned the area with wide eyes as if searching for familiar faces. "That's Catherine's parents over there." He pointed at an elderly couple with several people surrounding them. Some were hugging, and some crying. The elderly couple looked to be doing well, given their circumstances.

For one of the few times in his life Alex looked conflicted and nervous. The man was a boulder, and not just physically speaking but his rough upbringing had caused him to build walls around his personal life. As a result, he let very few people inside. I could see him hiding his nervousness, yet he seemed eager to meet Catherine's parents.

"Would you both like to head that direction?" I asked. The tension on their faces made me question whether today had been a good idea. Maybe this was too much for them. Maybe this was too much for *me*.

The instant I saw Emily across the lawn, my heart skipped, and I had to remind myself to be patient. It was no doubt the wrong time for me to run up and put my arms around her.

Matt must have noticed my expression had changed. "I take it you just saw Emily over there?" He motioned to the crowd slowly gathering around Catherine's family.

"Yeah, that obvious?" I asked as Matt gave me a small nudge. I took a deep breath. Her body language and the weariness on her face had me worried.

"If I know Emily as well as I used to." Matt spoke as he looked in our direction. "She needs all the support she can get today. Let's get this over with. Alex, you ready?"

It was amazing how easily Matt fit into our dynamic. As if the three of us had always known each other and were in support of one another. Alex nodded, and the three of us made our way towards Catherine's family.

Chapter Thirty-Nine

EMILY

I woke before the sun and hated that the first thing I did was look at my phone. I was hoping Kai had responded to my text, but there was nothing. Only a couple of texts from friends in support of today. I knew today would be hard, and I was wishing for the small bit of confidence Kai could somehow provide. Seeing him last night made me feel like I could get through the day. How could I have forgotten to bring up the memorial to him?

Why had I been so rude and asked him not to come in the first place? I was only hurting myself. Frustrated, I threw my phone onto the chair in the corner of my room and went to check on Tillie. She was sleeping peacefully in her crib. I tip-toed out of her room and went to get the coffee started when I heard my mother-in-law quietly enter the kitchen.

"Good morning, sweetheart." She came up from behind and gave me a quick hug. "How are you holding up this morning?" she asked through teary eyes.

I turned and put my arms around her as she broke down.

"I'm sorry hon, I thought I would be better than this. It just feels so surreal, doesn't it? I still can't believe this is happening. Even though we always knew this day might come, I just never thought it actually would. I almost miss living in the *what if* stage." She looked up at me as she sat in the chair nearest the coffee table. "Do you know what I mean?" she asked.

"I do know what you mean, but living with so many questions it wasn't really living. I feel like I haven't been able to breathe for years. Ever since I got that first call, time just stood still. The only indication time was still moving-on around me was the fact that Tillie was growing faster by the day. She's been such a blessing, Denise. She looks so much like him, it's not even silly." We both laughed. It was a precious moment between the two women who loved Evan the most in this world.

"You're right, Emily. As soon as she was born, it was as if I could see my son again. Sometimes I forget how beautiful his eyes were, how sincere they looked when he spoke. The moment I see Tillie, I can see him again."

I set a cup of coffee in front of her and checked the baby monitor.

"Do you need anything for today, Emily? Can I help with anything?"

"Honestly, everything is all set and ready to go. The caterers are doing everything food related, the florist knows where everything will be placed, and the venue will take care of all that's left. I didn't want any of us to have to really do anything except enjoy each other's company and spend time with the people that mattered most in Evan's life."

She nodded, and together we sat sipping our coffee and looking over the photos of Evan that we'd gathered over the weekend. We had placed our favorites in beautiful frames, and others were arranged on a display board. Tillie had decorated the board with her two grandmothers help before we added the pictures, and it turned out adorable. Evan would have loved the hearts she drew around each little photo. Today was Evan's memorial! My Evan was really truly gone! It wasn't just a *what if* anymore, it was undeniably real life now, no more ifs, ands, and buts.

Yesterday, when his remains were delivered, along with his uniform and dog tags I couldn't be near them. I couldn't even touch the container, but what I really couldn't do was explain to Tillie how her daddy was in such a small box. Instead, I had my parents take his remains to their house and there would be plenty of time later to figure these things out.

I set my empty cup near the sink. "I'm going to get ready now. If I'm in the shower when Tillie wakes up, would you grab her for me?"

"Of course. You go get ready, and I'll take care of Tillie." She was smiling at the photo in her hand. "It's going to be beautiful Emily."

I nodded, it was going to be beautiful, or something, there wasn't a word for what today would be.

A couple of hours later I hustled around the house searching for the new white tights I had bought for Tillie to wear. Finally, my mom found them, and we rushed to my parents' car. On our way to the venue, I realized I'd left my phone on the chair in my bedroom. "I forgot my phone at home! Should we turn around?" I asked.

"No, everyone you care about will be at the memorial, sweetie. It's probably best if you don't have the distraction," she replied as we kept driving. She was wrong, there was a certain someone I had grown to care a lot about that would *not* be there today. I had missed inviting him in time. "You're right, I guess. Thank you, guys, for driving. When you get there, the venue said the first five parking spots are reserved for us. Just leave room for—"

"Okay, honey. You can relax … just let me handle the driving, you focus on Tillie and getting those shoes on." my father lovingly cut me off from my ramble.

Tillie, who was typically easy-going, seemed to sense the tension in the air. She was throwing one fit after the other. I finally got her shoes on and smiled at my beautiful little girl. She looked absolutely adorable in her little pink dress and matching shoes. There were going to be friends here today that had never met her, and I was thankful she would be kept entertained.

As we pulled into the venue, my mind was all over the place. There was no way this was happening. Except it was. Reality hit me square in the face when I saw Evan's picture on a large easel. It was my favorite picture of him, we had just gotten married, and his expression was so care-free. His warm and inviting brown eyes were like a dark roast freshly brewed. His curly locks were always a mess, but in this particular photo he had just had them cut, ready to begin his military career. If I could just look into those eyes one more time. One more time would quench this hurt bubbling to the surface once again, although it never left.

The poster board Tillie made was proudly on display next to Evans' photo, and a flag was draped over the table. Next to the table was a guest book on a pedestal for friends to sign. The knot in my stomach tightened.

I didn't want Evan's memorial held at a funeral home. That wouldn't be his style. So instead, we were at his favorite winery, and the funeral home staff agreed to assist. I wanted this to be as casual as possible. A few people were going to speak, and there would be a slideshow towards the end. The winery had asked if we wanted live music to be played for the day, and in true Evan style, I said *yes* and gave them a list of his favorite songs. Maybe it was selfish on my part, but I didn't want Tillie to have any more depressing memories revolving around her father, so we made today a celebration of life.

People steadily trickled in and within minutes the large outdoor patio was filled. Tillie began playing with some of my friends' children, and they offered to watch her while I made my rounds. I was grateful for their help and relieved to see Tillie in a better mood.

I had only seen pictures of Catherine's parents online and spoken with her mother on the phone a couple of times. But when I saw them arrive, I slowly made my way over to them. They both smiled when they saw me approach.

The woman spoke first, her voice seemed nervous and rushed. "You must be Emily!"

"Yes, I am. And you must be Catherine's mother Sarah." I smiled and extended my hand.

"Yes, and this is my husband, Frank. We're so grateful that you invited us here today!" Sarah smiled as she spoke but still appeared distracted, as she hastily eyed the expanding crowd.

"Of course, I wouldn't have it any other way," I said as tears filled my eyes.

Sarah reached over and gave me a warm motherly hug. For some reason, she was stronger than I could be in this moment. "Thank you, Emily. Evan was our little girl's guardian angel. He risked everything for her safe return." Her arm was still around me when she lowered her voice. "And because of him, our Catherine ... was able to be returned to us."

Confused, I gave her a questioning look. "I'm sorry, I don't think I heard that right. What did you say again?" I had to have heard her wrong. I thought Catherine's remains were never found.

She looked around then slipped a piece of paper folded several times into my hand. She looked up and stared so deeply I thought I might break apart. "We will talk later after you've had a chance to read this over. Read it when you're alone, please."

A minute later she was back next to her husband with his arm around her waist. What could be so important that she had to write it down? I needed to find a quiet place, and fast.

I scanned the crowd and was pleasantly surprised as well as relieved to see those gorgeous piercing blue eyes that had captivated my sleepless nights of late. Kai! It was just the two of us there in that entire place the instant we made contact. Kai, Alex, and Matt all three made their way towards me. Within moments they were at my side. "You came!" I beamed, forgetting everyone else around me. Matt and Alex looked at us, then turned away and began making small talk between the two of them.

Kai's eyes never left mine. We were locked on each other, and for too brief a moment it was just us again. As Kai moved his hand through his hair, his ready smile quickly faded. "I thought you wanted me to be here?"

"Of course, but you didn't respond, so I thought …"

He placed his hand over mine and gave it a small squeeze. "I'm so sorry about that- I'm horrible about checking my phone sometimes. and with everything recently, I guess I just got sidetracked."

I wished I could just reach out and let him take me in his arms. That was until I remembered the note in my hands. With Kai's strong hand still over mine, the folded note dug into my skin. I fidgeted underneath his hold.

"I'm sorry," he whispered as he pulled his hand away. "Did I hurt you?" he asked, as his eyes went straight to the paper creased in my hand.

"No, it's just this note that Catherine's mom gave me. She was acting really strange and said to read it when I was alone." I looked again at the large crowd closing in. A large older man trying to squeeze by pressed me closer into Kai. "We're definitely not alone here."

"No, definitely not," Kai added. "Would you like an escort to find you a place to be alone?" There was no mistaking his devilish grin.

Alex cleared his throat and Matt gave Kai an elbow. I was brought back to my surroundings and remembered it was not just Kai and me standing there on a remote island.

"Matt! Wow, look at you! I can't believe it! No crutches! You look great!" I shrieked, finally noticing he was standing next to us. He smiled back, and I could see Evan's best friend in there once again.

"Yep, Doc got me fitted for a new leg … it was long overdue." Then he looked down at the ground and said, "I'm sorry, Emily. I'm so sorry that I've kept you from knowing for so long. It's my fault this memorial took so long to happen. You and your family have every reason to hate me. But with that said, I thank you from the bottom of my heart for letting me be here today."

Matt looked so broken, and I needed him to know all had been forgiven a long time ago. "Matt, we could never hate you. You did everything in your power to help Evan, and he loved you so much," I whispered as I went in for a hug and was met by his newly pressed suit. I had never seen Matt in his Service Uniform, but he fit them nicely. Any woman could easily appreciate the way his dark blues lay against his warm brown skin. His thick curls had been tamed and brushed into a handsome style, and he looked like the Matt I used to know. It was a good reminder that things were falling into place and life could eventually feel normal for us again. Hopefully.

However, this note in my hand was begging to be read and I needed to find a quiet place. "Listen, will you guys come with me? There's something I need to read, and if anyone should be there, it's the three of you." All three looked as if I'd just lit a firecracker that was about to go off.

"What is it you need to read?" Alex asked with a look of concern.

"I honestly have no clue, Catherine's mom said something pretty vague and then handed me this note and said to read it when I was alone. I don't know what I should be prepared for. But I do know I don't want to be alone," I admitted.

Matt took the initiative and began maneuvering through the crowd as the rest of us followed. Within moments, we were at an arch near the back entrance to the venue's dining hall. The four of us gathered under it as we looked around to make sure we were alone and far away from the crowd on the other side of the building. I quickly opened the note and began to softly read aloud.

It read:

Emily, I don't know how to say this exactly, but we've decided it's time to tell you. It's time that you know the truth. First, we have to tell you that because of Evan and his bravery, Catherine is alive and in hiding. Before you get too upset, please know that Catherine never meant for this to hurt anyone in any way. Catherine never left the base for vitamins; she was on a single soldier mission to find the location of a well-known organizer that had plans to bomb the base. Her mission was to befriend the man, gather intel that night, and report back to her commander. Unfortunately, they discovered her identity and held her captive... you know what happened next. The commander did not want Evan and Matt to go because they knew exactly where she was, and Catherine had signed a search and rescue agreement. They were waiting on the agreed time frame to call for the search. We understand as Catherine's friends, Evan and Matt could not just sit by and wait. We know their heart was in the right place, and she wishes every day that she told them ahead of time of the mission. When Catherine was captured, she was beaten so badly she can barely recall those few days she was in the holding cell with Evan and Matt. The last thing she remembered was being dragged out of the cell and driven to a new location where they left her to die. The search party that was searching for the missing three found her just in time. She was then airlifted back to the base, and once she had somewhat recovered, Matt had already been rescued and escaped the base. Catherine was then made aware of the situation, and she could not forgive herself for how everything had turned out. Her commander instructed Catherine to go into hiding for at least five years. The organizer behind the abduction had been notified that she made it out alive and had a hit placed on her. As far as the rest of the world knows, Catherine is dead. If things go according to plan, Catherine will come out of hiding in the next year or two. Everyone involved has always wished you knew the truth. Catherine's been made aware that Matt made it out of there alive, and all that he has done to protect Evans's wishes. She felt it was time you knew the entire truth. The truth about everyone involved. Evan has always been our guardian angel, and we wish you could find it in your heart to understand why we've kept quiet all these years. If you have any questions, please do not hesitate to call. Please discard this letter with caution.

All the best,

Catherine, Sarah & Frank

By the time I'd finished, I could barely hold back the tears falling from my eyes. I couldn't discern what I was feeling. So many emotions ran wild in my head. Anger, resentment, loneliness, fear, hurt.

This entire time Evan didn't really need to rescue Catherine at all! Why wouldn't they just fill him in on the truth behind her disappearance from the very beginning? They knew Evan and his savior complex; they knew he could never *not* go and search for her. I was angry, yes, but mostly hurt that there had been another coverup to this dreadful, ill-fated situation.

The entire time I was reading Kai had his arm around me and had been rubbing my shoulders. Just knowing he was next to me was the only thing keeping me from collapsing right there. I couldn't focus. I felt as though my world was crashing down on me again. Was there anything believable that I could trust anymore? Was everything around me a lie?

As if he had heard my thoughts, Matt placed his arm around me, turned me around and looked me straight in the eyes. "Emily, look at me...I'm just as shocked as you. Hell, I have a million questions after that letter. But this doesn't change anything Emily. Evan would have risked everything for a friend. You and I both know even if he knew of this contract, he wouldn't let them sit by and wait for some contracted date. He just wouldn't."

It was as though Matt knew Evan better than I did. I knew he was right. Evan wouldn't just sit by and wait, no matter what the contract said. That didn't change the hurt pounding inside me for hearing yet another lie.

"Matt, you were there. Is this even possible?"

He shook his head and shrugged. "I knew I was lucky to be alive, I knew I had it easy compared to them. I just never knew why. But that last night with Catherine in there with us, things were not looking good for her. She'd lost so much blood. Evan and I both tried talking to her, but she wasn't responsive. We just assumed she …" He caught his breath and stared down at the ground.

I could see there was so much we didn't know, so much they all had been through that was not written down in that tattered notebook. "It's okay, Matt. You couldn't have known. If you want to talk to them, please go." I motioned toward the large crowd on the other side of the venue.

Matt looked up now and shook his head. "I don't think that's a good idea. If this whole thing is as top secret as they're making it out to be, I don't plan on getting involved. At least in public that is," he whispered to the group.

It took me a moment, but just then, I thought of someone other than myself when I spotted Alex. Kai was two steps ahead of me.

"Alex, are you okay? This is a hell of a lot to process, isn't it?" Kai asked, as he looked at Alex who had been particularly quiet.

He looked as though he'd been hit by a giant freight train of information and couldn't catch his breath. Now that all eyes were on him, he straightened, and within seconds he was Senator Greyson again, not the vulnerable man standing before us mere moments before. "Well, I wasn't expecting *that* if that's what you mean. I understand her need for privacy, but I'll need to speak to her myself. If you will excuse me, I have to have a conversation with Catherine's parents." He pivoted sharply and began to depart our small group.

Matt sprang into action and grabbed Alex's shoulder. Alex swiftly pulled away and shot him an obnoxious glare. "I don't think that's the best idea," Matt said through gritted teeth. "If they have surveillance on her, I wouldn't be surprised if they have someone here today … seeing as how this is a memorial for *her*. This isn't a time to play the hurt senator card!"

Alex was silent, and you could see he didn't like the way Matt spoke to him. Finally, he nodded his head. "Okay, I'll wait till we're alone with them. Kai … I trust you can make the necessary arrangements. As for me, I can't be here another second longer!" He looked at me with sorrow in his eyes and I could tell that his presence of mind was hanging by a thread. "Emily, I'm sorry, but I need to–"

"I understand, Alex. Just do what you need to and don't worry about today." I cut him off, for if anyone could understand the feeling of being lied to, it was me.

He gave me a modest smile and turned his back to us once again. As Alex disappeared out of sight, I felt Kai's hand on my lower back. Had it been there this entire time? I didn't know or care at that moment I just knew I needed Kai, and most importantly, I needed him in my life. I turned and reached my hands to touch his face. I looked into his steely blue eyes and sensed the passion they held. Kai compassed me in his arms, and I was once again swept off my feet.

Matt cleared his throat and we quickly stepped apart from each other and looked in his direction.

"What would you like to do next? Matt, what time is it?" Kai asked.

"We have about thirty minutes," Matt answered.

"I should continue to make my rounds. Matt, you should speak with Catherine's parents, even if you already know about the letter. They're expecting to see you today." I spoke just above a whisper.

Matt rolled his eyes and took a deep breath holding it in. "I don't know how they can look me in the eyes and keep lying to me like this! It's one thing over the phone but when I'm standing right there in front of them? Catherine should never have let this happen! Not after everything!" He looked at his watch again.

I moved toward Matt. "We can all speak together after the memorial, Matt. For now, let's all head out there. For all I care, you can avoid them today, you'll have time to speak to them later." As I took my first step away from Kai's arm at my waist, it was as if his touch had become a fundamental need for me.

The second I returned to the crowd there were a dozen pairs of eyes looking in my direction. I felt them closely watching my every response to their sentiments. Some said they were sorry for my loss, some mentioned how Evan had died a hero and how proud I must be. I was anything but proud. I was hurt, and angry. And again, completely and utterly confused.

Chapter Forty

KAI

Watching Emily make her way through the crowd was mesmerizing. I tried to stay within earshot of her. The grace and confidence she held with each conversation was a new level of finesse. From the brief time I'd been blessed to spend with Emily, I could sense now when she was weary every time someone had a new assertion of how she should be feeling or how she should continue to live her life. One woman even had the nerve to tell her not to worry about the future ... that she was young, and she was lucky Tillie wouldn't know anything different than how things were now.

That was when I decided to step in and interrupt. Matt knew a few people and was off mingling on his own.

"Emily, your mother asked me to find you. Do you have a minute?" I asked, as I looked into her sad eyes. Emily wasn't just grieving; she was fervently holding back tears through every conversation. She nodded her head. And as if the woman hadn't completely offended her already, Emily still told her it was great to see her. The woman smiled and started to chat with the next unfortunate soul.

"I'm sorry, but your mom didn't ask me for anything," I confessed as I whispered in her ear.

She nodded and glanced about the crowd once again. "I figured as such. That woman was awful," she mumbled.

"She really was. I'm sorry for what she said. No one has a right to say any of that."

Uncovered

She looked up at me through her long, wet lashes and gave me a flicker of a smile. "It's nothing I haven't heard before. I've lost count over the years how many people have told me I was lucky that Tillie never knew what she was missing. If they only knew! I feel anything *but* lucky in that scenario."

I wanted to take her hands in mine, but again, I knew the timing wouldn't play out very well. Instead, I just gave her the best smile I could. "Emily, you're the strongest person I know. I won't pretend to understand what you're going through, or what you've had to do to become the strong woman I see in front of me, but I'm grateful for our paths crossing, and I'm happy to have had a part in uncovering your truth."

With the smile she gave me, I thought just then, she looked as though she could actually get through this day in one piece.

"Thank you, Kai. I'm just glad to finally have all the missing puzzle pieces. At least I hope that's all the pieces. I should go find Tillie, the service will be starting soon," she whispered. As she took a step away our fingers grazed, and in that instant, we both felt the fire between us reignite. She looked back at me. "I'll find you later."

And just like that this absolutely beguiling woman disappeared into the crowd. It took me a few minutes to realize I had a goofy grin on my face from our short encounter. I quickly wiped the smile and remembered where I was. Quite possibly the worst place to be walking around with a smile on your face.

Soon I found Matt and was glad he took the situation more seriously. He'd been good about checking in with me and I respected him enough to give the man some privacy. As I neared him without interrupting his chat, he turned around to include me in the conversation.

"This is Kai Taylor. He's the man behind getting the ball rolling for Emily. You could say he knocked some sense into me, as well," he added with a laugh.

It was good to hear Matt's laugh as it let me see what a fun guy he could be and probably was in his earlier life. His smile lines had returned. "That's quite the introduction, Matt," I said, as I reached out my hand to the woman he had been speaking to.

"It is, but it seems necessary. My name's Linda, and I'm Emily's mother."

My throat may have closed up a bit as I shook the woman's slender hand. I wondered if she knew anything about what all had happened between Emily and me. "It's so great to meet you, Linda. You have a wonderful family. It's been my privilege to help assist Emily," I managed to mutter.

"And we can't thank you enough for taking this on and getting us all answers. We've needed this ... Emily really needed this. She's been stuck for too long," she answered, as she looked over at Matt.

"Linda, I'm so sorry for playing this role in your pain and suffering," Matt interjected. "I only hope you can understand why I had to do what I did. The reasons look foolish and wrong now. But at the time they were all he had. Evan's last thought on this earth was to protect Emily, and as his best friend, I had to honor his wishes,"

Linda nodded her head and patted his back. "Matt, you were Evan's best friend. He was so lucky to have you. You did what you needed to do, and we are not holding it against you. We want you to know that just because Evan's gone, that doesn't mean you need to be gone too. There are too many people in this world that love and care for you. It'd be a shame for Evan to die and for you to pretend to do so as well. You lived through a horrible situation. Would Evan really want you to hide out and be *dead* as well?"

Matt looked as though he had been reprimanded by an old teacher. He hung his head low and said, "I'm eternally grateful that Officer Kai here pulled me out of my hole and made me tell the truth. It's a burden I will not miss, because Evan's story needed to be known."

Matt swung an arm around me, and I gave him an easy smile.

A few moments later we heard a woman speak into a microphone. "If I could have your attention? Please find a seat as we are about to begin the service. Thank you."

The woman left the stage and stood next to a few others of her staff. The crowd made their way to the rows of chairs, and as they were all taken, a small group of us stood in the back. I saw Emily and Tillie at the side of the stage, and Linda was now with family off to the side as well. A couple, that I assumed to be Evan's parents, were next to Emily. Tillie then jumped into the woman's arms as Emily made her way to center stage.

Just moments ago, this group was as loud as a football stadium, but now with Emily standing before us, you could hear a pin drop. She looked absolutely radiant and even though her eyes were red from crying, they were as beautiful as ever. Her soft blonde curls fell right below her shoulders, and her lips were touched with a natural pink glow. The blue dress she was wearing clung on her body like it was tailor made for her. In this vulnerable moment, she was simply stunning.

"Thank you all for coming. We feel so blessed to see you today. Evan was always better at public speaking, and he always knew the right words to say. So, I hope I can live up to all that," she cleared her throat and began reading from a piece of paper she was holding.

"Evan was what some would call perfect. I called it Evan being Evan. He had a loyalty about him that could surpass any expectation. He was happiest when he was helping others. In fact, I can recall a fight we had once because I didn't stop in the middle of an intersection to give a homeless person some spare change." A few people laughed in the crowd, and I could see Emily loosen up.

She continued reading. "Evan's first passion had been helping those in need. Therefore, he always knew he would someday join the military … or in some capacity. I don't think there was ever a question about that, as he knew where he could be the most helpful and that was where he went. I've always been so proud of Evan. Not only for his bravery and dedication, but for his compassion and drive. Evan's second passion in his life was family." Emily's voice broke and she wiped an eye with her hand. I instinctively took a step towards the stage only to be stopped by Matt's arm preventing me from going anywhere.

"Not the time to be her rescuer, Kai," he firmly whispered beside me.

Reluctantly, I nodded in agreement. Linda walked up on the stage and stood by Emily with her arm around Emily's shoulder.

As Emily blotted tears from her face and regained her composure, she spoke softer now. "Like I said, Evan was always better at this than me. Evan would have loved to see all of you today … to catch up and hear about your lives. If you were a friend, you were family. A couple months before his deployment, we were lucky to finally begin the dream of starting a family, as it was something that we wished and prayed for. I can remember when we found out we were having our sweet Tillie," she said as she smiled over at her little girl.

"We were both so thrilled to be starting this new chapter of our lives, but unfortunately, the excitement was short lived as we found out Evan would be deployed a few months before Tillie was born. It was tough those first few nights. I wanted to relish in the excitement of our upcoming new addition, but the idea of raising a child while Evan was deployed had me nervous as hell. Evan had a way about him that with just a look you would know he was up to something. The day after he got word of his deployment, Evan set up an appointment with a 3D ultrasound center. We were able to see our Tillie almost perfectly, and we both fell even more in love with not only our new addition, but with each other. We even got this cute little bear that had Tillie's heartbeat in it for Evan to take with him. It was a beautiful moment that I'll cherish forever. I couldn't fathom him missing Tillie's birth, but he promised he would be back for it. He promised he would be there beside me when the time came. Well, time came for him to come home, and he ... he didn't ..."
She trailed off. She wiped another tear trying to escape her weary eyes.

It was all I could do to stand there and watch her agonize over the memories she had to share with everyone, but I knew there was nothing I could do to take this sort of pain away...at least not yet.

Once ready, Emily continued. "Evan always put others before himself, it was both his worst and yet his greatest flaw. I am so thankful for the time I was able to have with Evan, he was my everything. I've promised myself to keep Evan and his dreams alive, no matter how silly. This world needs stories of the good, stories of the good people that make us all better for simply knowing them. One of his wildest dreams in particular was to send Tillie to Game of Thrones Camp. He thought it would be and I quote 'beneficial to learn the art of sword fighting and arrow shooting.' So, I'm sure someday you will all see pictures of little Tillie with a bow and arrow."

It was great to see her end with a laugh as she spoke of more fond memories they had made together. Once she sat down and had Tillie on her lap again, her mother-in-law stood up to say a few words. She was obviously heartbroken but seemed to have always believed this would be the outcome. A few more people took the stand and shared their memories.

At that point, the woman who first got us seated took the mic. "If anyone would like the microphone to say a few words, please stand and we will assist you in doing so." She looked around and no one stood up. But then to my surprise Matt raised his hand and I instinctively took a step back to give him his space. A couple of venue staff made their way over to us and one of them handed him the cordless mic.

Matt looked to me with questioning eyes, and I felt as though I could be of no help at all. "You got this, say what's on your heart," I muttered, hoping to support him in some form.

He took the microphone and held it to his chest. He shuffled a bit on his new leg and finally began to speak. "You may not know me, but my name's Matt Stone. Evan was not only my best friend, but he was nothing short of a brother to me. We knew almost everything about each other, and the one thing I knew for certain was his passion. Evan lived his life for others, and I'm fairly certain there was not a selfish bone in his body. Everything he did was for the greater good. Over the past three years, I've been selfish enough to make up for his lack thereof. I wanted my best friend to be remembered for the light he brought into this world, not the way he left it. I was lucky … no, *blessed*

... to spend those last few days with Evan. I would give my life if it meant he could be here today."

Matt took a pause and looked up to realize all eyes were solely on him. He went on. "Evan thought of others before he thought of himself. He taught me things you could only learn from someone like Evan, He was truly one in a million. We are all better people because we knew him. I am here today because Evan risked and sacrificed it all for someone that meant something to him. He ... he is, was, my best friend, and I will always fight for him and his memory."

He handed the microphone back to the attendant. I caught the strange look he gave to Catherine's parents. They noticed it too as he stepped back next to me.

A few others stood and shared their memories and condolences. After the last one finished with a tearful poem, the woman attendant again took to center stage. "Thank you all for sharing your memories. The family asks that you join them in about fifteen minutes for food and drinks in the courtyard.

People stood around quietly as one by one the area began to clear. I watched several people approach Emily, and I was eager to be at her side to shield her from the stares and possible misguided comments.

Matt caught my gaze and tugged on my suit. "You know it's written all over your face what you're thinking, right?" he mumbled loud enough for just me to hear.

"I hoped I had a better poker face than that, but I can't help it," I smiled as I continued to stare at Emily and her family.

"I think as Evan's best friend, I should want to punch you in the face and beat the shit out of you, but for some reason I don't. Maybe Evan's finally rubbing off on me. Or maybe you're actually a pretty okay guy, and if Emily *was* to meet someone else, you'd be a good contender."

We looked around and both realized we were the only two left in the area besides Emily and her family who were now heading toward us.

Emily's mother-in-law, Denise, was the first to approach us. "Matt, I'm so happy you were able to be here today." She went in for a big bear hug.

As they parted, the father reached out his hand and firmly shook Matt's. "Thank you for all you did for our boy. I know it wasn't easy keeping that to yourself," he said as he looked straight into Matt's eyes.

Matt didn't flinch, and for a moment I couldn't read him. "I would do it all again sir, I'm sorry for the way it all went down ... it wasn't my intention ... he just couldn't have people remember him like that. He wanted his memory ..."

Unable to finish his sentence, Evan's father stepped closer and put his arm on Matt's shoulder. "We know. We understand that now." They both looked at each other, and in that moment, there was a silent understanding.

I finally gained enough courage to look into Emily's eyes as she was now so close to me that I could have touched her. To my surprise, she was already looking at me, and when our eyes met, I was reassured by the fact that we were here together. And although I wasn't able to reach out and comfort her the way I wanted to, I think she knew I was there for her and her alone.

I noticed that Emily's mother, Linda, was watching Emily and me as we stood silently reading each other. "Emily, I'm going to show everyone where we'll be sitting. Don't worry about us. I'll take Tillie while you talk with your friends." She was smiling as she walked away with the rest of the group.

Matt, Emily, and I were now the only three left standing in the large outdoor patio.

Matt looked awkward and shuffled a bit until he made eye contact with an old friend in the distance. "If you two don't mind, could you give me a moment to say hello to an old friend?" He looked me in the eyes with a questioning stare. "I promise, you will never lose sight of me, Kai. I'll just be right over there," he mumbled as he walked away.

"Matt, I trust you. No need for the play by play," I called out to him.

I then turned my sights toward Emily who was wrapping a loose curl around her fingers. Without thinking, I reached up and cupped her cheek.

Emily looked at me with the most innocent yet alluring eyes. "Kai, I was so worried I pushed you away for good," she sighed as she looked up at me and then down at the ground. "I know this isn't the time or place to discuss whatever this is going on between us, but I can't help what this is I'm feeling ..."

I interrupted her rambling. "Wait, hold on. There's an *us?*" I asked, hoping my smirk wasn't too obvious.

She looked confused, and I could tell that I had hidden my sarcasm too well.

"No, no, no, that's not what I meant. I would love for there to be an *us* ... at some point. I agree today is poor timing, but you need to know I feel the same way." I quickly whispered.

Emily's face instantly brightened, and my day was complete. She stood up on her tiptoes and gave me a quick kiss on the lips, and without a second thought I deepened the kiss and could feel her tongue graze my lower lip. I let a low growl escape from within, and in moments we were practically tangled up in each other.

"Okay, let's not make a scene. That's the last thing I need here today," she murmured as she pulled away from my grasp.

"Of course, but I would like to finish this exact conversation at a later time." I breathed as I laced my fingers in hers.

Chapter Forty-One

EMILY

It had been hours since the memorial had ended, hours since Kai had placed his hand in mine. His smile every time I introduced him to those closest to me became imprinted on my brain for the rest of the evening. Unfortunately, the memorial was not entirely a success. Catherine's parents left quickly after the memorial and left us all with more unanswered questions. Alex was upset and for great reason, and there at the end, Kai had to return Matt to the hospital in order to assist in Alex's newest endeavors.

My parents had taken Tillie to their home afterwards so that I could pick up around the house and finish my night with a hot bath. The knowledge that my biggest questions were finally being answered took me to a place I hadn't fully expected. On the drive to my home, I could barely see the road through my tears. It was as if I had just received the news of Evan's disappearance. My heart was torn.

I was angry at myself for wanting something more with Kai, more with another man on the very day of my husband's memorial. I kept telling myself he had been gone for years, but the fact that I had just heard the news of how and why, could not escape my questioning mind.

The hot bath water was heaven but couldn't cure my tears. As I soaked in my vintage claw foot tub, I remembered the time Kai had been here, and I knew we were lucky to share something that to many was uncommon. The ache I had for so long would always be there, but I knew I had no choice but to keep moving forward. Every cell in my body told me Kai came into my life to keep me moving toward that goal.

My heart picked up speed as the phone resting on my towel next to me beeped.

KAI – *How are you doing? I can't stop thinking of you, and how you must be feeling after a day like today, is there anything I can do?*
EMILY- *Hello to you too. It's good to hear from you.*
EMILY- *I'm okay at the moment, just enjoying some quiet time in a warm bath while Tillie is over at my parents. How did things go with Alex?*

The phone grew silent for a few minutes, and I thought I may have overshared. My heart continued racing as I saw a new text come through. I couldn't help but smile.

KAI- *Well, there's an image that I won't be able to get out of my mind all night…*
KAI- *Alex is good… for now, we're arranging a meeting time for the two of them… virtually… for the time being. Seems to be safer for now. He's convinced she has the child, but we think they would have mentioned the child if there was one.*
KAI- *Sorry for the overload of information… it's been a hell of a night over here. Once Alex heads off to bed I will be leaving here and finding time to relax as well.*
EMILY- *If you would like some company, you're welcome to come over here.*

Again, there was silence, and I couldn't believe I had just asked him to come over for a second time. He was probably trying to find a nice way to turn me down. We both had had long grueling days … the last thing he would have wanted to do tonight was to be another shoulder to cry on.

EMILY- *Sorry… long day, we can chat more tomorrow. Have a great night!*
KAI- *Emily!*

Kai had texted back, and then there was nothing. I felt my cheeks flush hot. Had I offended him? Did I make things awkward between us so soon? Just then my phone began to ring. I saw Kai's name and my heart started to race yet again. "Hello?" I answered, trying not to give away my embarrassment.

"I'm just finishing things up here, and I'll be right over. Is that okay? Does the offer still stand?" he asked, his voice rough and maybe a bit intense.

"Of course. I thought I freaked you out … of course the offer still stands," I laughed.

"Oh babe, it would take a lot more than that to freak me out."

He breathed a husky sigh into the phone, and my bath water seemed to have gone up a few degrees.

"Give me a couple more minutes, and I'll text you when I get on the road. Emily, I can't wait to see you," he breathed heavily.

"Sounds great," I managed to mumble as I tried cooling myself off.

"Are you okay, Emily?"

I choked on my sip of pinot noir. "I'm doing okay, surprised is all. It's just been a while, Kai …" I trailed off, unable to say the words aloud.

"A while for what?" he asked as I became mortified to have to say the words aloud.

"Having these feelings for someone, and … and …" I stuttered.

"Emily, I understand what you mean. Believe it or not … it's been a while for me too," he confessed.

I was silent for a moment but knew in my heart Kai had come into my life when I needed him most. I couldn't let my fear of how things would look push him away from me and miss out with someone or something so great. "I believe you Kai, that's the crazy thing. I trust you more than I ever thought possible. You've been such a strong support to me these last few weeks, that I feel like we've known each other for so much longer," I sighed.

His breathing had grown heavier, and I wished I could see his face. "I'll be over in twenty minutes. Please let's finish this conversation in person. I need to be able to see your face when we do." He exhaled heavily. "I'll text you when I'm on the road okay?"

Now it was my turn to breathe heavily. I could not believe what I had started. "Okay, I'll see you soon then." I hung up the phone and took a deep breath.

I quickly began the primping process that I had not done in years. I chugged the remainder of my glass of wine because I knew what tonight could lead to, and I would be lying if I said I wasn't completely uneasy about what could or could not happen as the night progressed.

Moments later my phone notified me that Kai was on the road and heading my way. I put on one of my favorite summer dresses, freshened my hair, and brushed my teeth just in time for a knock on my door. I looked in the mirror one last time just like I had that very first day I had met Kai. The only difference now was that I knew who I was opening my door to. I was completely enthralled with Kai, and so eager to see where things could lead to with this amazing man. I opened the door to see him facing me with a look of longing and need.

He had the bluest eyes and the steadiest gaze. His eyes were taking me in as if he could read my thoughts and all my deepest desires.

Within a moment his hands were around my waist, and I was caught in his arms. The overwhelming urge to press my lips to his was instantly satisfied when his lips crashed into mine. I smiled as my lips moved over his. I wanted to memorize the feel of his body demanding mine. The second we simultaneously parted for air, we gazed into each other's eyes. I studied his expression, and that was when all the strength I had been holding onto fled. I reached up and wove my fingers through his wavy brown hair. He leaned into my hand, and I pulled him closer to my level. I placed both hands on his cheeks and brushed my fingers over his five-o-clock shadow.

He smiled, and my heart skipped a beat. "Hi," he finally muttered through his warm full lips.

"Hi," I replied, sure that my lips were swollen from our heated kiss. "That was unlike any other greeting I've ever received," I laughed, as he held me in his arms.

The warm embrace Kai provided was something I wanted to get used to. We had met only a short time ago, but from the very beginning we had shared this common feeling together, and I was excited to watch it grow.

"Can I come in?" he asked, as I felt a shiver run up his back.

"Of course, I'm sorry. I got so caught up."

We both smiled as he followed me into my living room. The entire time his hand never left my lower back. We sat next to each other on my loveseat, and my eyes were drawn to where our thighs were touching.

"Thanks for coming over tonight. How were things with Alex before you left?"

Kai laughed long and loud. "You want to talk about Alex after that kiss?" he finally was able to ask between laughs.

I blushed as it dawned on me that I had been trying to change the subject. "Yeah, I guess that's silly of me." I looked into his eyes.

"Alex will be fine; this is all a lot for him to chew on, but he's a big boy … we'll get it figured out," he sighed. "But what I'd really like to talk about is what you mentioned earlier over the phone." He had a worried look as if my feelings could have changed in the last hour.

I collected my thoughts. "I meant every word I said. It's been a while for me, as you very well know, but I trust you, Kai. I'm done convincing myself I don't need you. I need you. I need you so badly that I can't imagine never not knowing you. I'd miss the way you twiddle your thumbs when you're thinking for the next thing to say, or how you continue to surprise me with your never-ending patience. Or, how your lips perk when I look your way. You've gone above and beyond for me these past few weeks, and if they've taught me anything, it's that I want you by my side. I've had to learn to live my life without needing anyone, but I need you, Kai … and that scares me. But right now, I know this is the best kind of scared, and if you somehow feel the same way, I will be the luckiest woman alive." I looked at the floor as I finished laying my heart out for him and felt my cheeks turning red. I almost wished I had kept it to myself. In the same moment, my regret turned to complete and utter joy.

Kai reached for my hand and pulled it up to his mouth. He placed his lips to my hand and kissed me softly. "Emily, I would love nothing more than to be with you through the tough times, the exciting times, the difficult times, hell, I want to be there for all of it. Please don't question yourself, especially when it comes to me. Since the moment you first opened that door for me, I knew you were someone special. I knew you were someone I couldn't let slip away." Kai leaned into me, and his lips once again captured mine.

He kissed me with everything he had, and then laid me back on the sofa. I couldn't help but smile as he whispered gently in my ear. "I want all of you Emily, every fear, every laugh, every inch … I want it all," he breathed as he placed his body over mine.

My mouth met his again, and I could not think. I could only react to his touch. Kai's hands grazed my cheek as he looked into my eyes. "It's going to get better," he whispered.

"What is?" I asked, trying to decide what he could be referring to.

"Moving forward, I guess," he stated as he shrugged his shoulders.

I nodded, and even though I only recently was able to know what had happened to Evan, I always knew the news could be crippling. He didn't deserve this fate. I wanted Tillie to know Evan was a fighter, and that he fought for what was right. He fought with his life for a friend.

"I'm honestly just trying to be a good example for Tillie. I want to show her that even in the hardest of circumstances you can be strong. That no matter what life throws at you, you can persevere. Evan did everything he could to push forward, but in the end it just wasn't enough. I won't let his death be in vain. I know things will get better, they must."

Kai nodded and gave me the warmest smile. No words were needed. There was something about this man, something that just made it all make sense. We were brought together for this. Kai leaned down and our lips met once again. I relaxed into the kiss and slid my fingers through his hair.

I caught myself laughing when I felt his tongue flick around my mouth, and again I was lost in our newly entwined exploration of each other. Kai put his arms around my waist and pulled me onto his muscular thighs. His lips found their way to where the lace on my dress met my collarbone. The feel of his wet lips on my neck was driving me wild. He gently ran his fingers down the slope of my breast and soon found their way to my nipple. Where his fingers once were, his lips now claimed. I moaned as my cheeks instantly flushed. I wanted to stay like this forever, knowing I could lose myself in the safety of Kai's warm, strong arms.

"Emily… what are we doing?" Kai asked, with a hoarse tone.

"The last I checked, this was called foreplay, Kai … and you seem to know what you're doing. So, I take it this isn't your first time?" I laughed as I looked into his cool blue eyes.

"Not like that, what are we doing here … tonight … now." He stared at me now with a wanting, piercing gaze.

I hated that I needed to define my intentions. I liked where this was going, and I didn't want it to end if I gave the wrong answer. "I don't know what to say, I really like where this is headed … emphasis on the *really*. Do I have to know right now where to go from here?" I asked, worried I may not get the answer I wanted.

"Well, if you really like where this is headed, can we head to the bedroom?" he breathed heavily.

I tensed at how straight forward Kai had become. I liked it. It was sexy and all together masculine. It was something I had grown to appreciate about Kai. He knew what he wanted.

"You really know how to sweep a girl off her feet, don't you?" I laughed as I slowly wiggled off his lap.

"Hey! Where do you think you're going?" he playfully asked as he pulled me closer and back into his arms.

"I thought we wanted to take this to the bedroom." I shrugged as I pulled far enough away to start making my way down the hall toward my bedroom. Kai was quick to follow.

Before I could second guess what we were doing, Kai was behind me and had somehow managed to take his shirt off while following me.

His voice was husky and raw. "Breathe, Emily. You're holding your breath."

Kai was right, he had that effect on me. His voice was intoxicating, and I couldn't help myself from pressing my lips to his· and tracing his lower lip with my tongue. I slowly sucked his lower lip into my mouth and gave him a gentle bite. I wanted to kiss him forever. I blocked out the world, as the only thought coming in loud and clear was … oh god, the taste and scent of this man had brought my senses back to life.

He then began to glide his hand behind my neck and pulled me close so that our chests were pressed tightly against each other. Kai gently fumbled with the buttons on my dress and began to slide it to the floor with his rough hands. I then felt his lips on my chest, and my skin tingled where his lips trailed to my ear. Shock rolled through my veins and a shiver ran through my body.

"Are you cold?" Kai gently asked as he brushed his thumbs over my newly exposed skin.

"Not at all, I don't think I could get any hotter than this," I murmured as I stepped closer towards his warm chest. He held me there for a few minutes before his large rough hands pulled me completely out of my dress. He lifted his hand from my chest to my face, I leaned in closer, wanting to be as close to him as possible. I'd guiltily thought of this exact scenario for days, but now that I was actually kissing him, feeling him, my imagination was but a poor substitute for the real thing.

Kai's eyes were practically eating me alive as he watched me walk to the bed. As I lay there on the bed, Kai joined me, closing the space between us in one swift move. My lips found their way to his, and I couldn't stop from smiling. My hands found new and exciting places to explore, and his moan was my reward. A smirk teased his lips, and I couldn't help but keep exploring. The passion of this moment was more than I could have ever dreamed it would be. The hunger in which we moved together only confirmed how badly we both wanted each other. His body was strong, but his touch was gentle. I turned against him as our bodies were pressed tightly together. I was trapped between the bed and his solid frame, there was no escape, and I couldn't help but love the dizziness of it all as I lost myself completely in his touch. Kai took me in his arms and pressed his fervent body into mine, and for the next few hours he showed me just how much he cared for me.

Chapter Forty-Two

KAI

My lips were pressed against Emily's back as we woke the next morning. I brushed my lips to her neck and began teasing the sensitive skin beneath mine. As her body instantly pressed closer, it was then I could truly appreciate the feel of her naked body beside mine. I brought her closer to my chest. Emily's soft curves now nestled against my body were like nothing I had felt before.

Emily turned around, and I placed my lips to hers, kissing her long and hard. It shouldn't have felt so wonderful, considering how little time we'd actually known each other. But instead, lying there kissing Emily and smelling her intoxicating scent felt undeniably right.

Her hands reached over to my chest and gradually made their way lower down my frame. The further she got, the more confident I became as she swirled her tongue with mine. I wanted to lose myself in her body … again … but I needed to remind myself that I had decided to take this slow and steady.

"Good morning, beautiful," I smiled as Emily wiggled closer to me.

"Good morning. I wish we could spend more than just a night together, but I have to get Tillie soon," she said with a smile that made its way all the way to her eyes.

"Of course, I understand. Do we have the morning, at least?" I asked, hoping we could spend at least some of our morning together. "I make a mean omelet."

"I think I could make that happen if an omelet was involved," she laughed as she pressed her lips to mine.

"You better watch yourself there, beautiful. A man could get used to mornings like this."

"Well, why don't you? I meant what I said ... I want you by my side Kai ... I'll admit I kinda like having you around," she teased as she gave me a playful wink.

"Say no more, lovely. I am officially here to stay," I said, as I wrapped my arms around her.

We stared at each other briefly when all too soon, she started to make her way out of the bed. I was met with the beautiful sight of her climbing out of bed wearing nothing but her naked body.

"If you keep this up, you'll get more than an omelet this morning," I laughed, as she peered over her shoulder and into my eyes.

"You are wicked, aren't you, Mr. Taylor? Before I consider your invitation, I'm going to get the coffee started." She hummed as she wrapped herself in a pink and yellow floral robe.

I didn't mind admitting to myself how good it made me feel to have been the one to put that gorgeous smile on her face.

Once Emily was out of the room, I checked my phone to see if there was anything from Alex. He was in a bad place the night before, and to be honest, as his friend, I felt a tad guilty for leaving him. There was one text and two missed calls from Alex.

ALEX- *Hey, we just booked a flight for late next week to visit Catherine and her parents. As of right now ... we have no other details. Thanks for listening to me whine like a baby. Where did you head off so quickly last night?*

I had to tell Alex about Emily and me. I didn't know exactly how yet, and I sure as hell wouldn't be telling him details. I decided to shoot him a quick text to get him off my back and stop calling for the time being.

KAI- *Sounds like you were able to get it figured out. I hope you get your answers. We should talk about where things have led with Emily and me. I'll have time to talk later if you have the time.*

I set my phone down and began getting dressed. My phone made an incoming text noise, and I was surprised that Alex was taking time out of his morning workout to respond so quickly.

ALEX- *HAHA! You think you need to fill me in about all that? I've known you long enough to know when something's up, especially when it comes to a woman. You and I both know you've never been this way about one before. Good for you man, you both deserve this.*

Reading Alex's words made the situation feel all the more real. I was one lucky man to have met Emily, because I don't think we would've ever met if in a different situation. My heart ached for the loss Emily was dealing with and there were no doubts in my head that I would make it my responsibility to try and help fill the void. No matter what that may look like. I heard footsteps draw closer to the room as I began to pull on my pants.

"Well, don't get dressed on my account," Emily sighed, as she watched me button my pants.

I knew if we kept this up, we wouldn't be leaving the bedroom anytime soon. "That omelet isn't going to make itself," I laughed, as I leaned over and kissed her forehead. My gaze fell to her roaming eyes. She was hungry, and not just for an omelet. I closed the space between us and kissed her swollen lips. I wanted her to know I desired her as much as she so obviously desired me. I desired all of her, not just her beauty, but her scars, the pain she had been through, her past, and all the lies she had had to face. I needed her to know I was hoping to be her future, and I had accepted whatever that may look like.

When I finally released her full alluring lips, she was dazed. As I began to pull back, Emily grabbed me by the waist and pulled me closer. Her curves softly nestled against my body, and the sweetness of her breath drew me in. She reached her hands up to my chest as she drove her body straight into mine. I wasn't expecting the sudden push and stumbled back to the wall to hold us up.

"Sorry!" she whispered in between breaths.

"Don't be, this is the best morning I've ever had." When Emily kissed me, it was as if her hands and body took complete possession of me and my entire being. I let out a low moan.

"We should get breakfast started, or I doubt we'll ever leave this room." Her voice was low and sultry, and it didn't help the overwhelming urges growing inside me. Going against all my urges, I leaned over to grab my shirt on the bedroom floor.

"Aw, that takes the fun out of everything," she groaned, as I pulled my shirt over my head.

"If we keep this up, you won't be getting your omelet," We both shared a laugh.

We made our way to the kitchen. I quickly grabbed four eggs from the fridge and started preparing omelets for the both of us as

Emily poured us each a cup of coffee. It felt as though we had done this a hundred times.

"That was amazing, thank you!" Emily sighed, as she took her last bite.

I was mesmerized watching her pull the fork from her mouth. "I'm glad you enjoyed it. I'm useful for more than you think," I gave her a quick wink.

"Oh, I already knew that." We were laughing when her phone began to ring.

Emily looked at the caller ID with a smile. "Hello?" she answered. I couldn't hear the voice on the other end, but I guessed it was Tillie by the tone of her voice. "You did? WOW! That sounds like a lot of fun! Did you thank Grandpa for doing that? Good job honey. I'm so proud of you ... sure, we can do that. I think that sounds like a lot of fun. I'll be over soon. Bye, honey, I love you too!"

Emily smiled as she hung up the phone. "I hate to cut our breakfast short, but I should get going. Tillie wants to go to the park," she smiled, as she looked deep into my eyes.

I tried to find the words to see where we would go from here. "When will I see you again?" I asked, hoping my voice was not as desperate as it felt.

"Would you like to go with us? I mean, of course you probably have other things to do, and no worries if you can't, but I just thought..."

"I would love to go, that is, if you want me there," I replied, cutting her off from her rambling, I knew she was nervous asking me to join them.

"Of course, I want you there. If we're going to see where this goes between us, I'll need to involve Tillie." She smiled, as she reached for my hand. "Also, I think my mom already knows there is something going on between us," she admitted.

I felt like a teenager getting caught by the parents. "Should I be worried?" I asked, assiduously.

Emily laughed and squeezed my hand harder. "Not at all. My parents have wanted to see me happy again for quite some time. I just couldn't move forward until my last chapter was closed. Or as closed as it could ever be." She looked toward the living room and would not meet my eyes.

I stood up and stepped closer to her as I reached out and pulled her close. "Emily, I would never ask you to close that chapter of your life. It's part of you, it made you who you are today, it made you the woman I've fallen completely head over heels for. He was your first love, and I'm not here to diminish that. That's your history. That's your story, and I'm just happy to be a part of it. He was your first love. I'm here today hoping to be your last."

Emily looked up into my eyes, and within a moment her mouth was again on mine. I could think of nothing more than holding her in my arms and never letting her go.

"Thank you, Kai. Thank you for always keeping your word and making me trust again." She closed the gap between us and once again she was right where she belonged. Firmly wrapped in my arms.

EPILOGUE

EMILY

One Year Later.

"Tillie don't forget your jacket, please," I yelled down the hall as we began to make our way out the door.

"Don't worry, babe." Kai whispered, as he leaned over and sweetly kissed me as we both stood in the doorway. "I grabbed one for her, and it's already packed in the car."

Kai's kisses had become my favorite necessity this past year. He had a way about him, that with just the touch of his lips, I became calm. The way he grinned could make my heart skip a beat. To this day, I couldn't believe that this man had chosen to be with me and all my baggage. My scars had taught me to never take love for granted, feel the feels, take the chances given, and most importantly open your heart to change. Change didn't always have to be scary; change could be a wild and awesome adventure you wouldn't know you needed until you took it from life's grasp. I had pushed away the walls that were so easily built, but crucial to tear down. With Kai by my side, he somehow made the task less intimidating, less daunting. Kai reaches around my waist to pull me closer; I'm firmly pressed against his chest as I realize this is the man that has completed my shattered pieces, he's put me back together again, better than I ever thought possible. It took me longer than expected to come to the realization that you have to revive a broken heart before it can ever love again. Kai was my resuscitation.

Kai's bright blue eyes still twinkled when he looked at me, and that amazing smile had won me over yet again. "What's that look?" he asked, as I gazed at him in amazement.

"You have that look again." He smiled as he wrapped an arm around my waist and pulled me closer.

"I just can't believe that I'm so lucky," I said, as I pushed myself deeper into his arms.

"I'm the lucky one. Look at this beautiful woman I have here," he mumbled in my ear as he gave it a quick nibble.

"Moooommmmyyy, I'm ready now. I have all my stuffies ready to go," Tillie shouted, as she came running toward us and straight into Kai's arms.

Kai swooped her up as he had been doing for the past year, and they both smiled as they made their way to the car. Kai and Tillie had gotten so close that if you hadn't known any better, you'd think they were father and daughter. In fact, I hadn't quite minded when at a park the other day a lady assumed we *were* a family. I tried not to notice as Kai made a face, one I couldn't quite read. It had been on my mind all week, but I decided not to mention it or bring it up, especially right before our first big trip together.

I finished triple checking the locks as we all piled into Kai's large SUV. My small sedan rarely saw the three of us these days. If we were all going somewhere, we would take Kai's vehicle. I pulled out my GPS and typed in the hotel where we were headed. Luckily it was not too far of a drive. My parents would be meeting us at the hotel the next day and agreed to watch Tillie one night to give Kai and me some time alone on our first weekend getaway.

Kai jumped in the driver seat and looked over at me again with a silly grin. "What do you want to bet, Tillie's asleep thirty minutes into the drive?" he said with a grin.

"You know her well, but not well enough. I bet she lasts an hour. Loser has to accept a dare of the winner's choosing," I smiled, as I looked into the deep pools of blue staring back at me.

"Bet accepted. You have no idea what you just signed up for," he laughed again.

We had just under three hours until our arrival at the hotel. I felt lucky Tillie was such a good toddler for car rides. I'd let her use my old tablet, and she was quickly entertained by watching some silly cartoon. I found it adorable that Kai was making bets on her sleeping through the car ride. Over the past year, we had taken enough of them together for him to actually know her and her patterns.

A couple months after the memorial, we had been driving back and forth to each other's house almost daily. We got to the point that Kai was basically living at our place without actually living there. I had talked to my best friend about having 'the conversation' and asking him to move in. But every time I almost did, it felt childish to need a label slapped on our relationship.

We were happy, and that's all that mattered to me. Since Evan, I never thought I'd feel this way again. Kai had helped me *love* again. I was pulled from my thoughts by a small tap on my arm on the middle console.

"So, when can I claim my prize?" Kai whispered, as he nodded towards the backseat. Tillie was already asleep! We had only been on the road for twenty minutes.

"No way!" I said, as I took a look at my sleepyhead in the back seat. I shook my head in disbelief. "I can't believe you actually won that one ... I'm impressed!" I practically growled.

Kai only smiled wider. "I'd like to think that after a year of driving with the two of you, I've caught on to some things," he said, as his hand makes its way onto my thigh.

"I've also caught on to the fact that you get nervous when we leave the house for long periods of time, so I hired a guy to watch the place while we're away."

"Wait, who? I don't want some stranger in the house, Kai. I have some sentimental stuff in there. What if ..."

He cut me off before I had a chance to continue. "Babe, it's just Matt. Is that okay? I'm sorry I didn't run it by you first, but I can call him now."

Kai looked worried, and I couldn't stand seeing the poor guy squirm. "No, Matt's perfect, honey. No need to worry. Thanks for thinking of me and doing this," I said, as I squeezed his warm hand on my thigh.

"Are you kidding me? I'm always thinking about you. It's become my favorite pastime," he said in a low growl as he leaned closer to me.

I was thankful for the patch of traffic we hit, and that Tillie was unaware and snoozing in the backseat. As Kai leaned closer, I reached over and grabbed a handful of his curly locks. I loved when he left his hair natural and unbrushed. My fingers turned the curls around, and I gently massaged his neck as he concentrated on the road. "There's a million things I wish we could be doing right now, and driving is not one of them," I muttered, just loud enough for Kai to hear.

His eyes lit up, and his smile grew wide across his face. "You can't say those things and think they don't have any effect on me ... I am not immune to your charms. How much longer till we get there?" he asked, as his hand went higher up my thigh.

"We've only just started, Mr. Taylor." There was a long pause as we both laughed, keeping our hands on each other's lap. These quiet intimate moments were what first made me visualize a future with Kai. I had come to the point in our relationship that I couldn't see a future without him in it, and that scared me. I knew better than anyone how easily someone could be taken from you, and how a future you thought you may have had snatched away from your hands. I hated the fact that at any happy moment, my scars could so easily be ripped open once again.

"What's that face you've got going over there, babe?" Kai sighed.

"Oh, it's nothing. Don't worry." I whispered, hoping to not raise any red flags, or wake Tillie so soon after she fell asleep.

"Emily, we've got a long drive ahead, you should know me better than that, you know I won't just let you off that easily. What is it?"

"Kai, it's really nothing, I'll get over this in a minute or so, it's really nothing to even bring up. I promise, I'm good."

"I don't want you to just get over something, if we're going to be together, I want to be there for you through the good, the shit, and everything in between." Kai growled.

He actually growled, Kai didn't get upset often, but you'd know when he did. He had a way of getting me to voice my insecurities, never letting them sit and linger for too long in my mind.

"I see a future with you Kai, and that scares me more than anything. What if you get tired of this, what if it's easier to be with someone that doesn't have a screwed-up past, what if you want someone without a child, or I don't know, someone that has their life established and put together. You know me, I live my life day by day. I love you so much… so much… I can't imagine."

"Are you done rambling, or would you like a few more minutes to think of more insane ideas?" Kai laughed.

"Are you laughing at me? I'm a nervous wreck over here, ever since you made that face at the park. I don't know what you're thinking anymore." Kai's expression was more confused than I'd ever seen on his perfectly chiseled face.

"What face did I make at what park? What are you talking about?"

"Kai, it's nothing." I breathed, hoping to end the conversation.

"It's obviously nothing if some face I made you question how I feel about you." He countered with a look of irritation. My heart was aching, why was I doing this, why was I making something out of this, I promised myself I wouldn't bring it up.

"I didn't want to bring it up, because again it's probably nothing. But the other day at the park, this lady assumed we were a family and the face you made, I don't know what it meant. It made me think maybe a family isn't something you want with me … with us." I shrugged; I wasn't able to put it all into words in this heavy moment.

"I wish you would have said something sooner, I hate that you've been sitting on this for what a week?" He asked as his eyes were full of concern.

"Yeah, it's been a few days. I'm really sorry I even brought this up, it's so immature to get upset about a face."

Kai shook his head. "Babe, whatever face you saw, you very clearly didn't know what was going on in my head. I wish for nothing more than to be a family with you and Tillie. You both have become my everything. That face, to be quite honest, was hoping you weren't offended, I don't know if it bothers you that people assume I'm Tillie's father."

Vulnerability. plain and simple. We were both laying it all out there for the other to take. For the other to digest.

"I don't have the perfect answer for that, but I know you're the best father Tillie could have. You've stepped in and done everything and more. More than I ever envisioned we *could* have. You've made us more of a family than we ever were before you came and knocked on my door Kai. You awakened me when I didn't even know I was asleep." My eyes fell to my lap. I was feeling more than exposed.

"Emily, my love. Look at me," He breathed just louder than a whisper.

"You're driving Kai, we can talk later once we get to the hotel."

Kai began to laugh. "It's funny you think I can wait till the hotel to say this to you." He quickly pulled over at the first opportunity and put the car in park. His look was purposeful, and I couldn't help but notice how fast his breathing had become. "You want to know my dare for you?" he asked, as he began to twirl his thumb around my inner thigh.

"What are you talking about, what dare?"

"I won the debate on when Tillie would fall asleep, so I'll ask again, would you like to know my dare for you?" He had a mischievous grin forming.

"Can't this wait Kai? We were kind of in the middle of something important back there." How could he think of playing games right after I laid my heart out for him?

"Just trust me, okay? I know you do, so show me right now, right here, how much you trust me." The longing in his voice, he knew better than anyone how much I trusted him.

Of course, I trust you Kai, tell me, what is your dare?" I tried not to roll my eyes, but I just couldn't understand how this could be the right time for this.

Kai smiled a pure, genuine, brightens-his-entire-face smile. His fingers are now coming dangerously close to my most intimate space. "Are you sure you want to know, maybe you're right, maybe later will be best," he smirked.

"Kai, you can't do that! Now I'm eager to know what you have up your sleeve. I definitely want to know," I managed to say, as his touch was growing more sensual.

Joy tugged at the corners of his mouth, and his eyes continued to shine. "Alright, Emily Decker, I dare you to make an honest man out of me. Marry me my love! I can't have another day of you second guessing my intentions, I want you to not only know but *feel* how much I love you."

This couldn't be real. Yet the look on his face told me that this was no joke at all. "Kai don't joke around with me," I managed to say, just loud enough for him to hear.

"I'm not kidding Emily, this isn't how I planned it, not by a long shot, but with what you're doing to me ... inside and out ... I have to get this off my chest. There's not enough room in these pants for two packages." He laughed, as he reached in his pocket and pulled out a beautiful black box.

"Emily, you may think I'm crazy, but I'll say it again. I knew I was in love with you the day we met. I couldn't get you out of my head then, and I sure as hell can't get you out now. You are the best thing to ever happen to me, and I hope you'll do me the honor of becoming my wife, so I can prove to you each and every day of our lives together that you mean more to me than life itself. I love you, Emily. I love Tillie, I love those amazing cinnamon rolls you made on Christmas morning, and I even love your crazy old bungalow that you so desperately need my help fixing. Please say something my love," he pleaded, as I sat there with my mouth wide open.

I knew my answer, I knew it as plain as the words he spoke. For I too knew we had something special from the very beginning. My silence must have been killing him, for he began to nervously twirl his thumbs again.

"Emily, please say something," he whispered as his eyes pleaded for an answer.

"Kai I could never imagine my life without you. Now that you've shown me what this life could be like, my only wish is growing old with you by my side. I would love to marry you, Mr. Kai Taylor!" I practically screamed, as I flung myself out of my seat and into his arms.

We both anxiously checked to see if my sudden act of excitement had woken Tillie, and to our amazement, it hadn't. That's when all the composure I'd held in escaped. I leaned over and pressed myself into Kai's hard, warm chest. I press so close I feel I may sink into him if I push any closer. We held each other there for a moment, and found our lips pressed together once again. And in that moment, we were teenagers hungry for more. Kai's hands skimmed up both sides of my body as he then cupped my face in his large hands. I closed my eyes. My head swirled as I placed every little detail into memory. I wanted to remember everything about this moment.

Kai put a finger under my chin and tilted it up as he gazed intently into my eyes. "Say it again, please," he begged, as if his life might depend on my answer.

"Kai Taylor, I do! I would love nothing more than to be your wife!" Staring down at my left hand where not too long ago, a different ring lay, I knew I was ready. The ring was breathtaking, it had four thin bands delicately wrapped into one central oval diamond. The ring was unusual, but then again so was our story. I knew Evan would want this for me and for Tillie. I was excited for this new beginning, and I couldn't wait to see what our future held.

And at that moment, Kai placed the beautiful ring on my finger.

The End

Uncovered Playlist

Let It Hurt by Daniel Saint Black

High Hopes by Kodaline

I Found by Amber Run

These Memories by Hollow Coves

Oceans by Seafret

Incomplete by James Bay

Wrecked by Imagine Dragons

Wait by M83

I'm With You by Vance Joy

Hurt For Me by SYML

Perth by Bon Iver

Happiest Year by Jaymes Young

You're The One by Luca Fogale

ALEX GREYSON

The day was here at last, the wedding I never thought I would attend. And not just because my wingman, Kai, had recently taken a new job closer to Emily's side of town, no, *that* I could stomach. What I couldn't stand was finally getting to see the woman who not only once, but twice uprooted and wrecked my entire life.

Shortly after we read that ambiguous letter at Evan's memorial, I scheduled a flight to see Catherine once and for all. But, before I had a chance to even board the plane, I was met with a cease-and-desist letter. The woman had taken legal action against me! This shit only made me more skeptical of the entire situation.

Three months ago, Emily heard from Catherine to everyone's surprise. Sure! She could show up over the phone and face Emily, but *me?* Wouldn't happen! Guess it was too risky for her to meet in-person until closer to her contracted time away in hiding. She would have to wait to see anyone in person, especially a senator.

That day had finally arrived. Today I will see Catherine after almost five years. Even though I've been waiting for this day since the very beginning of the whole ordeal, I am more nervous now than when I was sworn into office.

"Can't believe the big day's finally here!" Matt screamed as he threw me a small shot-sized bottle of whiskey. My love language, alcohol. If I was to get through the day in one piece, I needed this, and lots of it.

"Thanks, buddy." The warm burn my comfort provided was vastly welcomed. "You got more of these ready for me?" I laughed as I tossed the mini container back.

Uncovered

Matt's eyes widened as he swished the remnants left in his bottle. "Take it easy, best man, or you won't be so *best* come twelve o'clock." He scoffed as he continued to fidget with his prosthetic leg.

I rolled my eyes at him and scanned the spacious room for something to drink. My gaze landed on a large bottle of Crown. *Jackpot!* "Can't make any promises." I sarcastically growled as I walked over to the refreshments.

I recently bought this old historic hotel to add to my never-ending ventures. This dump had been deteriorating faster than it was being managed. But thankfully, we finished the exhaustive remodel just in time for the wedding.

Now, with its designer interiors and modern finishes, this place was now fiercely sought after. Having my name attached to a luxury hotel didn't hurt business either. We only kept *some* of the historic charm, wanting to give it some contemporary industrial touches. The goal was to make this place my retirement plan, and I was rather pleased with the results to say the least. A perfect place for Kai and Emily's big day.

Matt always had to talk shit, and I'd had enough of him getting into my business for today. I knew my limits. I would never ruin Kai's big day. We worked too hard to get here. He and Emily deserved a perfect wedding, and I wasn't going to let my messed-up life do any damage to it.

"You know I'm just messing with you right? I know you won't overdo it." Matt eyed my latest swig as I swiftly chugged it back.

"Yep, we're good." I forced a grin his way.

You could hear the commotion in the hall before the door barreled open and the rest of the groomsmen entered our private suite. We had Davis, our smart-ass techie friend from college, and not far behind, Brannon, my burley security guard. Then came Kai, whose smile was permanently plastered on his dopey face since dinner rehearsal the night before. The man was the happiest I'd ever seen him. I envied him more than I cared to admit.

"Here, here! We got two hours till this man's officially whipped!" Brannon roars, while he pops the champagne. *Good thinking,* it was time for another drink. I knew I hired the man for a reason. I walked over to Brannon with five flutes and helped him prepare for a toast. Of course Matt glared as I handed him his glass, the guy was always full of judgmental angst.

Across the room Davis cleared his throat and prepared to speak to the group. "I personally would like to say thank you to you, Kai, for having me here today. I saw this day coming the second I heard about Emily. If I'm being honest, there was a time however, I thought your wedding would be to Alex since you two were attached at the hip." Without missing a beat, the room erupted in laughter.

"Ha ha, shut up!" I belted over all the laughter thundering through the room.

"As I was saying, Emily's great. Man, I couldn't be happier for you two. I'll leave the rest for the reception later, but let's toast to years and years of wedded bliss!" Davis cheered as we all clinked our glasses.

'Can I say a few things?" Matt muttered awkwardly as he stared at the tiles below his feet.

"Of course, we'd love to hear from our newest member of the group," Brannon bragged.

"I know I haven't known Kai as long as most of you, hell, I'm definitely the odd one out in this group. But I know a good guy when I meet one, and I'm grateful that for Emily's sake I like you, Kai. It would've really dampened the mood if things weren't as easy as it was between us. We all know the weight that today not only brings, but exchanges. I couldn't think of a better man to marry someone as special as Emily. Thanks buddy, for always making me feel welcome in your group, and I'm excited to see you finally become an honest man." He laughed, as we each drank from our glasses.

As everyone in the room finished their drinks, Brannon poured us each a new glass. I watched Matt as he looked around the room once more, his sights landing on a bag in the corner of the room. He walked over and gathered up a brown package. "There's something I need to give you, Kai. I gave this a lot of thought, and I think it's for the best."

I diverted my stare, careful not to look too eager to know the contents of the questionable package. Brannon sensed my unease and we both took a step closer to Matt. Even though we had both accepted him into the group, we knew he still had deep-seated issues to work through. Maybe today was too much for Matt. Maybe seeing his best friend's wife marry another was too much. Maybe this was his breaking point.

"You can stop eyeballing me Greyson, and that goes for you too Brannon. I'm not about to wreck the day or anything. It's just something that rightfully belongs to Kai now."

Without a moment to give his words thought, or for Matt to hand off the package to Kai, there was a loud knock on the door. Brannon looked at me and I shrugged my shoulders. The door began to slowly open as a hotel attendant poked their head around the small crack.

"Hello, sorry to interrupt, but I have a guest looking for Matt Stone?"

Matt stepped forward and walked over to the attendant. "I'm Matt," he answered.

"Oh, great, I'll let her in."

As the attendant ushered in the guest, Brannon howled, "Go Matty Boy! Who's the lucky lady?"

Into the room stepped a petite woman with curves made to be appreciated. Her emerald, green dress was so tight it appeared she was either extremely confident or unaware how tight it clung to her body. Every curve appeared to be sculpted by Da Vinci himself. As the woman looked up, her eyes roaming the room searching for the man she came here to see, her bold hazel eyes landed on mine.

I inhale sharply as I return her stare, shocked at the uncomfortable awareness. It takes me a moment, but the beating in my chest picks up speed as it registers who is standing in front of me. Catherine is facing me at last, and the room seems to have fallen silent. As all I am able to hear is my glass as it drops to a shatter on the tile floor.

COVERED COMING SOON!